A WORLD
OF HURT

A WORLD
OF HURT

A WILKIE JOHN WESTERN

TIM BRYANT

PINNACLE BOOKS
Kensington Publishing Corp.
www.kensingtonbooks.com

PINNACLE BOOKS are published by

Kensington Publishing Corp.
119 West 40th Street
New York, NY 10018

All Kensington titles, imprints, and distributed lines are available at special quantity discounts for bulk purchases for sales promotions, premiums, fund-raising, educational, or institutional use. Special book excerpts or customized printings can also be created to fit specific needs. For details, write or phone the office of the Kensington sales manager: Kensington Publishing Corp., 119 West 40th Street, New York, NY 10018, attn: Sales Department; phone 1-800-221-2647.

PINNACLE BOOKS and the Pinnacle logo are Reg. U.S. Pat. & TM Off.

ISBN-13: 978-0-7860-4229-6
ISBN-10: 0-7860-4229-X

First printing: December 2017

10 9 8 7 6 5 4 3 2 1

Printed in the United States of America

First electronic edition: December 2017

ISBN-13: 978-0-7860-4230-2
ISBN-10: 0-7860-4230-3

CHAPTER ONE

My name is Wilkie John Liquorish, and I'm here for to rob you," I said.

The trip from Mobeetie to Fort Worth was a fool's errand. It's an angry hot ocean of sand, full of snakes and scorpions, Tonkawas and Comanches and maybe even ghosts, and when you're herding eight hundred head of cattle, it's akin to swimming the Colorado with a bale of cotton under one arm and a pig under the other. By the time we got to Comanche Texas, speaking of Comanches, our cattle were skin and bones, completely unsellable, and half our boys were jealous of them, because the boys were bones only.

I buried my brother Ira Lee in Meridian, and that was it for me. I had lost all my taste for cattle driving. Far as I could see, we were driving them straight into hell itself. I was ready to repent of that life. When I walked away from it, I walked from there clear to Fort Worth. It was slow and hot and lonesome. I walked mostly by night and slept by day, and, when I wasn't walking, I was riding a mule named Bird. Not my favorite way to go, but more about that later. In between all of these things, I became my own man. When I arrived on the edge of town, I had no past and no great future either. The sun meant nothing and the moon meant less. Hell's Half Acre opened its arms.

Three days after arriving, I pulled a robbery. I was dead hungry and didn't have any coin on me. Tubbs's General Store at Sixth and Main seemed to have plenty. I'd been watching long enough to know their banking schedule. Another man I couldn't identify would come in at four o'clock to spell Mr. Tubbs, and he would take the day's earnings down to the Fort Worth National Bank on Eighth and Main. Way I figured, 3:30 would be just about right. Any earlier, the pot would be smaller. Much later, you might run into that second fella and have more trouble on your hands.

"Well, my name is Bill Tubbs, young man, and I hate to tell you, but you're doing nothing of the kind," the man said.

He was standing behind the counter and seemed to be set on staying put. I was in a quandary. If I backed down now, my outlaw days would be over in a hail of laughter instead of bullets. They would most likely throw me in the hoosegow just for trying. They might feed me there, but in general the thought wasn't appealing.

"Don't reach for nothing but sky," I said.

I pulled Ira's .44 Colt out of my holster and waved it once. I knew I didn't have the luxury of time.

"You say your name is Liquorish?" Tubbs said.

I could tell by the way he said it, he was thinking

of the candy. It isn't spelled that way, but I didn't have time for a spelling lesson.

"You're wasting my time," I said.

"No need to do anything hasty, Mr. Liquorish," he said. "That's an awful big gun you got."

There was something implied there, and it was something that didn't need saying. Being barely five foot tall and a hundred pounds when packed down with holsters, guns and ammo, I can tell when I'm being poked at.

"You saying I'm little," I said. "I get that. I get that a lot. But you know what? So's a bullet, and I got six of them right here."

I leveled the Colt good and steady at his face, taking in the waxed mustache, the sweat that glistened on his nose, and those eyes, blue as the Gulf of Mexico and every bit as full of crap, and I fired twice. Tubbs fell in a huff and a puff against a shelf full of flour and meal, a cloud of white rising around him like a quickly fading halo.

He left a trail of blood and flour across the back of the store as I dragged him into a mop closet, where I traded him for the mop and went to cleaning up. I pulled thirty dollars from the money box to cover expenses up until that point. Leaving more than that behind would show it wasn't personal and I wasn't greedy. I was just about to be on my way when the front door opened. In walked the High Sheriff of Hell's Half Acre.

"Bill not here?" he said.

I scanned the back of the counter and found an old rag, which I quickly dried my hands on.

"Not at the moment, Sheriff."

The sheriff scooted across the floor at me,

squinting like he was looking into the sun. The man easily made three of me, and none of the three looked particularly friendly either.

"Who in tarnation are you?" he said.

"Wilkie John Liquorish, sir," I said.

He had a big Colt Navy Revolver. I knew what it was because I had seen one like it on a sailor back in my San Antonio days. I had offered the sailor three head of cattle for it.

"What the hell am I going to do with three cows on a ship?" the sailor said.

I regretted letting that damn gun get away.

The High Sheriff was a little slow on the draw. Maybe he didn't see me being all that formidable. If that's the case, it was a mistake. I shot him right in the teeth. That brought out such a holler, I was afraid the whole neighborhood was going to come running. The next two shots shut him up real good.

The sheriff joined Bill in the mop closet. Seeing as I only had one shot left, I decided it was closing time. I locked up the store and grabbed three boxes of bullets from the top shelf behind the counter. Nobody laughed when I climbed the ladder to get them. Nobody laughed when I crawled out a back window and slipped into a side street, two blocks away from the whorehouse where I was keeping a room. I was seventeen years of age, but the Madam there didn't believe it. In that instance, it was all for good, as she took pity on me and took me in. An hour after I turned Tubbs's General Store into one more crime scene in the middle of the most crime-infested town west of the Mississippi, I was sleeping like a baby in the Madam Pearlie's big feather bed, her best girl, a caramel-skinned redhead named Sunny, keeping watch over me.

Waking the next day and heading downstairs, I was surprised to hear the news being whispered from ear to ear to ear. Mr. Tubbs, the city commissioner who had muscled his way into the Acre with the plan to clean up its dirty image, had been gunned down in his own store. The High Sheriff, who had been using the store as police headquarters in enemy territory, was shot dead too. The Madam called for a day of celebration. Call girls were going for half price and so were the drinks.

CHAPTER TWO

I thought about taking credit for the killings, but it wouldn't have done me any good. It would've been taken as a plea for attention, which I had no need of, or, more likely, for a joke. Then I might have had to shoot somebody else. I could see it was a vicious cycle, and, anyway, I sure didn't want to shoot up the madam's establishment, a right genteel place called the Black Elephant Saloon. And yes, I had been instructed right from the get-go that there was a White Elephant Saloon on Main Street where I might better belong. But Madam Pearlie had welcomed me like a son and told me to pay no mind to any such talk, I belonged right where I was. I liked being the only white man in the Black Elephant. It made me feel important. And I liked Madam Pearlie.

It was during that half-priced celebration, while the Black Elephant's six girls lined up the men in the back and the bartender lined up the drinks at the bar, that I first met Gentleman Jack Delaney, whom Madam Pearlie said was known, to close friends and family, as Jack Rabbit. That was the only time I ever heard her refer to him in that manner. Others said Gentleman Jack had once been a slave on a plantation somewhere north of New Orleans. They said he managed to save up money from blacksmithing and bought up his own freedom a few years before the war. Then, somewhere along the line, he went into business as a bounty hunter.

"I'm here strictly on business," he said.

I thought maybe he was referring to the Tubbs store murders as they were being referred to in the *Fort Worth Chief*. It's what everyone was talking about, inside and outside the saloon, me included. We would sit around the Black Elephant half the day talking about who might have done it, how they could have pulled it off and got away. It was such great fun that, every once in a while, I'd have to remind myself that my latest thought on the matter wasn't at all how it had happened.

The barkeep, a one-eyed man from Missouri named Black Price Hardwick, was taking bets on who did it and whether they would ever be found out. Even Madam Pearlie got in on the action, which she said was unusual for her, putting a fifty-dollar banknote on the authorities never fingering anybody.

"If they was somebody here in the Acre, we'd already be knowing," she said. "Whoever it was that done it, they're already east of the Mississippi or else west of the Rockies."

I had heard of both of those places, but they seemed far away from me as the ocean and maybe farther. I had no plans on ever seeing either of them. To me, Fort Worth was far superior to Mobeetie and the God-forsaken desert that made up most of the stretch between. I was staying put, at least until more reasonable weather arrived.

Gentleman Jack had a room at the colored hotel right across the street, so we saw plenty of him. Each of his days, as he told it, began with a breakfast of six eggs, salt pork bacon, biscuits, and brown gravy, all delivered up to his room and eaten off of a silver tray. Then he had his beard trimmed by one of the hotel staff while he watched in that same silver tray. After that, he was on his way. He would gamble at one of the poker tables or one of the blackjack tables in our front room until the clock over the bar showed noon, smoking and swearing up a storm and collecting his winnings. He always seemed to win. Then he moseyed on a little after noon.

"I've got to get about my work," he would wink. "I'm strictly here for business."

I wasn't too naive to know what a bounty hunter was. I'd run into a few of them in San Antone. Still, it was an occupation of mystery, and I didn't have the first clue how it all worked or how a person would become such a thing. It was partly out of natural inquisitiveness and partly out of suspicion that I decided to follow along after him. I'd heard enough talk from Madam Pearlie and others to pique my interest.

Hell's Half Acre wasn't so different from places in Mobeetie or San Antone. The biggest difference, San Antonio's Sporting District was mostly filled with military boys, and its girls spoke mostly Spanish. As a result, it was something between alarming and downright embarrassing to hear pale-skinned girls calling out from their ratty little cribs, telling you specifically what they could do for you and how little it would cost you. If you had to walk down a block, you might hear two or three of them calling out and then arguing amongst themselves, trying to undersell each other. It was all a guy could do to get to the other end of the block with his dignity intact.

With Feather Hill in Mobeetie, on the other hand, it was all a matter of scale. Whatever Mobeetie had, Fort Worth had fifty of. Fort Worth was an overabundance of abundance.

It was easy enough to follow Jack through a crowd though. He stood a good head taller than most of the men in the street, which meant he had two heads on me. He also wore, as a habit, a dark red top hat with a feather stuck in it—surely one he had purchased down in New Orleans—that made him tower even taller. I couldn't help but admire his ability to wind his way through the girls, who all called even louder to him, caught as in a spell by his appearance.

He was heading in the direction of Main Street, and I began to wonder if it was foolishness or fearlessness leading him there. A colored man might move among the white people on that street if he kept his head down and didn't call attention to himself. Neither proposition seemed likely with Jack. With each storefront he passed, it became more obvious that he had no plan to turn back. I considered calling out to him, just as a friendly warning. I stopped against a hitching post right

square in front of Tubbs's General Store and
watched him go.

He ducked into the back door of Mary Porter's
house, the biggest, fanciest brothel in all of the
Acre. It wasn't uncommon for well-bred colored
men to enter through the big two-story house's
back door, but I watched as his silhouette made its
way from window shade to window shade, and, suddenly, out he stepped through the big red double
doors in the front, stepping down from the wrap-
around porch and continuing on his way as if the
whole house had been no more than a puddle to
step through and then shake off.

Down Main Street he paraded, barely slowing
down to doff his hat at a couple of the townspeople
along the way. Finally, he removed his hat and
ducked into a small building I had never taken
notice of. I had just come off a disastrously star-
crossed cattle drive, so I was dressed as the other
ninety-nine percent of the crowd, and my white
face, sunburned as it was, blended in well enough
that I could walk right up to the old clapboard
building built against and leaning noticeably
toward the constable's office. I meant to make a
pass-by, take a quick glance into the two big front
glasses, and try to identify the proceedings within.
What fell on my eyes, I must admit, staggered me
in my steps.

The man was dead. That was the first and fore-
most thing that sprang to my mind. There wasn't
any question about that. He was dressed in a fine
looking suit. The kind you have shipped in from
St. Louis or somewhere via stagecoach. He had a
derby on his head that seemed too small by a size

and determined to sit just a little off center. The man's face seemed contorted into an expression that said, "I'd rather not have my photograph taken in this condition," but that's exactly what they seemed intent on doing.

One man stood behind the camera, his left hand on his hip and the other on the contraption that made the bulb flash. Another man had what looked like a woman's powder puff in his hand, dabbing at the dead man's cheeks and repeatedly trying to level out that devilish derby.

"What you staring at?"

There was a gentleman standing outside on the small porch, and it took a moment to realize he was talking to me.

I gathered myself and moved on without answering his question, although I could have told him plenty. I knew more about what I was staring at than he did. Sitting inside the little shop, waiting to have his picture made, gussied up like he'd never been in all his live-long days, was my old cattle-drive coach driver. A man named Leon Thaw, he had been born and raised in Mobeetie, Texas. The best shootist far and wide, his reputation had been sealed by getting tossed out of a Wild West Show in Amarillo and warned against ever coming back for getting up and outshooting J. B. Hickok. Twenty-six years old and getting no older, he was the husband of a seventeen-year-old Emeline Thaw and father of baby Millie. The last I had seen him, he was skinny as a broomstick, but swearing that he would make Fort Worth before I would.

"You take off on your own, Wilkie John, you'll be lucky to ever see me again," he said. "But if you do, I'm sure to be sitting up in some fine hotel sipping whiskey and waiting for you."

I walked by the building again on my way back to the Black Elephant, and I could see Gentleman Jack, the Jack Rabbit, standing next to my unlucky friend Leon, jotting down notes in a little brown book. Talking to the photographer, he leaned over and rubbed on Leon's face. That's when it hit me that he was truly good and dead, for Leon would have never allowed such a thing. Not that I had any tears to give him. He hadn't been like a brother to me. Truth is, he had tried to kill me on one occasion, and I couldn't help seeing his current predicament at least partially as being well deserved.

As I walked along Main Street and made my turn on Fourth, I couldn't help shaking the feeling that the tables had turned and it was now me that was being followed. I watched in the glass windows of the passing businesses. I saw nothing but my own reflection, looking thinner and older and maybe a bit more worried than expected.

CHAPTER THREE

"Wilkie John," Gentleman Jack said. "Must it be both? Why can it not be Wilkie? Or John? You can even pick."

We were sitting at the third blackjack table on a slow Tuesday night, which meant the dealer was at the bar chatting up one of the girls and we were sitting alone. My appearance at the table had been requested by the Jack Rabbit himself, earlier in the afternoon. I had been beside myself since then, standing in front of the mirror in Madam Pearlie's room, practicing answers to every question I could think up. Now, I was sitting three feet away from the man, he was looking me dead in the eye, and all my cool had suddenly evaporated.

"I've always just been called Wilkie John," I said.

That actually wasn't true at all. I had been called all kinds of things. Wilkie. Will. Wilkes. John. Johnny. Liquorish. Whiskey. I was in the *Texas Panhandle News* under the name John Liquorman and Whiskey John, so Wilkie John would do just fine, thank you. I didn't see what the big problem was.

"Okay, Willie Boy," Jack said, "you expect me to believe you did not come into town with the coach from Mobeetie, the same coach your good friend Leon Thaw showed up dead in."

I had never been called Willie Boy, and I didn't like it at all. On the other hand, part of me was fascinated by this man, and his calm manner worked to keep my hot head in check.

"That man is no friend of mine," I said.

If I hoped to trick the system, he was having none of it.

"Willie, I'm willing to give you that one. You know why?" He leaned across the table and lowered his voice from steady, quiet lilt to full whisper. "I don't guess good friends put bullets in each other's noggins, do they?"

So it turned out that the derby hat was tilting because some part of the top of Leon Thaw's head had been taken off with a bullet. I only knew two things: One, Leon was more the cattleman's hat type. Two, it hadn't been me that pulled that particular trigger. Last time I saw Leon, he was fully intact and talking back.

"The two drovers on the drive were located. One was dead and buried just outside Meridian. Fella named Ira Lee Liquorish, I believe it was. Now ain't that a peculiar thing?"

I was a balloon and he was a pin.

"The cook, from what I can tell, seems to have died before you even hit Wichita Falls. Why, it's a wonder even two of you survived."

I wasn't sure if he was amused by the story he was unfolding or by my reaction to it. Either way, I didn't like the way he was smiling at me. I figured by the way he was telling it that Simeon Payne had survived and was back in Wichita Falls. That made some sense, because last I had heard from him, he was turning back and heading for home. Still, I could scarcely imagine Simeon hanging around in Wichita Falls.

Things had already been going south for the cattle drive when we reached that damned spot in the trail. Our cook, a Mexican named Jacobo, had come down with food poisoning just days out of Mobeetie. Tainted chili, he said. The whole bunch was thrown out. Rivers of chili. Jacobo talked about going back over the border to his family, but he needed the dinero.

"I will go on to Wichita Falls and see," he said. "If I'm better then, I continue with you. If I'm not so well, we find a new cook, I collect my pay and get out of your way."

We even discussed turning the whole drive back to Mobeetie. How things might have changed if we had. It all came down to Ira Lee and Simeon. The *Jefe* and the *Segundo*. Ultimately, it was Ira Lee's drive. They conferred and decided to push on for Wichita Falls.

"Jacobo will be fine by then," Simeon said.

"If not, he's right," said Leon. "There's bound to be cooks in Wichita Falls."

On we went. You know, there are times in life when you have to make decisions. Sometimes it's a fork in the road. Sometimes it's a dancing partner. You choose one, and if it proves out, you become something you weren't before. You're a successful business man, or you're the husband of the prettiest girl in town, or you're a cattle driver. You

choose wrong, you're every sad son of a bitch
drinking his life away in every bar and brothel between Boston and Austin. I was well aware of this.
I was also aware that I was sitting in a brothel with
a very bad hand of cards and a poker face that had
just betrayed me.

"Ira Lee Liqourish was my big brother," I said.
"He was twenty years old."

I didn't feel like admitting to this was admitting
to anything important to Gentleman Jack. Whether
it was important to me wasn't any of his business,
and I couldn't see how it was any link to the dead
stage driver with the tilted derby.

"Let me ask you two more questions, Willie Boy."

It seemed like as good a time as any to
remind him.

"Wilkie John Liquorish," I said.

He kicked his chair back at an angle and rested
one big black boot on the chair next to me.

"If I were to prove that a certain man pulled the
trigger that shot the bullet that took our friend
Leon Thaw's head off," he said, "do you think that
man ought to hang for his actions?"

I knew that old trick. I had seen the same approach play out in a courthouse in Mobeetie. If the
man on trial said "no, that man shouldn't hang," it
made him look either morally suspect or just plain
guilty. If he said, "yes, that man should hang," he
was tossing the dice on his own mortality. Not
many men could do it with any air of confidence.

"Yes, that man should absolutely hang before
sundown," I said.

I don't know if Gentleman Jack was expecting that response. His boot wiggled, but he kept his calm. I didn't smile, but I didn't cry either.

"That he should."

He nodded and said it again. I looked him square in the eye and willed myself not to blink. After some looking back, his eyes moved down to the table, perhaps imagining the hand he was playing had become just a little less copacetic. If that was the case, I knew the feeling.

"And what if he killed fifty, sixty, more even. Men, women and children, free men and slaves, preachers and sinners alike? What might be due a culprit like that?"

That boggled the mind. I had once run into John Hardin in Gonzales, and even he couldn't boast numbers like that. It seemed biblical.

"I suppose only Jehovah himself could do numbers like that, sir."

Jack seemed satisfied enough with that.

"I suppose that's right."

He was stone cold and still, but his foot was twisting in its boot next to me, like it could barely keep from giving me a swift one in the side. It hurt my feelings that this most interesting and engaging man from New Orleans had taken such a strong disliking of me. I made note that I should do what I could to rectify it. I also thought it might be prudent to look into moving on out of town, even if I had developed a bit of an attachment to it.

CHAPTER FOUR

I had lived in Mobeetie long enough that some people called it my home. I never called it that. I was born in San Antone in '64, the second child of Noemi de Salina Liquorish. Noemi had begun life inside the walls of the Alamo, just four days before Santa Anna's army arrived. A Texian soldier had invited her mother there, ironically enough, for safety reasons. She was released as an infant civilian noncombatant after the battle, along with my grandmother and two aunts. I never knew my father Henry, who came to Texas with the New Orleans Greys. Henry stuck around long enough to marry and pass the Liquorish name to Ira Lee and then me. He then died at the hands of Comanches on the ride home from Fort Phantom Hill, where he had gone to set up a refuge against those same Indians. Irony at work again.

Henry John Liquorish was a hero around our house. Hell, I thought he was a hero around the world until I went to school and found out nobody else had a clue who he was. By then, it was too late. The die was cast, and Henry was someone to measure myself against. A constant reminder of what I wasn't. Tall, strong, heroic. And, to be fair, dead.

I stayed in San Antonio, getting a few years of schooling before I took a job as a photographer's assistant. We took Rip Ford's photograph after the War between the States, and we took Oliver Winchester's too. Winchester, who might actually be responsible for more deaths than anyone south of heaven, had insisted on posing with one of his rifles on his shoulder, like he was just returning from battle or maybe a possum hunting expedition.

We took quite a few photographs of soldiers. Most of them were alive, even if they were missing a limb or two, but the first dead person I ever photographed was a Confederate soldier whose body had been returned from a Yankee grave in Ohio. The dirt had turned him just a shade or two lighter than Gentleman Jack, and his lips had tightened into a smile that came back to me when I viewed Leon Thaw in the store window.

"Apply more color to the cheekbones," said the photographer, a man named Neely who came from South Carolina. "Comb his hair this way. Try doing it that way. Be careful. Don't mess up his smile."

I couldn't see what the color did for the camera, but if I could make Neely think the guy looked alive again in some way, my job was done. More often, it seemed to give the appearance of an actor at a minstrel show.

Truth is, that dead man's smile had followed

me from that job in San Antone all the way to Mobeetie and Fort Worth. It hadn't been the worst thing I had seen on that job though. Mangled boys my own age made me feel uneasy, as if I had something to answer for, but it was the dead babies that finally drove me to unemploy myself from Neely and look northwest.

There is something about a dead baby that turns on such lamentation inside of me, it became both a hindrance to the job and considerable embarrassment. When a cholera epidemic came to town, the coffin makers only rejoiced until it hit their own families. As for me, the line of tiny coffins was more than my constitution could stand. One morning, I didn't go in to work. I liked the change so much, by the week's end, I was on my way to Santa Fe, New Mexico. I was going to join a cattle drive.

"What makes you think those cattle have any need of you?" my mama said.

It was more out of a desire to keep me home than any concern for the cattle. My brother Ira Lee had already left, heading the same direction, and she wanted me around mostly to plow the tiny field behind our house and bring the handful of crops in. We didn't have much—just enough vegetables for us and maybe a few of the women around us— but it was more work than she cared to do.

"Ira Lee can get me on a drive," I said. "We might go up to Kansas."

I promised I would send for her if we ever got there. I never made a more sincere promise. Next morning, I lit out before she was even awake, knowing goodbyes did her the way dead babies did me.

I rode through the market full of people setting their goods out for the day, me, my Saddlebred, Roman, my Colt Sidehammer, and the clothes I had on, and I never glanced back. My San Antone days were behind me.

I had three greenbacks in my pocket, half of what I had saved from my photographer's-assistant job. The other three lay on the kitchen table for mama to find, a last gratitude to her for raising Ira and me best she could in difficult circumstances.

On the days ahead, Roman was usually all I had to talk to, and we talked plenty. We discussed hillscapes and waterfalls, cold nights in the hills and various sounds we suspected to be either wolves or Indians working their way through the sticks around us. I cooked rabbit one night, rattlesnake another. Roman ate with me when there was food and starved quietly with me when there wasn't. We crossed paths with a German family in a wagon drawn by two mules. They claimed to have land waiting for them somewhere on the Pecos River. It was a notion I didn't put much stock in, but they were kind and let me have enough salt pork and biscuits to last a few meals.

I also crossed paths with a Kiowa Apache boy named Long Gun on his way to Fort Griffin, a place I had never heard of.

"It's halfway between San Antonio and Indian Territory," he said.

It was the general direction I was going, so I invited him to ride along.

"I'm going to be a scout for the Americans," he said.

I had known Apaches in San Antonio. I had

even helped photograph a few in their war dress. I wasn't afraid of Long Gun, even if he did carry a rifle that was longer than I was. An Apache with such a gun would be a good companion on the trail.

"It's called a Whitworth," he said, holding it out on his palms for my inspection. "Made in Britain. Taken off a dead Confederate in Nacogdoches. It can hit a rabbit at five hundred yards."

My plans for Amarillo were subverted in time, and I wound up going to Fort Griffin with my new companion. I don't know how my life changed because of that impulsive decision, but, at the time, I was glad for the company. From what I could tell, Amarillo was north and west some distance from the fort, so I could move on and find Ira Lee in time. If I chose to.

"The United States Army settled the fort to protect white settlers from the Comanche," Long Gun said. "I speak Apache, Comanche, Tonkawa, Spanish, and English. That should give me value."

I could understand enough Spanish to follow the general idea of a conversation. I couldn't speak it worth a damn. Long Gun taught me a few Apache words, but they were the kind of things that would stick in the mind for a while and then be gone when you reached back for them. Eeya meant to eat, deeya meant to go. For some reason, I remember those.

Between the salt pork and whatever critters we could kill, we ate well the rest of the way to Fort Griffin and got there on the seventh day after I left San Antonio. I entered Fort Griffin weary from traveling under the hot sun and sleeping on the hard ground. I was ready to join the U.S. Army and help fight off the Comanches if they would give me a bed to sleep on. That was to last about as long as my career in photography.

CHAPTER FIVE

I was sitting in my corner room upstairs at the Black Elephant talking with Sunny. It was a Sunday afternoon, which meant things were slow.

"I mailed myself here from Waterproof, Louisiana," she repeated, lying across the end of my bed and tugging at one stocking and then the other. "People mail their kids by the Pony Express all the time. I just mailed myself."

I had heard of the Pony Express, and I knew stagecoach lines criss-crossed east to west and north to south, but I had never heard of anyone mailing themselves anywhere.

"Waterproof, Louisiana?" I said.

All things being what they were, I would have given even odds she was putting me on.

"It's on the Mississippi," she said. "There were war boats coming down the river, banging and booming through the night. You couldn't sleep for the racket. And the days were just as bad. The local battalion would fire on the boats till they drove them back upriver, then it would all start over again after nightfall."

"Didn't you have any family?" I said.

I wasn't naive as all that. I knew more families that had been pulled apart by the war than not. Southern families, much like the South itself, pulled limb from limb by Union soldiers, by disease, by their own deeds.

"My parents were slaves," she said. "When the Master saw that the war was coming, he sold my mother to a bigger plantation. Out of pure spite. Then, when the Union got to Waterproof, he freed my father. Freed all the workers and took a stagecoach west. Daddy, he didn't know what to do with hisself. Last I saw of him, he was threatening to jump into a river he couldn't swim out of. I didn't want to say it, but, way I saw it, he was already there."

There was a knock at the door, and I figured it was Madam Pearlie coming to find Sunny. Most likely a customer had come in requesting her. She had her regulars, colored folks and a few white ones too, who liked her smooth, caramel skin and the way her red hair worked against it. It wasn't hard to see why she was one of the most popular girls in the house. I was saving up money for her too. Mostly I was saving up nerve.

"Wilkie?"

It was Pearlie. She knocked at the door again, and I reached out to pull it open. I hoped she wouldn't be mad at Sunny for being there with me. Not because she would think I was sampling the merchandise, as she called it, but because I was keeping others from doing so.

"Sorry, Madam Pearlie," I said.

Looming over her shoulder was Gentleman Jack. My first thought was that he had asked for Sunny's company. It was the first time I ever considered socking him.

"Wilkie, Mr. Delaney here needs to speak with you for a moment," Pearlie said.

He had a piece of paper in his hand, and he looked at it as if he was about to read a telegram. Sunny came up next to me and put her arm around me.

"Wilkie John Liquorman," he said. "I am putting you under arrest for the murder of sixty-five men, women, and children, including one Leon Thaw who was the driver of a cattle drive for which you were employed, and over eight hundred head of cattle, all in and around Wichita Falls, Texas. The High Sheriff of Hell's Half Acre being deceased and no Texas Rangers being available in the Acre, you are to be remanded into my care until such time as you will be tried for your transgressions. If you are found to be guilty, you will be hung by the neck until you have joined your victims in the Good Lord's vengeful arms of death."

Sunny pulled me backward, as if she could pull us away from the reality of what was going on. Madam Pearlie looked stunned, as if she'd been under the impression she was escorting Gentleman Jack upstairs to sing happy birthday to me.

"Why, he's just a boy," she said.

I could have pulled Ira's .44 Colt from its holster. Had Jack reached down to draw his gun, his lanky arms would have had farther to go to get there, farther again to lift it up. I would have caught him just as he raised the barrel. Madam Pearlie would have stepped aside so as to allow the big man to fall unhindered, his pistola maybe firing off a single shot into the roof. As if to prove to myself that I wasn't always impulsive, I did none of this.

"Eight hundred head of cattle?" Sunny said.

I couldn't tell if she was horrified or impressed.

"I've never killed an animal in my life," I said.

"An ex-associate of Mr. Liquorman, a man by the name of Simeon Payne has testified that this man was responsible for bringing a cattle drive infested—I believe that should read infected— with red water fever to the town. That he traded sixty head of said cattle to a meat packing operation in exchange for goods and services while on the outskirts of the town. That those sixty head of cattle were infested with the fever. That he had, in fact, buried his own cook, a man named Jacobo Robles, on the outskirts of Wichita Falls because he came down with the fever. That he recklessly and wantonly transmitted such illness to both man and beast before leaving Wichita Falls and is responsible for what took place as a result."

Why, I had never accomplished so much with so little effort in all my days.

"The name is Liquorish," I said. "Wilkie John Liquorish."

I wondered why he was reading the paper in the manner that he did, as if he were reading it to Madam Pearlie and Sunny and not me, standing right before him.

"He was jailed in Mobeetie under the name John Liquorman," Gentleman Jack said.

He pulled the paper down and, for the first time, seemed to acknowledge that I was present.

"How is it that you are John Liquorman and your brother is Ira Lee Liquorish. You are a liquor man and he's only a little liquorish?"

I told him John Liquorman had been nothing more than a newsprint error. Nothing more. My mama named me Wilkie John Liquorish and that was what I answered to. He didn't seem that interested. His head was back into the paper.

"Shall we tell the ladies here what that little jail sentence was all about?"

It had been my first time in jail.

"I was only trying to expand my vocabulary," I said.

It's not what it sounds like. I didn't call the deputy sheriff names or curse him in Latin or anything. The sheriff had split town the previous year, heading for Alaska to mine gold, and the Deputy had his hands full enough without making trouble for me. He was also the local judge, and he preached at the Methodist church on Sundays.

"He was jailed for refusing to turn over his copy of the *Encyclopedia Britannica*, sixth edition," Gentleman Jack said.

Madam Pearlie laughed. It wasn't a troubled or shocked laugh. It sounded like a mother laughing at the hijinx of her child. It sounded like home. Safety.

"That true, Wilkie?" Sunny said.

My right hand moved to the holster at my hip, but Jack saw it and silently shook his head. Pulling his duster back, he made sure I could see the Smith & Wesson hanging ready at his side, hand already in position. I relaxed, content that I wouldn't have to kill him there in Madam Pearlie's corner room.

"It contained the words beer and alcohol in it," I said. "Even reading about them was against the law in Mobeetie."

What took the cake was, it was perfectly legal to drink in Mobeetie, so long as you did it in a saloon, of which there were four. If I'd kept my dictionary in the saloon too, I'd have probably made out alright. Truth is, I never felt a speck of guilt in Mobeetie, and I didn't feel guilt in Fort Worth either. I didn't feel guilt over killing no damn cattle or no people in Wichita Falls. That whole notion was nothing but foolishness. If it had happened, it was God's work, and I had no hand in it.

I felt guilt-free of killing the High Sheriff and Mr. Tubbs too. Why would I not? Folks were celebrating in the streets over that, and I had been selfless enough to not even take credit for it. Didn't matter. The thanks I got for it was a summons to appear in front of the courthouse two days later. It promised to be a hell of a show, and Gentleman Jack did love a show.

"They're building a stage especially for it, just so everyone can come and get a good look at you," he said. "And I've asked them to build a special door in it just so you can make a grand exit."

I looked at Sunny and smiled like none of it worried me. Inside, I was thinking I needed to figure out who really killed Leon Thaw.

CHAPTER SIX

Long Gun and I reached Fort Griffin just as it was being fortified with additional troops from Oklahoma Territory. They had a sawmill built on a creek just southeast of the fort, which was the first thing we laid our eyes on. Part of a corps of soldiers was there, loading logs onto a mule train and pulling them up a hill into the fort. They shouted out to us, not appearing to be the least bit thrown off by this skinny cowboy and his Indian companion.

"You boys look like U.S. Army material to be sure," the lieutenant, a man named Granville Hanley, said.

Long Gun introduced himself and said he was hoping to find employment working as an Indian guide. Hanley didn't seem to put much stock in the idea.

"Only need I might have far as redskins go," he said, "is that long gun you've got strapped to you. How is your aim?"

Long Gun told him the story about shooting at rabbits from five hundred yards, which suitably impressed Hanley. He nodded appreciatively and turned to me.

"What about you, son?"

I don't like being called son, unless you're my mother. I overlooked it.

"I can't compete with hitting rabbits at a quarter mile," I said, "but, last I heard, we wasn't at war with no rabbits."

Hanley seemed to like my reasoning.

"Go up to the fort and tell Colonel Dolon to feed you and your horses. We'll talk more after dinner."

Colonel Marcel Dolon had all the warmth of a root cellar. Even so, he was wearing his dress coat on a day that the sun had traveled from one horizon to the other without a single cloud to cool it down. He had the jittery disposition of Napoleon at St. Helena, but he did see that we were escorted to the kitchen and that our horses were watered and fed.

Fort Griffin turned out to be not much more than half a dozen small buildings scattered around on a plain just above the winding stream they called Mill Creek. There weren't any trees to speak of, and it seemed like a poorly chosen spot to fortify against groups of wild Indians. We were afforded a sleeping space separate from the soldiers on that first night, and I confess I slept like the dead. At first light, we were shaken awake by a reveille bugle call, which stirred feelings of home, as I'd heard it played so much around the barracks back there that I considered it my own personal wake up call.

If the truth of it is known, it very well may have been that reveille bugle that determined what would happen that morning. After the breakfast call, the soldiers all went on fatigue duty, which meant Lieutenant Hanley took his men back down to the sawmill and Colonel Dolon oversaw the building of two new barracks at the back of the fort. With duties dispatched, he soon turned his attention to me and Long Gun.

"So you fellas want to join the U.S. Army?"

I might have had no interest in it twenty-four hours before, but, at that very moment, it seemed clear enough that my whole life had been pitching toward that very decision. Part of me saw it as taking on the unfinished work of my father Henry.

"I would like to work either here or at Fort Phantom Hill," I said.

He didn't seem the type to be moved by emotional pleas, so I gave no reason, and he asked for none.

"Fort Phantom Hill has been abandoned," Dolon said. "You're stuck with me."

Long Gun reiterated his ability with rabbits and said he wanted to be an Indian scout.

"He speaks five languages," I said, sure that the colonel would be impressed.

"There are over one hundred Indian languages," Dolon said.

Long Gun looked dispirited.

"I speak Comanche and Apache," he said.

Dolon reared back in his chair and peered over a pair of reading glasses at him like he was inspecting an animal in a trap. I wondered why they didn't have Hanley in the fort and Dolon down at the mill, as it seemed Hanley was much better with people. Then again, the U.S. Army wasn't in the business

of getting along with people, especially if they were
Indians.

"Hell," Dolon said, "I can pretty well speak Comanche myself at this point. All you really have to
know how to say is 'get a move along before my men
put so many bullets in you, you'll just be a big hole
in the middle of the happy hunting grounds,' son."

We didn't have anything else to do that day, and
we weren't in any hurry to get back on the trail, so
we joined the United States Army that morning
and were part of the kitchen help by lunch time,
spooning out plates of beans to soldiers who didn't
look much different than me. By the time bugle
call sent everybody back to work, I was starting to
wonder if I had been hoodooed.

"The beans taste good," Long Gun said.

It was his way of telling me to stay put. For the
next week, I think he was afraid I was going to
abandon my post at any moment, and, with it, him.

To be truthful, the beans were good, and so was
the cot. We spent less time with Dolon and more
time with the cook, a Mexican who knew enough
English to tell stories of when he was a cook for Emperor Maximilian and Empress Carlota of Mexico.
Me and Long Gun were never sure if he was saying
that he cooked for them or he knew the man who
did it.

"How did the emperor's personal cook end up
cooking beans for a bunch of soldiers in Texas?"
I said.

After a week of beans, we considered that maybe
he had been banished for only cooking that. Finally,
it was Long Gun who put the question to him.

"How I wound up here?" he said. "The emperor

killed many, many people during his reign. Finally, the opposition party gain enough strength, they run Carlota out of the country, then they come for the emperor. Emperor Maximilian tried to escape, but they catch him. He and all of his people executed. All of them. They want to kill the cook too. Can you imagine? A lowly cook like myself."

Seeing him there in the little kitchen, he seemed too lowly to have ever made beans for an emperor.

"They tried to execute you?" Long Gun said.

He shook his head.

"President Juarez, the man who take over Mexico, I tell him, let me cook you a meal. If you like the meal I cook, you let me go, and I will leave Mexico. You don't like it, you may shoot me. I will not even run."

To believe this man's tale or not?

"And you cooked him beans?" Long Gun said.

He laughed in response.

"Yes, beans. And corn. And meat. Much meat. I use French breads. Custard. I cook a feast. And the president tells me, you are a good man. Go. Go away, Jacobo. Never let me see your face in Mexico again. And so I leave, and I come here."

And that is how I met Jacobo, the Mexican cook who made the best beans a Mexican emperor ever ate.

CHAPTER SEVEN

Gentleman Jack afforded me my freedom, if you can call going through your daily chores with a tall colored man in a suitcoat and red hat freedom. For the most part, it beat sitting inside a jail cell, a fact he reminded me of at regular intervals. My room was moved from the upstairs corner of the Black Elephant to a downstairs storage room directly off the bar, so the Jackrabbit could spend his time and money in the bar and still keep an eye on me. The room, having been a broom closet, had no windows and no exterior exit, so the only escape was through the bar.

Not to say I was a constant prisoner in the cell. Jack still went on his daily rounds, and he paraded me around with him as he did.

"We're going to town," he would say. A funny thing, because we were right in the middle of town. By that he meant, more than likely, we were going to Main Street, to the bank to do business, to the Post Office to check for telegrams, to the White Elephant for more business and pleasure.

It was during a visit to the White Elephant that I discovered a relevant piece of information concerning Mr. Jack Delaney. Of course, I could walk into the White Elephant and cause less commotion than him, even if I did look like I'd just gotten out of school.

"Stay with me," he said. "Get five strides away from me, I fire one warning shot over your head. I can promise you won't hear the second one."

The crowd in the White Elephant—and there were always longer lines there than in the Black Elephant—could easily be divided. A large portion looked at Jack like they were seeing Bigfoot Wallace himself walking in. The others stiffened up like children caught passing notes in church.

"Mr. Delaney," the barkeep said from across the room, "your usual?"

Jack nodded, and, by the time we strolled across the floor, a shot glass of whiskey was waiting. Gentleman Jack knocked it back and pushed the glass back across the bar.

"We're going to have one hell of a show, noon tomorrow," he said.

The barkeep shook his head.

"Twelve o'clock, sir. When I open up for business. Gotta be behind the bar."

Jack leaned into the counter and pulled me with him. I wanted to take one of the open stools, but the nearest one was a good four paces. I decided not to chance it.

"People will be out, looking for something to eat," Jack said. "I'm going to feed their taste for excitement."

The barkeep studied me closely.

"How old is he?"

Gentleman Jack wasn't happy with the question. "Old enough," he said.

The barkeep turned to me. He didn't look like the kind who had ever questioned a patron's age. He didn't say anything, but he didn't have to.

"Seventeen," I said.

Jack didn't seem to care much for the answer either.

"Old enough for a whiskey," he said.

He nodded at the glass sitting there between them. The barkeep pulled a bottle of something called Moral Suasion and poured. You can choose to disbelieve this, but I have to say, it was my first time to ever swallow whiskey. I had once imbibed a single glass of gin and almost immediately heaved it back up. I never went back in that particular bar again, and I steered clear of most hard drinks from that day on, afraid I might recreate the scene. No big loss, as there were bars on every block around the District, and they offered everything from potato beer to coffee for the less adventurous.

As a result, my first fear was vomiting onto Gentleman Jack's fancy leather shoes from New Orleans. The whiskey tasted like gold, and I could feel it mining its way deep down into my gut.

"I got something for you to see, young Mr. Liquorman," Jack said.

I wondered if he had compiled a list of things to call me that weren't my true name. As far as the Liquorman name went, I had indeed been listed under such a name in the *Panhandle News*, but it had been nothing more than a typo; one of several within the article itself. I decided to pay a return visit to the White Elephant and ask for another taste of the Moral Suasion.

The walk down Main Street was almost the same as it was when I had followed, and I wondered if I was due a visit to the photographer who had Leon Thaw on display. I tried following behind Mr. Delaney, but he seemed to prefer me walking in front of him. This made our progress slightly awkward, as I had no idea where we were going and had to be pushed along like a mulish child.

We did pass the window of the photographer, who had a new dead body in his parlor. This time, it was an old woman, framed by a simple wood casket and surrounded by a handful of other women who seemed just as old but not quite as dead. Sisters, maybe, or cousins. Too old to be her children. Or maybe they were; grief doesn't wear well, and it photographs poorly too. I knew from experience.

"Look yonder," Gentleman Jack said.

We were standing on the corner of Main and Houston. If there were two thousand people in Fort Worth—which is no more than a rough estimation—at any given time, it seemed that eight hundred of them were within sight of that particular spot. Fort Worth was like a pregnant lady in her ninth month. And everyone knew the baby was going to be trouble.

"I see a bunch of people," I said.

I could also see coaches and horses. The post office. The courthouse. A restaurant. Hotel.

"Exactly," Jack said. "And tomorrow, at noon, all eyes will be on that spot right over there."

People were passing each other in the street,

moving around us and anyone else standing still. It looked like a great river winding its way down Main Street, then branching off, much but not all of it into Hell's Half Acre. Down the street from the stagecoach station, immediately past the platform where freight wagons pulled in and unloaded goods and supplies, there was a great wooden stage of a different sort.

"What's coming to town?" I said.

I wasn't dumb. I sure as hell wasn't innocent.

"You are, Mr. Liquorman."

I was naive, thinking first of medicine shows and circuses.

"All the world's a stage, and this is where you will play out your role," he said. "Tomorrow, every eye will be on me and you, and you will answer for your crimes in Wichita Falls."

The stage was in front of the courthouse. I counted the steps leading up to it. That's when I realized the seriousness of the situation.

"I didn't kill anybody in Wichita Falls," I said.

He put his finger to lips and sushed me.

"No," he said. "Save your part for tomorrow. It's much better that way."

Part of me wanted to believe it really was a big play. An act by Jack to scare the tar out of me and then laugh and let me be on my way. Maybe even an act for all the people. Some kind of debate or show like I'd seen from vaudeville players traveling through Mobeetie. If it weren't for the thirteen steps leading up to the stage. If it weren't for the trapdoor right in the middle of the stage floor.

"Some say that little theater came straight from Governor Davis down in Austin," Jack said. "I'm here to tell you, Willie Boy, it came straight from hell. Straight from hell, no stops."

What was hell was getting to sleep that night. I laid in my little bed in the broom closet for half the night, turning one way and then another, staring at the ceiling and imagining faces in the wood. Not the face of the High Sheriff or of Bill Tubbs. Not the face of Leon Thaw. Not even the face of Gentleman Jack. It was a face from a little farther back. A time that seemed, like the ceiling itself, so close I could touch it.

CHAPTER EIGHT

We weren't the Three Musketeers, but Long Gun, Jacobo, and me became something of a team. That was mostly due to Long Gun and me continually being assigned to kitchen duty, even though Long Gun pled daily for an assignment with the soldiers who rode out and ushered settlers into or out of the fort. Dolon wouldn't even entertain the thought.

It didn't bother me so much. There were several families living among us, most of them waiting to be taken to Buffalo Gap. One of the families, the Lusks, had come to America from Scotland. The father, Bricky Lusk, was a wall of a man, standing a full head over Dolon, one and a half over Hanley, and as wide as both men side by side. Lusk had been a shipbuilder back in Scotland, living on the River Clyde. Then one day, he had enough of building ships and watching them sail off into the blue. He told his wife and three kids to pack up their things, and away they sailed for North Carolina, U.S.A.

One of the horse soldiers said Bricky had got

himself into trouble somewhere back east and left town rather than deal with it. The specifics were vague. He talked of bashing someone about the ears with his Welsh comb, which I believed to be a literal thing for a considerable time. How was I to know? I had trouble making out half of what he said, and he was likely having the same trouble with me.

Whatever, I had no quarrel with Mr. Lusk. But I confess I lusted after his daughter, an eighteen-year-old brunette named Greer who had the palest skin I had ever seen. I half-heartedly shuffled along behind Long Gun on his requests to join the soldiers on horseback, but I tried my best to look uninterested. I was more than content to sit in the kitchen and peel potatoes and onions with Jacobo, just for that five or ten minutes each day when she would come through and ask for a meal.

"Where are y'all going?" I finally said one day after several silent passes.

She spooned at her plate of beef stew and studied me, as if trying to determine if I was worth any answer at all. Maybe she was working out my Texian accent.

"First, Father wanted to see Texas. We came to Wichita Falls for a year. Then he decided he wanted to get a look at Mexico. Mother is tired of traveling."

They had come a lot farther than Long Gun and me, and not for much of a pay-off as I saw it. There was little between Fort Griffin and Mexico to get excited about, unless you were aiming for San Antonio. I had no desire to return there, although

I might have followed her back, if only she had asked.

It was established within the next twenty-four hours that a group of soldiers would escort the settlers to Buffalo Gap at the end of the week, when a new relief unit arrived to hold down the fort. Long Gun was determined to get a spot on the escort. I was ambivalent.

"You like Greer," he said.

I was a rabbit in his sights.

"Doesn't mean I want to escort her out of my life," I said.

She was little more than a daily glimpse into another world, a world I had never known or even imagined, but I closed my eyes and there she was, her big brown eyes, her small nose, her smile crooked in just the right way. Suddenly, my own world seemed insufficient without her. I might not have ever summoned up the courage to talk to her if I hadn't just been inducted into the U.S. Army. I took the situation on like it was a battle.

"I'm from San Antonio. I'm planning to go north and work cattle drives."

I didn't dare mention my brother. I had heard one of the soldiers mention she was eighteen. Just a little older than me. Maybe I had little to offer her that Ira Lee couldn't better, but I had seen him talk to the girls in the District at home. At my best, I was a better than average mimic.

"Tell me about the cattle drives," she said, nice enough to play along.

I checked to see just a couple of the sawmillers left to come through the line and quickly abandoned my post.

"It takes ten or twelve men to drive maybe three or four thousand head of cattle, if they know what they're doing. Take 'em up to Kansas City, fight off the Comanche, the Blackfoot. Blackfoot Indians are the meanest. It's hard work, but you can make thirty dollars for four weeks of work, turn around and do it all again."

It sounded like I knew what I was talking about. Like I had done it all before. Of course, everything I knew, I had learned from Ira Lee and wranglers in San Antone.

"How did you end up in the United States Army?"

I had lain in our tent on a night or two imagining conversations with this new arrival in my life. Now that it was happening, I was thrown off by questions I hadn't worked through. Thankfully, I was quick on my feet.

"I brought my friend Long Gun here," I said. "He's a Kiowa Apache. He wants to be an Indian scout."

"An Indian scout," she said.

I heard Jacobo call my name, but I couldn't tear my attention away just yet.

"Help the soldiers to communicate with the wild Indians in the area," I said.

"Señor Wilkie."

I turned to find Jacobo and Long Gun standing in front of Lieutenant Hanley. Jacobo seemed to be sending hand signals with his right hand and shielding them with the left. It was to no avail. Hanley wasn't amused.

"I'm leaving this place soon," I said, "if you'd care to come along."

Even today, I don't know why I said it. It was as

much for other people's ears as it was for Greer's. I was embarrassed, but I wouldn't allow that of myself. I was angry, but I wouldn't let anyone else see that. I paid for it too, of course. Immediately taken off kitchen duty, I was put to work helping to build one of several new cabins on the backside of the fort. Bricky Lusk was head of the crew. It might have been him or it might have been my guilty conscience that worked at me so hard, but it went well past nightfall, and when I finally went to bed that night, every muscle in my body fought sleep.

I finally fell asleep, long after everyone else around me. I kept building that damn cabin all night long, with Bricky Lusk breathing down my neck. Every once in a while, I tried my best to make it Greer herself, but, each time when I turned around, it was Bricky. If it wasn't Bricky, it was Lieutenant Hanley, with Long Gun standing by helplessly and Jacobo still trying to send me hand signals. It was a long night, even if morning came too soon.

CHAPTER NINE

The High Sheriff of Hell's Half Acre, before I retired him, had done his utmost to bring a little order to the disorder that was the Acre. When they found him dancing with the broom of death, no one doubted he'd been done in for his troubles. One of the most visible changes was the gallows built in the most conspicuous place on Main Street.

The sheriff had refused to call it a gallows. According to Madam Pearlie, he insisted that it was a law court, built to enforce the idea that justice had found its way to town.

"Of course, he didn't have so much to say about that door in the middle of it," she said. "What soon came clear: every scoundrel he brought up on that stage escaped kicking and screaming by it."

Madam Pearlie was furious. She'd been happy enough at hearing of the High Sheriff's demise to put all her girls on sale in celebration. Now her newly adopted son was scheduled to go on trial, and it was that blasted New Orleans bounty hunter in charge of the judgment.

The fact that the bounty hunter was sitting right across the room, drinking up the house's whiskey, wasn't helping matters.

"Don't Wilkie get nobody to stand up and speak for him?" Sunny said.

It occurred to me that the only people willing might not be the best qualified to do so. At the same time, if I was going to be the special guest at a neck stretching party, I would rather have Sunny up there to hold my hand and whisper into my ear than to stand there truly alone as the mouth of death opened and swallowed me up.

"I can speak for myself."

True or not, it sounded good, so I said it. When it came right down to it, there were always two separate things going on inside my head. One was some semblance of truth, and the other was something else. Something that captured my interest, that sounded like the character I was playing. Trouble is, a good portion of the times, I couldn't tell the two things apart. I had become the character. Truth was irrelevant.

"Wilkie John Liquorish, you will do no such thing," Madam Pearlie said. "I'll look all over Fort Worth to find someone to represent you. And if I can't find anyone willing to take the job, I'll get up there and do it myself."

No doubt Madam Pearlie knew more people than all of us combined, so I went about my meager business feeling slightly better about my impending doom. That sliver of hope was magnified when Pearlie went to Gentleman Jack and announced that she would arrange my legal representation for the case the following day.

"We must do this by the law, or we won't do it at all," she said.

Jack hemmed and hawed, but, in the end, he consented, taking the news as a personal challenge. Later, I would wonder what Pearlie meant when she said . . . "or we won't do it at all."

Did she have the power to put an end to the matter? What were they holding out from me?

Jack, although he held his cards close to his chest, made it apparent that he had what he thought to be a winning hand. This unnerved the first man Pearlie brought in, a young fellow named Gagnon from somewhere up north, whose eyes twitched back and forth over a pair of spectacles like he was watching an imaginary fly dart back and forth between us.

"Gentleman Jack is going to argue that you're responsible for the deaths of sixty-five people and eight hundred heads of cattle. That calculation would put the largest price on your head of any outlaw in all of Texas and the Indian Territory as well."

I kept looking in vain for that fly.

"I didn't do it," I said.

I don't know if he didn't hear me or just chose not to acknowledge my plea.

"Knowing Gentleman Jack, I would suggest you give him the eight hundred head of cattle, just so he feels that he's winning something, and we'll make him prove that you were directly responsible for the human toll."

Gagnon was the guy who had helped Madam

Pearlie skirt the law on several issues involving the city, but he seemed to be lacking when it came to criminal defense.

"Give him the cattle?"

I wasn't sure what he meant. Soon enough I was.

"If you've got eight hundred head, you're maybe looking at an average of twenty, twenty-five dollars a head. He'd have a hard time proving they were worth any more. If we can get him to agree to twenty, that's a total worth of sixteen thousand dollars."

He stopped and looked at me like I was supposed to say something.

"I was supposed to make thirty dollars," I said. "I didn't even make that."

Gagnon wanted me to admit to causing the destruction of the complete herd of cattle and then hope that would strike a sympathetic chord in Jack which would cause him to overlook the sixty-five people. I sent him away at once. An hour later, I discovered him coming down the back stairs with one of Pearlie's girls on his arm. No doubt, he had made an incredible deal for her services.

Later, Pearlie told me that Gagnon had money in every bank between Fort Worth and Chicago and could have paid off the sixteen thousand without batting an eye. That much might be true, but he hadn't offered to wire me any money, and I didn't like admitting to doing something I hadn't done. On top of that, I wasn't even close to comfortable with laying the deaths of those sixty-five other people on the mercy of the court, even if one of them was Leon Thaw.

I knew the cattle. I wanted to know who these people were.

The second person Pearlie sent my way was a colored man from Hog Eye, Texas, named Kitch Howard. Pearlie was getting into some meticulous thinking, picking Mr. Howard. Kitch knew Jack Delaney, although I wasn't clear on how. He seemed confident he could outsmart his friend, whom he referred to as "the Rabbit."

"How is the Rabbit doing?"

"Does the old Rabbit still call New Orleans home?"

"Is the Rabbit keeping a residence here at the Black Elephant?"

He wasn't, although it might have been easier on all of us had he been. He locked me into my room at night, being sure to keep the key with him when he left. I could move around the hotel while he was there, always with his eye on me and his gun at the ready.

When he saw Kitch Howard in the house, he re-acted as if he was seeing the ghost of a long lost family member.

"Kitchen Boy!"

Kitch made the kind of face that told me there was a past there. It looked to be a past he had hoped to keep in the past. He walked across the room, straight up to Jack, and stuck his hand out. I couldn't help noticing that he looked like a student approaching a teacher. Maybe a student who didn't complete his studies and was trying to soften the punishment.

"Rabbit, I'm surprised they let you into an establishment like this," he said.

I couldn't think of any student who would get away with calling his teacher Rabbit.

"Any establishment that would let the kitchen boy run rampant through the halls has low enough standards, I suppose," Gentleman Jack said.

He slapped Kitch on the back, and Kitch dug his heels in so as not to be dislodged from his stance.

"It's just like you to be picking on kitchen boys, Rabbit," Kitch said. "And now trying a young drover on such trumped up charges as these? I can't see any evidence this boy ever swatted a mosquito."

When Gentleman Jack laughed, it felt like he was laughing directly at me. He'd removed my Colt Sidehammer, and it was a good thing too. I likely would have tried my best to kill the two of them with a single bullet and then used some extras if that didn't work out. Thing is, he knew it. As for Kitch, I wasn't sure whether he was more interested in winning a philosophical debate or saving my hide.

"Was he really a kitchen boy?"

I had no idea how Madam Pearlie knew the guy. Far as I knew, he might have met Jack when he was cooking right there in the Black Elephant. It did have its own kitchen, and there were a few boys working away behind its swinging doors. I wasn't convinced I wanted to leave my life in the hands of

a man primarily known for his work in front of a
stove. Had he cooked for royalty too?

"My lands, no," Pearlie said. "That's just Jack's
way of putting Kitch in his place. It's all sport to
them."

Turns out, Jack Delaney and Kitch Howard were
cousins by marriage in a competitive family that
didn't like each other. Kitch was from the Texas side
and Jack was from the Louisiana side. Jack considered himself to be a self-educated man, having
dabbled in everything from Greek and Latin to law
to blacksmithing, all by way of the public library in
New Orleans and a few nice old Creole ladies in
the eighth ward. Kitch, whose real name was actually Kitch Corentin Howard, was among the first
colored men in the Dallas area to go north to get
an education, having crossed the Mason-Dixon five
years before the War of Northern Aggression did.
Howard's father, named Corentin but without the
Kitch, had been granted his freedom, mostly because he was in too bad of shape to be much value
to his owner. Corentin had, one by one, bought
the freedom of his four children, sending two boys
up north for school and two girls up north for
marriage.

Kitch asked a lot of questions. Some of them
seemed to have nothing whatsoever to do with the
situation at hand.

"Wilkie John Liquorman, when and where were
you born?"

"November 30, 1864. The District in San Antonio. And it's Liquorish."

"Like the candy?"

"No," I said. "Like the drink."

I spelled it out for him, but he seemed to think I was joking.

"By the district, you mean the Sporting District?"

It wasn't a subject I had the most satisfactory answers for. I took a deep breath and tried to find one that would do.

CHAPTER TEN

First man I ever shot, it was because of his reaction to a similar question. He was called Gallo, and I had seen him playing billiards in a couple of the halls in the District where people would bet on horse races and pretty much any other outcome you could wager on. His father had been a well-known farmer north of town. When Lincoln freed the slaves, Gallo lost half of his workforce, and a year or two later, cotton worms did in what was left. The father sold off his property and became the town drunk, and it looked like Gallo was following in that family business.

He caught me in an alley along the backside of South Concho where me and mama lived. I was coming home from a late night selling cigarettes to soldiers, and never saw him until we were practically eye to eye.

"Your name is John Liquorish, right?"

People have been getting it wrong as long as I've had it.

"Wilkie John," I said.

What I knew of Gallo wasn't good. I was fifteen, he a good three or four years older, and close to twice my size. I was already running late and not in the mood for idle chatter.

"Your mama stays in the cribs on Concho, right?" he said. "She's the gorda I see you with in the marketplace."

My Spanish wasn't fluent, but I knew what *gordo* and *gorda* meant. Even though I was the youngest kid, I wasn't a mama's boy. There was a younger woman two doors down on Concho that had taken me in, given me her books and taught me to read. Still, mama was blood, and, especially with Ira Lee being gone, there was a bond. I took his words—or that specific word, anyway—personally.

I had a little four-shot Remington pepperbox pistol that the neighbor lady had given me for protection. I pulled it from my waistband and stuck it right between Gallo's eyes. He didn't even blink.

"Johnny, mi amigo, what are you doing?"

I felt like crying, and I wanted to kill him before he saw.

"You don't talk like that about my mother," I said.

He pushed the barrel of the gun away from his face like he was shooing a fly.

"I don't mean no trouble now, Johnny," he said. "You understand. Give me about an hour with that sweet mama of yours, I think everything will work out, muy bueno."

I understood all too well. The second time I brought that pepperbox up, I wasn't trying to make any lasting impression. I pulled the trigger once and hit Gallo square in the chest. It was enough to startle him, but he didn't go down. I pulled my aim up and shot again. The second one caught him right under the chin, and it must have lodged somewhere in his brainpan because I never saw it come out anywhere. I fired one final shot right between his eyes as he lay in the dirt looking up at the stars and seeing me in between. I watched as the lights turned off inside of him. I remember them all glowing brighter that night for me, like my eyes couldn't take it all in.

I was surprised what happened in the aftermath of that first killing: nothing. Nada. I never heard anything about it, never heard Gallo's name mentioned again. It took me a few weeks to gather the nerve to walk back through that alley, and, when I did, it was as if nothing had ever happened. It had all been cleaned up and washed away. I went by twice, thinking maybe I had gone down the wrong alley. I even began to wonder if I had dreamed the whole thing. Maybe Gallo wasn't even real. I asked people if they remembered seeing him around. They shook their heads and said no. People did go missing around the District like that though. Like Ira Lee did, and later I did too. Maybe someone remembered seeing me hanging around the cribs, in the bars and gambling halls, outside the Army barracks. But, other than mama and the lady with the books and one other girl named Ginny Hay, who will come into the story later, I suspect not.

CHAPTER ELEVEN

Long Gun and I finally got our chance to get out of the kitchen. Hanley put us both on the horse escort taking the Lusks and two other families the seventy miles from Fort Griffin to Buffalo Gap. It wasn't a long trek. A couple days there, a couple more back. Hanley undoubtedly had multiple reasons for changing our orders. He was getting tired of Long Gun asking to be given the assignment. He may have been equally tired of both of us and looking for a few days' respite. More than that, though, he wanted to punish us.

Lieutenant Lemuel Yost was in charge of the trip to Buffalo Gap, and he was less than thrilled to find out two tenderfoots were taking positions from more experienced soldiers.

"Granville, surely you'll rethink this," he said. "We're going straight into Comanche country. I need my best men. Not two unproven boys."

We had been called into the front office, which was a one-room stone building with two big windows that looked like they'd been created by shooting cannonballs through the walls. Inside, Lieutenants Hanley and Yost were doing their best to ignore our presence.

"The Indian knows Comanche, and he's handy with a rifle," Hanley said.

Yost looked unconvinced.

"I know Comanche," he said.

Neither could pull rank over the other, but Hanley had the comportment of an older brother to the younger looking Yost. This may have been because he had a full beard which lent him a more dignified look. It may have only been because we were better acquainted with him.

"The Indian has the added bonus of looking like an Indian," Hanley said.

Yost stopped and looked over at us, measuring Hanley's words against the shadow of a man standing next to me against the wall.

"And does he speak English as well?"

I looked at Long Gun, expecting him to answer. He looked at Hanley, unsure whether he was clear to speak or not.

"Well, of course, he can speak English," Hanley said.

"What is your name, boy?" Lieutenant Yost said.

We had been issued wool coats and hats— secondhand uniforms that were too hot to wear except when instructed, as we had been before the meeting with Yost. The uniforms made him look more like me and me look more like a Yankee. Long Gun had also trimmed his hair with a machete since our arrival. In the unlit room, I'm not sure Yost knew for certain who was who.

"The short version of my Apache name is Doho-son Tay-yah. I am called Long Gun."

My first reaction was to think he was fooling around. I had never heard him mention an Apache name. Then again, it seemed only natural he should have one. Yost didn't seem impressed. He walked right up to Long Gun who managed to avoid looking him in the eye. I wasn't as successful.

"And what's your Apache name?" he said to me.

I might have momentarily considered a better answer if I could have slowed things down a bit. I would live and learn to regret hasty decisions. This was one of them.

"Liquor Man," I said.

Hanley thought it was pretty funny. Yost didn't seem to agree.

"Long Gun and Liquor Man," he said. "You boys have some kind of minstrel show or something?"

Long Gun was keen to get onto Lieutenant Yost's escort team, so he tried to steer the conversation back toward that end.

"I'm a Kiowa Apache Indian guide."

By that point, I knew the script.

"He can pick off a rabbit at a quarter mile," I said.

You could see the lieutenant's gears turning, and it seemed to tax his brain enough that he had to shut his eyes to see what he was looking at. We stood there like school children awaiting our fates, until finally Yost turned to his friend.

"I can't take both of these boys, Granville. We're

dealing with rabbits that shoot back out there, with rifles and arrows and God knows what."

Hanley was quick to concede.

"Pick one of them. I'll put the other on mill duty."

I wasn't looking forward to them separating us up..I was used to being alone—that didn't bother me none—but I knew we put up a stronger defense against the lieutenants as well as the older soldiers when there were two of us.

"Give me Dohoson," Yost said.

Dohoson sounded more like Wilkie John than it did Long Gun, so, for a minute, I wasn't sure which of us had received the call. I knew I wasn't much of a rabbit hunter, and I only knew the few words of Cherokee, but it still stung that I wasn't chosen. I was already itching to get out of Fort Griffin. What I was really itching for was a little more time with Greer Lusk. If I could connive my way into the Buffalo Gap trip, I would be guaranteed a couple more, and they wouldn't be under the nose of Hanley.

"Okay," Hanley said. "I'm giving you the Liquor Man there along with him. You complain, I'll pull one of your boys and give you the whole minstrel show."

As it turned out, me and Long Gun both stayed in the same barracks as before, and nothing changed for another day or so. One night after dinner, two of the soldiers brought out little guitars and serenaded us with "The Bonny Blue Flag" and "Aura Lee" and "The Ship That Never Returned." It was one of those nights where the stars seem to shine a little brighter. I was sitting between one of the guitar players, a blond guy from Tennessee, and Jacobo, and looking straight across a crackling fire at Greer, hoping her daddy didn't think it was him I was staring down.

Later, I walked down to Mill Creek to do a little business, and when I was coming back, I saw that Bricky was up and singing something about the girl of his soul being in tears or something. With his accent, it was hard to prove that it was English. What wasn't so hard was to see that Greer was no longer in the light of the fire. I decide to make a wide path around the circle and head back to the barracks. Maybe Greer would be somewhere in the vicinity, and I could talk to her.

I walked along practicing what I would say if I ran into her.

"It's a beautiful night, and you make it more so."

"I love the way your accent plays with words."

"Come with me to Amarillo."

I hadn't quite worked that last one out yet. I'd pretty much decided I was leaving Buffalo Gap for Amarillo to join up with Ira Lee's cattle drive. I knew there was no room on a cattle drive for Greer Lusk, but if I asked her, and if she said yes, I also knew I was quite inclined to give up my career as a drover and become a farmer or a blacksmith or whatever was needed in Amarillo.

I was contemplating this possible change of direction when I turned the corner behind the Lieutenant's office and ran straight into Greer herself, coming back across the campground in the direction of the river.

"Oh, Wilkie John," she said.

She must have seen me jump straight up, scaring

me like she did, but she only smiled. I was in love at that instant, mostly because I loved the way my name sounded rolling off her tongue.

"Wilkie John," said just right. No one could have said it any righter. Part of my shock, other than running into her in the half dark in a place I hadn't expected, was for the fact that she actually remembered my name.

"You gave me a start, Greer Lusk," I said. "You shouldn't jump out of the dark at people like that."

We walked down to Mill Creek again, which became slightly uncomfortable when she led right up to the very spot where I had pissed only minutes earlier. Had she been spying on me?

"Is it true, what you said about Buffalo Gap being no place for a girl?" she said.

It was true that I had said it, though I had no idea if the statement was true. I had never been there. I only knew what I'd heard. That it was a stopover for people traveling to and from Mexico. That everybody was doing either one or the other. No one stayed in Buffalo Gap, except for maybe a day or two to rest horses.

"It's no place for anybody," I said. "That is, unless maybe you're an Indian."

In the background, I could hear Bricky launch into another song. Its melody line twisted and turned like a snake, and part of me wanted to shut up and admire the way he handled it.

"I'm planning on going to Amarillo," I said. "I expect you would love Amarillo."

I knew no more about that city than I did Buffalo Gap, but I was naturally optimistic, at least most of the time. She stepped closer to me. Close enough that I could see her pale freckles in the starlight. She touched her finger to her lip.

"Did you mean what you said the other day, about me traveling along?"

I never felt my heart beat inside my chest like I did at that moment. Not before, and not after. Not when I kissed a girl, not when I killed a man. I wanted us to go get Roman and leave then and there. My Army career was finished.

CHAPTER TWELVE

"Guess that explains why you'd find refuge in a place like The Black Elephant."

I didn't like the way Kitch Howard looked at me like some kind of puzzle he'd just solved. I knew what he was getting at. It was something I had mulled over myself on the first day or two in Fort Worth. I remembered a preacher passing through Fort Griffin talking about how a dog would return to his own vomit. I didn't care to think of Madam Pearlie's fine establishment as dog vomit, but, truth is, I don't suppose the dog thought of his vomit as dog vomit either. If he did, would he return so predictably?

"Madam Pearlie is good to me," I said.

Not the most enlightened utterance. Pearlie was the one who found Kitch and talked him into taking my case. If he'd thought she was no good, he wouldn't have been standing there. Come to think of it, he had never said anything equating her place with dog vomit either. Maybe I was being too hard on him.

"Jack is going to make you look like the biggest scoundrel that ever hit town," Kitch said. "For most of the white folks around here, all he has to show is that you associate with negroes. As a negro myself, I won't do you any favors, standing up there next to you."

I mentioned the fact that Gentleman Jack was also of that persuasion.

"And Jack will swear he frequents your company as well, if it helps to achieve his goal."

His tongue lolled out of his mouth and he made the sign of being hanged by a rope. I got the point. He looked at Madam Pearlie, then at me.

"You know any damn white people, kid?"

I thought for a minute.

"Most everyone I know is dead," I said.

I thought he was going to have a spell. Sunny, of all people, came to the rescue.

"I think I know somebody."

We looked at her as if she'd just materialized before us.

Fort Worth was, by and large, a Confederate town, and it had paid the price for it. By 1882, things were starting to turn around, but it had been bleak. Slaves had been freed and moved along, and most white folks had too. The only businesses that hadn't gone under were the ones that appealed to the basest of desires—saloons, gambling houses, brothels. The only kinds of people to stick it out were the type you'd find there. Hell's Half Acre had been born, and it received everyone with open arms when they started coming back.

Still, the whites and the coloreds mostly kept to

their own, except for a few who dared step across the lines into the other side's brothels.

"Why does that not surprise me?" Kitch said.

I knew what he was getting at. It was often the upper crust whites—doctors and lawyers and even lawmen—who could be found slipping down the back stairs and out of the Black Elephant. It was those lawmen, for the most part, that guaranteed that the saloon remained open for business. The girls kept quiet, and so did they.

"There's a man named Elijah Caliber," Sunny said.

Madam Pearlie sounded like she'd sat on a spur, she let out such a raucous sound. It took a moment or two to even identify it as laughter. I wasn't sure what the joke was, but I wasn't in the mood for it.

"Good lord but that man can talk," Pearlie said.

Kitch looked at me as if to ask if this was a good idea. I knew nothing about Elijah Caliber, but I was open to learning.

"Well, it's *Reverend* Elijah Caliber, to be specific," Pearlie said. "He was with the Methodist Church until they kicked him out for spending tithe money over at the White Elephant. He left town for a spell. Next thing you know, he's back at the Baptist Church."

"And he spends his time and money here now," Sunny said.

When the late High Sheriff of Hell's Half Acre had first come snooping around, trying to pass new laws to put places like the Black Elephant Saloon out of business, Madam Pearlie impressed upon Reverend Caliber to go into court and argue the saloon's case. His verbiage was of such a high degree that it was said he could even talk a little bit of the devil out of a saint. Of course, he had refused to take up the saloon's cause on account it would ruin his career with the Baptists too. But he'd promised Pearlie he would make it up some other time. It seemed his chance to repent had arrived.

"He's white?" Kitch said.

Sunny nodded.

"He's a preacher?"

Sunny and Pearlie both nodded.

"And you think he'll do it?"

This time, even I nodded, and I had no idea what I was talking about.

"Madam Pearlie, send out for this man, and tell him to come at once," Kitch Howard said. "If he will agree to do this, I will walk down the aisle of the Baptist Church my own self and drop a most generous offering into the plate."

I was so excited about the prospect, I almost forgot what was on the line.

"And tell him, if he can out-talk Jack Delaney and save the neck of our young Wilkie John here," he added, "I'll double the reward."

"Hallelujah!" I shouted.

I was ready to put my life into the hands of a preacher and trust that he would save me. Surely, Sunny had just delivered a small miracle.

CHAPTER THIRTEEN

Greer Lusk's mistake was in standing up to Bricky. At eighteen, she considered herself an adult. Ready to get on with a life of her choosing. Bricky wasn't so easily swayed.

I told her I'd been selected by Hanley, against all odds, to go with the group to Buffalo Gap. It had to be a sign that our plans were unfolding according to fate. We would travel to Buffalo Gap, and then, before her family left for the Mexican border, we would head north for Amarillo where we would be married and start a whole new life together.

"I'll go on a cattle drive with Ira Lee, just to get something started," I said. "We'll use the money to open a store. Maybe even a bank. There's always money in money."

Greer wondered if she should talk to Bricky.

"He might be willing to help us get started," she said. "He has two daughters, Arabel and myself. I'm sure he would be relieved to get rid of one of us."

Arabel, at thirteen, was the youngest of the three Lusk children, so it seemed logical Greer would be the one. Still, I wasn't so sure and thought she should wait at least until we made Buffalo Gap before bringing up the subject. She left on the final night in the fort with plans to see me at sunrise. I had, by then, met with Yost's men, all five of them, and been given my orders. As much as they doubted my abilities, they admired Roman. It was decided we were to ride along behind the families and keep check on anyone following our trail. I would ride alongside Yost himself, which gave me both some relief and some trepidation. I knew he preferred Long Gun.

I tossed in my bunk that night, unable to stop my mind from thinking of Amarillo, of Ira Lee, of Cherokee Indians lying in wait along the hard trail to Buffalo Gap. Mostly of Greer Lusk. I finally fell asleep long after a restless silence fell over the fort and awoke just a few hours later. I looked over to see Long Gun's bed empty. Thinking he'd gone out to take a piss, I hurriedly dressed and saddled Roman and then stepped out into the night. I was greeted by a stiff wind and widely scattered raindrops coming from the north.

Long Gun was gone. So was the entire Buffalo Gap party. Yost had taken his pick and pushed off early.

"Looks like your friend double crossed you."

It was Hanley, up in his shirt sleeves and having a first cigar. He seemed too amused to realize he'd been double crossed as well, or maybe he had been in on it all along. I didn't know and didn't much care. I'd heard enough talk at night between soldiers to know how to proceed. There was a reason Lieutenant Hanley and Colonel Dolon had been so quick to sign up two ruffians, no questions asked. Soldiers were deserting on a weekly basis, prodded first by bad food and equipment and then by a big cut in pay direct from U.S. Grant himself.

"I'm going to Amarillo," I said. "My brother has called for me."

If Hanley knew anything about Greer, he didn't let on. It occurred to me that he may have forgotten he'd selected me for the Buffalo Gap trip. He had bigger problems.

"I have the power to punish you for abandoning your post," he said.

I thought about mentioning that I was still only sixteen years old, but I knew Civil War soldiers younger than that, especially in the South. Hanley was from Louisiana or Mississippi. It was doubtful he'd be sympathetic.

"I'm not the only one," I said.

Might not have been the best thing to remind him of. He swished a mouthful of coffee around and spat beneath me.

"You might feel tall sitting up on top of that horse, but we both know better."

First call bugle call sounded as we faced each other, me several spans over the lieutenant. It was bad timing on his part. Hanley looked back to the south and made a half-hearted motion to salute. I acted on pure impulse, bringing the Sidehammer up and firing a single shot right into his ear. He slid into the damp dirt, the blood gurgling loudly enough from his mouth and eyes as the bugle faded into the morning. As Roman stepped over him, I saw his coffee cup still clutched tightly, its contents spilled out on the ground.

I left Fort Griffin to the north, away from the waking soldiers and followed Mill Creek for several miles before I circled back southwest. I figured I was at least an hour behind the Buffalo Gap group. If I made good time, I would catch them soon enough.

Bricky might be pretty sure he'd outsmarted me. I could guess that Greer, in an overly optimistic moment, told him of our plans. I couldn't blame her. Wouldn't have done it if I could. No doubt, Bricky wasn't keen to see Amarillo. Wasn't keen to have me as a son-in-law. As I made my way along the rocks and hills, I imagined Bricky sending for Yost and preparing to leave early. Get his daughter out of harm's way, get his family on their way to Mexico. There was rain coming in, and they would need to make good time to meet the Mexican party who would take them South into Mexico.

I could picture Bricky, as the group saddled up and prepared to leave, sending Yost for Long Gun.

"I don't want the white boy," he said, if only in my head. "Bring the Indian instead."

Greer would have fought it, but, when the fighting was over, she would've gone along. She had no other option. It was her father, her family, her life. She didn't know what might happen to me, especially if Hanley had been made aware of things. I might not even be allowed to leave. She certainly wouldn't have risked being left alone in the fort.

As I rode along, I didn't consider Lieutenant Hanley. I didn't consider that I had now killed a soldier in the U.S. Army. Didn't consider the danger I was leaving behind me or the danger I was riding into ahead of me. I was thinking about a girl who'd been born on a river called Clyde, half a world away, and was now headed for the Rio Grande.

CHAPTER FOURTEEN

I met Elijah Caliber on the morning of my trial. Because he said he was responding as a man of god and not a man of the flesh, he refused to meet inside the Black Elephant, and so me, Pearlie, and Kitch Howard trudged off to find him in a part of the town I'd never been to. The Methodist Church on one corner and the Baptist Church on the next, I'd be lying if I said the folks who filled the pews on Sunday weren't the same the perched atop bar stools the night previous, but it was a part of town that liked to pretend Hell's Half Acre was only for cowboys passing through. If they had ever seen Caliber creeping down the back stairs of the saloon with Sunny on his arm, they'd have been shocked. They would have lynched him just like they were about to lynch me, even if it was pointed out they were in the saloon as well.

Now I should state for the record: I'm not in any standard way of thinking a religious man. I've never believed in any kind of man in the sky waiting to hear anything from my lips. All the same, I wasn't against a little assistance, and if it came from above, I was willing to be shown the error in my thinking. I was willing to concede Reverend Caliber might be my ticket to earthly salvation, if not necessarily to the next world.

He wasn't as long as Gentleman Jack, but he was big, and his head of shoulder-length white hair put one in the mind of an Old Testament saint, if not Yahweh himself.

"Miss Pearlie," he said, "Jesus surely does love you, and so do I."

He flat out refused to call her Madam. With the Reverend, it was always Miss Pearlie. It sounded unnatural to my ear, but I reasoned that "madam" was a dangerous word in the mouth of the reverend, being so suggestive and all. Pearlie, who was usually quick to recognize bull corn, smiled in a way that made her look like a whole other person—a younger, happier, more foolish one—when he said that.

"Reverend Caliber," she said. "I need to remind you that the Good Lord hears you even when you're not praying."

He looked Kitch Howard over good.

"So this is the man I'm speaking for," the Reverend said.

I raised my hand up like a school kid who had the right answer. But my answer wasn't going to win me any prize.

"No, it's me."

He seemed shocked by the news. Maybe I looked too young or too innocent. More likely, I looked a shade or two undercooked.

"You're the big bad man everybody's talking about?"

He smiled big and wide like only a preacher or a snake oil salesman can. Maybe he thought his job was going to be easier than he'd been led to believe. I was hoping that wasn't the case. All I needed was a Baptist preacher with a false sense of security.

"I'm bigger than I look, but I'm not so bad, once you get to know me," I said.

It was a line I had practiced the night before, unsure if I'd use it on the reverend or the crowd at the trial or, to be honest, anyone at all. I tested it on Caliber, and he acted like he didn't hear it.

"Miss Pearlie, were you able to write down all the information I asked from you?"

I had the papers in my vest pocket, wrapped around a gold medallion I won at a carnival in Mobeetie a year before. At the time, I took the thing to be a token of good luck, having won it with a beautiful woman on my arm and a half moon of witnesses egging me on from behind. Now, it seemed tarnished. A false hope if any kind of hope at all, it had only survived this long out of spite. I believed in luck—both the good and bad variety—about as much as I did Reverend Caliber's little black book.

"Here they are," I said.

I handed him the pages, torn from a ledger in the Black Elephant. The medallion was transferred from my hand into his.

A veritable history of Wilkie John Liquorish, in detail not from the beginning of the cattle drive forward but from my days as a child in the District and even going back to my father's heroic deeds, was written out in one long scribbly scrawl that I couldn't make out for love or money. Sunny had read from it and assured me it was on the level. She read it like she was reading from a great book, which made me like her even more.

"Where did you get this?"

He turned the medallion over in his hand and looked closer.

"I won it at a carnival for knocking chickens over with baseballs," I said.

"Chickens?" he said.

I was embarrassed I had unloaded it on him. Knocking chickens over with baseballs wasn't the equal of shooting rabbits with a rifle.

"It looks like a magic coin," Sunny said.

"They weren't real chickens," I said. "Wooden chickens."

Reverend Caliber held the coin up to his mouth and tried to take a bite out of it.

"It's an Indian Peace Medal," he said. "I haven't seen one of these in years."

I hadn't been sure it was a real coin. I still wasn't sure. Could you walk into a general store and buy candy with it? Could you leave it in a church's collection plate?

Caliber had no problem reading the sheets of paper, and he asked me questions about what he was reading.

"Ira Lee and you had the same father?"

I explained that our mother hadn't been a whore until after Henry John Liquorish was killed. "She had to do something to put food on our table," I said. "She couldn't very well join the Army." By the time Ira Lee was old enough to make a wage, bad habits had settled in. She had no belief left in either herself or her ability to get along in a world outside the District. It defined her and confined her. I knew I had to get out.

"But you joined the Army and then what? Deserted your post?"

I'd conveniently left out the manner in which I left Fort Griffin. In the days between, a soldier coming through Hell's Half Acre told me it had been abandoned. I had seen that coming. Eaten up by a town immediately to the north called The Flat. Far as I was concerned, Fort Griffin was now a thing of the past.

"They don't have Fort Griffin no more," I said.

He was adding scribble scrabble to the piece of paper in front of him.

"So the whole fort abandoned camp then?"

Having no religion, I could lie to a preacher just as easy as anyone. Still I was happy when I didn't have to.

"You could say that."

All in all, Reverend Caliber was alright, at least for a preacher.

He asked me to tell him more about what happened after I left Fort Griffin, and I obliged to the best of my ability. I felt free to mix in a fib or two along the way, when it suited the story, but for the most part, I was straight up with him.

CHAPTER FIFTEEN

I wasn't a stranger to Indians. I had seen plenty in San Antonio. Some posed for pictures, noble, some even smiling. I'd gotten to know Long Gun fairly well. I had even seen a few Cherokees come by Fort Griffin, anxious to talk to Colonel Dolon. Most of those were worried about getting shot by overzealous soldiers. All the Indians I had come in contact with had been friendly and peaceful.

Now, we were out on our own, just me and Roman, and I was looking at evidence of wild Indians on the Buffalo Gap trail. When I say evidence, I was looking right at two groups of Blackfoot Indians, about a quarter mile ahead of me. There was no doubt about that much. The evidence indicated that they weren't out for a morning stroll. The rain had finally turned into a full blown storm, of the kind that discourages such activity among most people. The Blackfoot were a big problem in several areas around the middle of the state. They snuck up on families asleep in their farmhouses and scalped them all, grown men and women and babies alike. I was worried about the way they split off into two groups, as if to surround something. Mostly I was worried because I could tell they were Blackfoot.

The Blackfoot were big trouble.

The storm did benefit me by making it impossible for them to hear me behind them. I could see one Indian at the very back of the pack that took the north route through the rocky hills that began to grow up out of the ground. He would stop periodically to look back, and I thought he might have seen me once, but he moved on without incident.

There was no way I could follow both packs, so I chose the one leading south, mostly because there was more vegetation that way. More places to hide. It was noon soon enough, although you couldn't tell. There wasn't a piece of blue sky to be found anywhere. It looked like the rain would never let up.

When the Blackfoot stopped to water their horses, I did the same. When they suddenly picked up speed, I did too. I had the Sidehammer close by, loaded and ready. Every strange sound around me, I feared the worst. I'd heard tales of Blackfoot Indians circling around on their enemies, drawing the circle tighter and tighter like a noose. As I went along, I began to lose them in my vision. Where there had been at least a dozen, I now saw three or four. What were they doing?

And then the three or four became none.

I moved slightly to the north, thinking maybe the southern party had met back with the others. If not, I thought, maybe I would at least see a sign of the other group. I wandered through that area until night fell, and it fell early because of the thick cloud cover. Finally, it seemed impossible to continue on. I knew the Lusk party would be camping for the night as well. In the morning, with any luck, skies would clear and we would all sweep on into Buffalo Gap.

Everything was too wet to start a fire, and I didn't dare make myself obvious anyway. The Indians seemed to have moved on, but you could never be sure. Under a canopy of silent clouds, any sound, sight or movement out there in the dark could mean your death. It's no stretch to say I didn't sleep much either.

My eyes were wide open when I first heard the sound. It seemed like the earth shook. Maybe it was only me. I knew immediately what it was. The Blackfoot Indians. They were a couple miles due south of me, and they were whooping up enough dust that you could see a cloud rise above the horizon. I got Roman and took off under a sky that was so blue, so clear that, after the previous day's angry gray, almost didn't seem real. Less than a mile off, I could smell smoke and knew it hadn't been dust on the horizon. Soon enough, I could hear the crackling of fire swirling around the war whoops. I listened for the sound of Long Gun's rifle. It never came.

When I got to the site, I could see what had happened. The Lusk party, with its escort of soldiers and other folks, had stopped to camp next to a creek in about a half acre clearing. The problem— and they probably hadn't realized it in the dark of the storm—was that it was situated in a bottomland between two slightly elevated areas. The Blackfoot

waited on both sides and attacked just before dawn.
Just like the stories I'd heard from Hanley. And I
knew how they ended.

I took three shots from farther away than I had
ever shot at anything. The sound of gunfire caught
them unaware. They immediately turned and rode
away, leaving the smoldering remains of a camp, not
fifty feet away from water that coursed by unaware.

Long Gun had fallen in an area halfway up and
out of the camp area, as if he'd either been advanc-
ing toward the Blackfoot to fight them head on, or
maybe to try to talk to them. Alas, he didn't know
their language. They scalped him and left him
there on the ground, his blood pooling with yester-
day's muddy water. All under the bluest blue you
could imagine.

Yost was dead at the other end of the camp, his
rifle at his side. His men lay around him, all scalped,
most with their eyes open, as if they couldn't believe what had happened.

"Greer!"

I checked Long Gun's rifle and found it fully
loaded. I took a box of shells from his coat and rode
over to a row of four pup tents, ragged and far from
waterproof. I knew it was standard practice to bring
the tents for any ladies traveling, and there were
four in the company. Walking up and looking into
each of those tents may very well be the three hard-
est things I've ever had to do in my life, each tent
being harder than the last. The first one held the
remains of a lady I had only seen in passing at
the camp. She was a quiet lady who kept to herself.
She seemed to have died that way too, cut from
the throat down to the torso, like an animal. The

second tent held Greer's mother. I don't know why I cried when I saw her like that. Was it because you could see Greer so easily in her face? Was it because of the sadness there? The brutality of her death? What must it have been like to follow her husband across the world, only to die on a beautiful morning and be gutted like a deer?

Was there family back home on the River Clyde? Would they ever learn what happened or would they go to their graves imagining their loved ones far away in the streets of Mexico?

Greer's sister Arabel was still alive when I found her, curled up in the end of her tent. I pulled her out by her feet and tried to give her water. A deep stab wound spilled a trail behind her. She looked at me, but I could tell she was seeing something else. I listened to her insides sputtering and dying, growing softer and then more violent again as her body seemed to go into distress. I took a blanket from her tent and suffocated her. I sat there and waited. I knew why I was waiting, even if I refused to acknowledge it. I told myself it was because of Arabel, but it wasn't. There was one tent left. I couldn't see into it, and part of me wanted to keep it that way.

I wanted the rain to come back.

Finally, I crawled over to the fourth tent on my hands and knees.

"Greer?"

And then a little louder,

"Greer?"

I shifted to where my line of vision allowed me to glimpse the interior of the tent. It was empty. I stood up and called her name. It must have been eight, ten times. Maybe a dozen. I scoped out the area and finally found Bricky under an oak tree on the path leading toward Buffalo Gap. He had no gun on him. It had surely been taken from him. But he hadn't been scalped.

Looking more, I began to piece together the events, matching them up to the sounds I'd heard and the length of time I'd heard them in. It appeared that the Blackfoot had taken Greer as a trophy. Good old Bricky had put up a fight, chasing them as far from the camp as he could, before being shot dead and left to die. They were moving out, in too big of a hurry to do any more scalping or mutilating.

I would like to have buried everyone there in the perfect little spot by the river, but I had to follow. The Indians couldn't be far away. If they had Greer, and they didn't know I was behind them, I might be the best real chance for her rescue. And now that I had Long Gun's Whitworth, I might be able to do something.

CHAPTER SIXTEEN

Gentleman Jack was slick as otter snot, to borrow words from one of the Fort Griffin soldiers. A plan developed in his mind somewhere along the way, or maybe it had been there from the very beginning. We arrived at the town center on a Friday morning at ten, just as we had agreed. If we hadn't, he had announced that he was fully prepared to put a bounty on my head and wait for the townspeople to do his dirty work. Madam Pearlie, meanwhile, heard that he'd done something similar in a town somewhere in Louisiana, and the people had torn the man limb from limb to get a piece of the reward. I felt like, with Reverend Caliber behind me, I had a better shot.

I had a dream the night before, locked inside my closet of a room off the bar in the Black Elephant. I was back on the clearing by the creek, and there were now rows and rows of tents. It was night out, but the stars were shining and the tents seemed to glow from within, like there were lanterns inside them. I walked up and down the rows, my shoes sticking in the mud, and searched the silhouettes, looking for one.

"I know she's here somewhere," I said. "I have to find her."

A figure was walking along behind me, more out of duty than interest. He sighed and hugged himself, hoping each row would be the last, that I would either find this person or give up.

The sound of a reveille bugle call pierced the quiet of the night, and I turned. Lieutenant Hanley, his face suddenly plain to see in my sight, scowled.

"It's time to go, Wilkie John."

I turned to take one last look, hoping to find something. I woke up, and in that split moment between sleep and wakefulness, between forgetting what you were dreaming and understanding, I knew. I knew exactly what I had been looking for.

"Wilkie? Are you in there?"

It was Reverend Caliber, calling out from the other side of the door.

"I'm right here," I said.

I pulled myself up and into a seated position and grabbed for my shirt sleeves.

"It's time to go."

And so it was. Now we were standing behind the gallows platform in the middle of Fort Worth. A crowd was beginning to gather and ask questions.

"Is that the guy you're hanging?"

"What did he do? Is he an outlaw?"

I sat there and thought up answers and didn't say anything. Was I an outlaw? I didn't know any outlaws. To me, that meant horse thieves and train robbers. An entirely different breed. They had no principles. They did what they did for money. Even when I killed the storekeeper, Tubbs, I hadn't cleaned out his money box or even his pockets. I took some ammunition because I needed it.

No, I wasn't an outlaw. I hadn't killed eight hundred head of cattle. I hadn't killed a single soul in Wichita Falls. I was an innocent man, far as I could see. I would tell the truth and everyone would see it. I was not going to hang.

"You're going to hang, mister."

A little boy walked as close as he could and still hold on to his father's finger. The father looked first at his kid and then at me, smiled and nodded his head. They were there early. They would get a place right down at the front.

I was surprised by who I saw. Pretty ladies in soft blue and white dresses. Farmers bringing summer crops in and waiting around for a story to take back. A coach driver killing time before he headed out of town. Every ten minutes the crowd would double. At 11:30, a man climbed the steps to the top of the gallows and led a portion of the crowd through the valley of the shadow of disinterest known to more humble men as the Lord's Prayer. They weren't interested in it. I carefully recounted the steps from the bottom up, and then back down again, hoping I'd missed one last time I'd looked, but to no avail. There were still thirteen steps in all. I started to really worry.

At 11:45, I spotted Sunny in the crowd. Like her name, she was a bright spot in a sea of muddy brown and black, the red in her hair looking almost like flames. A fiery angel standing on the edge of the scene, taking it in but not participating.

She didn't want to be there, but she wanted me to know she was.

At 11:50, Gentleman Jack showed up with Simeon Payne in tow. To say I was surprised would be an understatement. I don't know why. I knew Payne had been located in Wichita Falls. He was low enough to do just about anything for money, and I was sure Jack had paid him for his services. I just wondered what he was prepared to say. Having anybody there at the trial to support the prosecution was bad news.

"Can I have anyone to defend me?" I said.

Caliber looked offended.

"I'm not here to lead the prayers, my boy," he said. "Speak the truth, the truth will defend you."

I'd heard tell it would set me free as well. I was only hoping it wouldn't mind if I let a few details slide a little.

By 11:55, the street in front of the gallows was full. The largest crowd I'd ever seen, including a pretty big one on the first night of the carnival in Mobeetie. It reminded me more of the eight hundred head of cattle when the drive into hell had begun. Only this time, the cattle were looking for blood.

At 11:55, Reverend Caliber asked if we could go ahead and have a moment of prayer anyway.

"I don't expect it'll hurt none," he said.

With me and Pearlie in general agreement, I lowered my head and shut my eyes, and the reverend strung together some pretty words, some of which I didn't quite follow. I could feel eyes on me, and something about hanging my head made me feel guilty so I put a quick end to it and looked at

Sunny instead. Then Gentleman Jack came over
and said he was going to climb the thirteen steps
and make a statement.

Through the whole process, I managed to keep
a level head. I had been in trouble before, I'd
gotten myself out of it. I had a knack for letting
bad news and trouble float along in the back of my
mind and not get to me. It was more of the same
until it was time for me to climb those damn stairs.
The first step was a little higher than I thought. I
caught my foot and pitched forward, barely catch-
ing myself before I fell face-first into the rough
wood.

"He's about to soil his trousers," somebody
yelled from the crowd. Laughter rose overhead
and scattered like birds. My knees grew unsure of
themselves. I wanted to sit down. I wanted to run.
I wanted my Sidehammer. It had been taken away
by Gentleman Jack, and I knew I wasn't getting it
back. I'd seen the gleam in his eye, and I knew
exactly what it meant.

I turned to the Reverend, my thoughts made
clear and grim in the moment.

"Don't bury me in no coffin," I said. "I don't like
small spaces."

Caliber smiled but said nothing. When I got to
the top of the gallows, I looked across the crowd.
All eyes were on me. I remembered something
Greer Lusk said when we were talking one night
in The Flat, due north of Fort Griffin but not to
Mobeetie. We were talking about how big the
world was, and how we were free to go anywhere
we could imagine. I think Greer was starting to feel
homesick. Maybe she just wanted to remind herself

that she could—that we could—go back to the River Clyde. I wanted to go anywhere but back to where I'd come from.

"Wasn't it Shakespeare who said the world is a stage, Wilkie," she said. "It's your stage to do what you will."

Now, standing on the gallows in Fort Worth, Texas, next to a New Orleans–born bounty hunter with a strong desire to see me hang, I wanted to shoot Shakespeare for ever saying such a thing. Gentleman Jack was at home up there, using every square inch of it. For me, it was starting to feel suffocatingly small. Still, I knew I would have to put on the performance of a lifetime if I didn't want to leave by way of the swinging door in the gallows floor.

CHAPTER SEVENTEEN

I caught up with a small group of Blackfoot Indians not an hour outside of Buffalo Gap. I kept a good distance and watched until I was fairly sure the rest of them had split off and dispersed for good. There was a leader riding in front of the party, wearing a Mexican hat and a blue coat that looked like a soldier's uniform. There was a second horse riding close behind and a body astride it, a blanket draped over it. I couldn't make out much else, but I was confident I had found Greer. Behind them rode a handful of others, probably as protection.

I had learned enough about Blackfoots to know they would steer clear of Buffalo Gap unless they were prepared for all-out war. I also knew they were known to camp out south of Buffalo Gap where the Concho met the Colorado. I wasn't surprised when they took a turn, and I was able to make up some time. By the time they hit the Colorado, I was a step ahead of them, traveling to their west but in a parallel line. If they were planning to stop at the Concho, I would be in a prime position to attack.

Riding along, just Roman and me, I had plenty of time to plan, analyze, and re-plan. I wasn't dumb enough to think I stood a chance against the whole group. Blackfoot were brutal and ready to fight to the death at a moment's notice. I would have to surprise them, outsmart them.

As much as I didn't want to think about it, I knew Greer Lusk was a trophy. The Blackfoot leader would take her as a partner, probably one of several. If I could be patient, I would find the two of them alone. That would be my only fair shot.

They stopped and cooked some kind of meat they were carrying. I ate nothing that first night. I couldn't afford to divide my attention and energy. I would find an opportunity to go in and rescue Greer, I thought, and I almost went a couple of times when the leader sat alone next to her, the nearest other Indian fifty yards away.

It appeared that he was talking to her, and I wondered if there was any common language they could find. I knew what he was wanting from Greer, and I could only imagine what she was thinking, having just seen her entire party attacked, scalped, and left for dead. Nothing happened that night on either side of Concho, but I watched and planned and, by sunrise, I'd developed a brash and somewhat reckless plan. With nothing to do but await the second night, hoping that they wouldn't pull up and move farther south, I retreated to a well-covered area and slept the hottest part of the day away.

Another night passed with me watching from a tree-lined hillside on the north bank of the Concho

River. An hour before daylight on the second day, I took a scrap of paper from my saddlebag and carefully handprinted: *lead him from the rest of the camp when it gets dark.*

I took the message and the Sidehammer—I didn't dare bring Long Gun's rifle on this escapade—and carefully circled the Blackfoot camp, quietly sneaking in from the back side, where the foliage along the river would give me cover until I was just a few feet from Greer. That gave me just enough time to quickly press the folded message into her hand.

I contemplated taking her then and there. I wanted to, but I knew my chances weren't good enough. I would've been forced to run toward the Colorado, which meant either crossing it or following it south. Neither option was good. I would take my time and deliver justice before I took her away from her captor.

I watched closely that morning for a sign that Greer got the message and understood what was happening. Sitting in the quiet and feeling the thumping against my chest again, so strong and hard that I could count the heartbeats, I knew I had to make a move either way. While leaving the camp, after leaving the message tucked against her palm, I had attracted the attention of one of the Indians upriver. He had come down and investigated the area where I made my entrance and exit, following it back through the undergrowth to the edge of the river. By the time I moved back into a safe position, he was standing in the middle of the camp, looking around and listening for trouble. A few minutes later, a snake wriggled from under a bush and slid into the lake. I couldn't see it in the water, but the Blackfoot fired several times at it and woke everyone around him. If I hadn't seen what these same people had done to the Lusk family and their escorts, I would have thought them somewhat wanting in comparison to their reputation.

That day may have been the longest of my sixteen-year-old life. I watched the Blackfoot eat lunch, and I ate the fruit from a patch of prickly pear cactus, as I had been shown by the soldiers at Fort Griffin. Just an hour later, the Blackfoot started loading up. They were moving out.

We followed the Colorado back north for a bit, then turned west toward Amarillo. I took it as a good sign. They weren't going toward Fort Griffin where there would certainly be a price on my head. Finally, I might run into Ira Lee and set up that cattle drive. I was feeling good enough about things that I decided to hang back a bit and wait for a better shot at rescuing Greer.

The Blackfoot leader was in his usual forward position, Greer hanging back with the one I recognized from when I'd snuck the note to their prisoner. That now seemed long ago. A wasted opportunity maybe. I followed on, and began to feel too confident.

"Mobeetie?"

Roman jumped sideways. I looked up and one of the Blackfoot, a boy in a yellow jacket, not much older than me, stood in front of us.

"Mobeetie?" I said.

Far as I knew, he was speaking Blackfoot. I knew nothing in Blackfoot. Eeya and deeya meant nothing to the boy.

"Mobeetie," the Indian said.

He pointed ahead to his party in the distance. I nodded at them. Greer never looked up. I don't think she had a clue I was there. I was there and she was not. The boy in yellow said something else in Blackfoot and the six or seven of them all parted, pulling their horses to the side. And they waited.

"You want me to go?" I said.

They looked at me. Finally, a Scottish lilt rose up.

"Sir, I believe they want you to ride into town ahead of them. Blackfoot Indians aren't always welcome around here on their own. I'm a woman so I don't count."

I felt shaky inside. Why, I don't know. My mind was racing, and maybe I was struggling to follow it. Part of me figured I could bring the rifle up and pick a few of them off. It still wasn't good enough. I took a deep breath and rode through the group, managing to tip my hat at Greer as I passed. Anyone might have thought I was thanking her for translating. I did wonder how she had done it.

"Nice to hear such a beautiful voice," I said.

I passed through to the front of the line and continued up the trail, the Blackfoot leader riding alongside me. Did he know who I was? One of us was riding into a trap. I couldn't say for sure who.

CHAPTER EIGHTEEN

"Ladies and gentlemen, good citizens of Fort Worth, and all Texans from the Sabine to the Rio Grande, from the Red River to the Gulf of Mexico," Gentleman Jack said, "today we are here to serve justice to a young man whose path of destruction, fortunately or unfortunately, led him into this great city. It's unfortunate for him but fortunate for us, because we have the power to put an end to his trail of death today. A trail of death that will only end with his own."

A cheer arose from the crowd. It was as though they were here to see a piece of theater. Maybe Jack and Shakespeare were right.

"I will show you how this mean and foolish young man, this man with no principles and no love for anyone but himself, came to be responsible for the deaths of sixty-five men, women, and children between Mobeetie and Fort Worth. I will show you how he is responsible for the loss of eight hundred head of cattle. Cattle that he was responsible for driving to Kansas. And I will call upon the expert testimony of his good friend and fellow cattle driver Simeon Payne to show you that this man has more blood on his hands and is responsible for more deaths than any Texan who ever lived."

I was brought up to the edge of the platform, where I was turned this way and then that, so every person there could get a good hard look at the terrible monster. After Jack was sure they'd got their fill of me, he grabbed me by the arm and marched me back to my place at centerstage. He stopped me one step shy of the trapdoor, which was painted black and adorned with the words Proverbs 6:12–19 scrawled on it.

Gentleman Jack motioned to Reverend Caliber that he was free to speak. Caliber walked up next to me, pulled a Bible out like he was pulling a gun, and held it up. I hoped he was about to explain what this sixth Proverb was all about.

"The Lord says vengeance belongs to him and him alone, my friends" he said. "I am here today to warn you. This young boy you see here is not guilty. You will hear a lot of words today. Some of them will be his personal story, the journey he's taken to our city. A journey which, you will learn, is filled with good luck and bad luck. Is he innocent? None of us are. We've all seen too much, we know too much to be called innocent. But he is not guilty of the terrible deeds he's been accused of. And if he dies here today, his blood will run through your streets. It will not wash away, and it will save no one. This boy's blood will be on your hands, Fort Worth."

Gentleman Jack stepped up from behind me

and tapped Caliber on the shoulder. Caliber turned to him and held the Bible up to his face in a fashion that brought a murmur through the crowd. I thought I saw a scowl cross Jack's face. Caliber, satisfied, brought the book down and stepped back. Jack sidestepped over to me and put his arm around me. He may have been hoping to portray a kindness, a fatherliness even. It felt like a spider wrapping up a wasp.

"Son, is your name Wilkie John Liquorman?"

I refused to answer. I stood there and, as the people began to shout out, pretended they were meant for Jack.

"Is your name Wilkie John?" he said.

My body felt as if I was already hanging. I couldn't suck enough air into my lungs.

"Yes."

He could barely hear me, and he was standing next to me.

"Can you repeat yourself and speak up, please?"

I launched a shout from the stage. It came out small and shaky.

"Yes, sir."

I immediately hated myself. For sounding small and shaky, for addressing him as sir. A sign of respect eeking its way from my mouth at a time when it wasn't called for. If he called me son, this man who was no father to me, I would not reply with respect again. I caught my wind, and it filled my lungs. I wouldn't die so easy.

"Were you born in San Antonio to a mother who makes her living servicing men in the Sporting District area of that town?"

The question was too complex for a simple answer.

"My father was one of the New Orleans Greys," I said. "He married my mother and sired me and my brother Ira Lee."

Jack wasn't happy with that answer. He held his hand out and stopped me.

"I was not asking about your father. I was asking if your mother works in the Sporting District in San Antonio, selling her body to the soldiers and men there."

I didn't see what it had to do with my guilt or innocence.

"She didn't do that when I was a child," I said. "I don't have any idea what she's doing today."

I scanned the crowd, shielding my eyes from the sun with my hand.

"Mom, you out there?"

The audience roared. I say audience because it was at this very instance that I saw it as more than just a crowd. I remembered mother taking Ira Lee and me to a puppet show at a children's theater one time when I was small. One of my earliest memories of mother and Ira. I sat watching Robin Hood and Friar Tuck and the Sheriff of Nottingham. At the end I threw a fit, wanting so badly to see it again.

"Son, you shot and killed Leon Thaw to keep him from telling authorities what you did on the ill-fated cattle drive that started in Mobeetie, did you not?"

I didn't want to answer. He was calling me his son again. I knew silence might come back to hurt me in this instance. I stuck my bottom lip out and pulled up my best six-year-old boy answer.

"No, daddy," I said. "I promise I never shot Mr. Faw."

A few people right up front were already playing along. I was playing to them, and every laugh made me want another.

"Are you known as Wilkie John Liquorman?" he said again.

I could sense some frustration already creeping in.

"No, I'm not him," I said.

Gentleman Jack pulled that old edition of the *Panhandle Times* from his vest and held it up as Reverend Caliber had done with his Bible. One seemed about as truthful as the other to me.

"So this is not you here?" he said.

I grabbed the paper from him and looked it over like I'd never seen it. I turned to my new friends in the front row and winked. Then I folded the paper and handed it back.

"I believe it is," I said.

Jack seemed not to notice the laughter. He was on a mission.

"So we've established that this is Wilkie John Liquorman, and that he was jailed in Mobeetie for causing a disturbance there less than a year ago," he said. "Given that small but important piece of information, I will thus be able to show how this same man, the man you see before you, is responsible for the greatest loss of life this side of the Mississippi River."

"Since when?" the Reverend said.

I wasn't sure if I liked his interjection, even if I was beginning to wonder if he ever was going to speak up again.

"In modern history," Jack said.

He was going all out.

"Including the Indian Wars, even?" Caliber said.

You could see Jack sigh for a block in either direction, even if you didn't hear it.

"Not including the Indian Wars, Brother Elijah."

Caliber walked up to my right side, putting me square between the two men. I was a wishbone, and one of them was going to win good luck. Either way, I was going to be broken.

"Including the terrible War between the States, Jack?" Caliber said.

I looked at one of them and then the other. Then I saw Sunny standing to the side of the platform. Looking at her cheeks, if she had been laughing at all, it had brought only tears. I wanted her up on the platform with me. That would be my good luck.

"Okay, I'll give you that one too, Brother Elijah," Jack said. "Not counting that terrible war."

It had indeed been terrible to Fort Worth as well as Mobeetie and San Antonio and most of the towns in Texas. Unless you were a coffin maker, you were lucky to have survived those years with anything at all.

Reverend Caliber—Brother Elijah—stepped out of that fight feeling like he'd gotten the measure of the man before him. If Gentleman Jack looked like a formidable opponent, it hid a vulnerability. Caliber knew he was beatable if he could get the crowd on our side. In that moment, Caliber's brain came up with a plan that neither he nor I had imagined. It was a plan that he hadn't dared contemplate. He looked at me, nodded, and winked. I

took it as a sign to continue what I was doing. I
nodded and winked back. There on the edge of
death, with Gentleman Jack placing a rope around
my scrawny, young neck, I had never felt so alive. I
wanted to be right there forever.

CHAPTER NINETEEN

Me and Roman rode into Mobeetie, Texas, with a company of Blackfoot Indians, three days after they had scalped and killed Long Gun and his fellow U.S. Army men along with two Anglo families who only wanted to see Mexico for themselves.

Any happiness that my girl Greer Lusk was still alive was somewhat tempered by the fact that the leader of the Blackfoot—if he had a name, it was completely unknown and probably unpronounceable to me—had taken her as his prize and was looking for a place for them all to hide out. When we arrived at Mobeetie, I had a good idea why this was their destination.

"Those Injuns with you, partner?"

Mobeetie was lawless. I'm not saying the sheriff was a bad guy or was outnumbered by bad men. I'm saying there was no sheriff, no deputy—no nothing. It was wild and raucous, and it was up all night. From the looks of the three-man welcoming committee standing in front of us, it never even closed its eyes and rested.

"We're looking for a place to rest for a day or two," I said. "I can vouch for them."

What I could vouch for was the fact that I wanted to keep an eye on them until I had a chance to make my move. If I could kill the leader and take Greer out of there, I didn't much care what happened to the rest. They were a snake that would be of little danger to me once the head was cut off.

We took three small rooms at the back of a bar. I took the room closest to the bar, not because I cared about it being close by but because I wanted Greer and her captor be as far from it as possible when I took my shot. They put Greer in the third room, way down at the end of the building, and all the rest piled into the middle one. Soon they had whisky brought in. Between their cavorting and the noise from the bar, I would be getting little shut-eye, but that was thought out too. I had other things I needed to be doing. Moments later, there was a knock on my door.

"Poker," the boy in the yellow hat said.

Not one of the things I'd planned. He was pointing at the door to the middle room. It wasn't hard to figure out what he had in mind. He had a .44 revolver at his side, and he didn't seem too anxious to use it, but I decided not to push the matter. I grabbed my Sidehammer from the table and followed. I knew how to play poker. I had taken many a soldier's hard-earned pay in the bars of the District. I had no compunction against taking a little of the Blackfoot's spending money before I stole their girl back.

It's a funny thing. There wasn't a lot we could

have discussed in the little room there in Mobeetie.
We could've compared the names of places we'd
been. Names of people we'd shot. Card games we
knew and liked. Beyond that, we found it fairly easy
to go through the motions of a poker game, and
they were soon emptying their pockets and pushing all manner of American and Mexican coins
across the table at me.

Half an hour into playing, the leader, whose
name seemed to have been something like Tata-
hami, left the group while I was busy reloading my
sarsaparilla. A few minutes later, I tried to pull out
of the game, but the others were eyeing me warily
and having none of it. They wanted another opportunity to win their money back. And then another.
I played through a couple games out of respect for
their wishes. By this time, the whiskey was impair-
ing their thinking enough that I was trying my best
to lose and winning anyway. I finally begged off,
saying I was sleepy, and went back to my room. It
was 2:30 in the morning, according to the clock
mounted on the wall next to the bed. I checked
the Sidehammer again and slipped back toward the
back of the building, past the room where I could
still hear voices and bursts of laughter, cards being
slammed down and coins clattering against the
table. Glancing back at the bar, I wondered when
the people of Mobeetie slept and if there were
women and children counted among its citizens. I
slipped along to the third door and tried the knob.
Against all logic, they didn't seem to put a high
appraisal on locks in Mobeetie either.

The room was laid out same as the other two, so
even with all lamps blown out, I knew my way

through the front room, knew right where the opening to the bedroom would be, right where to find the Indian and my girl. I unholstered my gun and stepped slowly, deliberately, breathing only through my nose. I was halfway across the room when I brushed up against the corner of the kitchen table, out of place by a couple feet compared to the one I'd been playing at. There was a scuffling sound behind me, somebody moving from the sofa under the front window. I suddenly knew why the lamps had been blown out.

"Greer?" I said.

There was a single step toward the center of the room and a single shot from a rifle. I felt the bullet miss me by inches. The flash from the muzzle fired up the darkness for a brief moment, but it was all I needed. I saw him lunge at me just as I brought the Sidehammer up and fired. I fired again and then a third time. He twisted slightly in his forward momentum, his hips thrown back for a moment, and then he pitched against me with a shudder and sigh that sounded like the propeller on a sinking ship. I backed up, and listened to his head ricochet off the table and onto the floor. I turned to the bedroom and caught Greer coming through the doorway with a candle in her hand.

"He had it worked out, you were coming, but I had no way to send word," she said. "He'd been sitting there at the window, up to high doh, playing with his wee pistol."

Her lilt was powerful, musical and intoxicating, but I had no idea what she was saying, and I was too green to see any sexual innuendo, if there had even been any intended.

"We need to get out of here," I said.

I did want to take her to my room, but I knew it wasn't possible.

"He had two of his men watching me," she said, "but I did what you said, and he sent them packing."

Even if he'd sent the two guards away, they wouldn't stay for long. There were a few things left back in my room, but nothing I wasn't willing to leave behind. I took Greer's candle and leaned down in front of the Indian, moving in closer and closer until the flame licked at his skin.

"Wilkie, don't," she said.

I suppose she thought I was going to set his body on fire before I left. While I wasn't as against it as she was, I had other ideas. As the candle singed his eyebrow, his eye opened and stared blankly across the room.

"He ain't dead," I said.

I cocked the Sidehammer and fired one last bullet into his head.

"Now we can go."

In the room next door, four other Blackfoot heard the gunfire and came to the aid of their imperiled leader. It really wasn't fair, standing in the center of the darkened room and waiting as they, one by one, appeared silhouetted in the door frame, the gaslight glow of the town giving me a perfect backdrop. I picked up Long Gun's rifle, still fully loaded, and fired off five shots. Only one of them managed to get a shot off. It hit a leg of the table and rebounded, piercing Greer's left shoulder and going straight through.

I went over to the poker game which was still in progress, the only two remaining Blackfoot too drunk to even notice when I walked into the room. I put the last two bullets in their Indian heads and they cashed out.

"Let's get you a doctor," I said to Greer.

And that's what we did.

CHAPTER TWENTY

Gentleman Jack loved being the center of attention. The way he dressed said it. The way he talked said it. The way he walked back and forth across the front of the gallows like he was walking a tightrope or a pirate's plank said it, even if I was the one dangling at the plank's end. Reverend Caliber, on the other hand, dressed and moved like a preacher who didn't want to be seen, by God or anyone else. He let his words do his work for him. And he knew how to make that happen, holding onto them when it was right to do that, letting the suspense build like a rain cloud over the heads of the townspeople until it broke and rained down either a cleansing and quenching shower or else a flood of righteous judgment.

The fact that neither of us felt beholden to it made it all the more fun. The Reverend didn't believe that man in the sky was going to deliver me from the hands of evil any more than I did. It was all up to us. We wouldn't have wanted it any other way.

"Wilkie, when you and your beautiful lady, Miss Greer, got to Mobeetie, was your purpose there to join up with a cattle drive?" Caliber said.

It was one of the few questions we had practiced on earlier. I knew what my answer was supposed to be. In the spirit of the moment, I embellished.

"Ira Lee was in Amarillo," I said, "and he'd sent word he could get me on a drive to Kansas. I was intending to go to Amarillo."

I was supposed to stop there and wait for the next part. Maybe I should have. We'll never know that for sure.

"I went to Mobeetie because a group of Blackfoot Indians asked me to go and vouch for them," I said. "Mobeetie wasn't too fond of Blackfoot Indians."

The way people laughed made me think maybe they didn't want to see my neck stretched so bad after all. I scanned the faces for the kid who'd told me I was going to hang. I wondered if he was still so sure.

Gentleman Jack walked across the stage, stopped and rested his chin in his hand.

"Blackfoot Indians are among the deadliest of Texian tribes," he said. "Interesting that you would join up with such a bloodthirsty bunch."

I suppose he was angling for that man-is-known-by-the-company-he-keeps line of thinking. It didn't seem like much to go on.

"I had it in mind to kill their leader, which I did in due time" I said. "He had scalped and killed a group of Scottish settlers and kidnapped Greer Lusk, the girl I later took as my wife in Mobeetie."

That drew such a loud reaction that Jack had to hold his gun up and threaten to shoot it off if we didn't all settle down. Blackfoot Indians weren't too popular in Fort Worth at that time either. I wasn't looking like such a bad guy after all. What was it about these sixty-five people I had left lifeless in my wake? Had they been Blackfoot too?

Reverend Caliber looked kind of like the floor had just been pulled out from under him. He still had plenty of questions left on his list, but they all seemed to need another lookover.

"So it looks like we've already added one more murder to the list," Gentleman Jack said.

I thought he was getting ahead of himself.

"That might be the sum total of the list," I said.

This wasn't satisfying the crowd. And it sure as hell wasn't satisfying Gentleman Jack Delaney.

"Ladies and gentlemen, I have three people who are prepared to climb up here and point out this man as the murderer of sixty-five Texas citizens," he said. "They will point out this man as being responsible for sixteen, maybe twenty thousand dollars' worth of cattle. That puts him ahead of the worst cattle rustlers we've seen, as well as ahead of most of the other men I've tried and convicted."

That was a lot of information to process. We knew Simeon Payne was going to say I was responsible for what happened in Wichita Falls. There was one problem with that. I had never entered Wichita Falls. The fine citizens of that city had seen to that. Payne, on the other hand, made himself a home there.

But who were the other witnesses? I hadn't seen any other familiar faces in the city that morning. Was he audacious enough to count himself?

The second thought I had was for the other poor bastards he had judged, convicted and sent off to their final rewards with less proof than he had against me. It made me look closer at the man standing there before me, and when I did, it wasn't pretty. I could see every dead man carved into the features of his face, as if each of us had taken a small piece from him and left him a little less whole.

This was a man who was so scared of death that he was bound and determined to put as many people as possible between it and himself. Maybe he thought they would cushion the fall. Maybe he thought if a seventeen-year-old boy could do it, it would give him a way to follow.

I looked at Reverend Caliber and saw a man so scared of living that he hid from himself, climbing back stairs to pay people to fall into strange beds, hold him and his secrets.

I stepped forward and, in doing so, landed dead center of the black square with its arcane message.

"Better you know a man, better you know his secrets," I said. "I know enough, I figure both of these men would scatter from the truth if it was to come their way. I give my word, I'll try my utmost not to do that. I will tell you my story, as fully as I'm able, and if you think it's of no value, you may decide this day to end me."

The you I was addressing wasn't you Gentleman Jack Delaney, and it wasn't Reverend Elijah Caliber. It was the crowd gathered there at the end of Main Street. I knew they were the key to me walking away or being carried off on a slab. They had the power—not Gentleman Jack—and the sooner I made him see it, the better.

CHAPTER TWENTY-ONE

Mobeetie existed in its own universe. There were colored slaves living there who had never been told they were free. Union soldiers in the jail who had never been told the war was over. Nobody just ever got around to it. That's the kind of place Mobeetie was. And it welcomed me with open arms. Indians were another matter. Unless they were there under the supervision of a white man, they weren't much tolerated, and they were eyed suspiciously even then.

I left the three rented rooms with six dead Blackfoot Indians stacked in them and moved to the other end of town, where I found accommodations much more to my liking. Greer Lusk and I took a two room place just over a livery stable, which was convenient. I had taken the best horse from the Indian party as a sort of peace offering to Greer. There wasn't a horse alive I would have traded for Roman. I was his as much as he was mine, and nothing was going to change that.

I also took a couple of keepsakes when I moved

to the new place. A Winchester rifle the Indian chief had carried that looked to be brand new and likely taken off a dead soldier anyway. A Colt Peacemaker that felt so good in my hand I couldn't find a way to put it down. And a lock of that damn Indian's hair. I didn't scalp him, though I wanted to. I'd never scalped anybody before, but I figured it was about like skinning a squirrel. Greer would have let me do it too, if I'd had more time and inclination. I kept a lock of the bastard's hair because I'd heard an Indian war fighter say, many years before, that if you cut a chunk out of their hair, they would walk around the Happy Hunting Ground forever, shamed and searching for it. That served him right, far as I was concerned.

I never heard any word about the dead Blackfoot Indians in the rented rooms. It's my belief they were scooped up and hauled outside of town where the trash was usually taken and burned. With that small problem taken care of, Greer and I decided we liked our new surroundings and quickly went about making a home.

There wasn't much peace at all in Mobeetie, but they did have a Justice of the Peace, an odd but likable fellow named Polidore Hews. Hews agreed to marry Greer and me. We jumped the sword, she became Greer Liquorish, and that small piece of happiness helped to console some of her sadness and calm her fears. Rarely would a week go by, though, without her waking me up shrieking about some unseen person in the house trying to steal her away. Usually it was one of them Indians, and I would make out like I was getting the Peacemaker and running them off, and it would, true to its word, restore peace for a little while. Other times, much rarer, the person coming for her would be Bricky himself, and those turned out to be trickier. I could only be patient, urging Bricky to return to the dark of her mind where she would eventually forget long enough to fall back into a slumber.

I decided to take a job digging holes for the undertaker, an old man named Grover Morrow. I needed the pay, and I was starting to think of my talents in a different way. Death didn't bother me none. If it was inevitable, I preferred it six foot down and well packed in to sharing retail space above ground. Of course, I'd shot those six Indians out of desperation. They asked for it, and that made all the difference. When they got it, I didn't feel a lick of remorse. If I had, I might have taken a different line of work.

"You got any kind of work here?" I said. "I don't have no misgivings being around dead folks."

I was dressed up and on my best behavior. It was one of the last chances to get anything, and, if I came up short, I'd either have to think about becoming a farmer or pulling up stakes. I didn't have what I thought of as a farmer's disposition, as I hated early mornings.

"Only people I hire on is gravediggers," Grover Morrow said, "and I got a man named Jolly does a fine job for me."

I didn't see any evidence of Jolly on the premises.

"Well, I don't see no Jolly, sir," I said, "but I'm here and ready to work."

I pointed out that I was well acquainted with Polidore Hews, and I had a new bride and a new home right there in Mobeetie. All of which got me nowhere. Morrow pointed to a door behind him, beyond which I could only imagine slabs and slabs of bodies awaiting their turns in the soil.

"No bodies, no holes," he said.

I found Joe Mack Jolly easy enough, living in a two room shack just a skip and a jump from Morrow's business. He seemed likeable enough. I didn't let on that I'd been asking for his job. Not exactly, anyway.

"I was talking to the undertaker," I said. "Says you're having trouble with the work."

Of course, he'd said no such thing. That didn't matter.

"Only trouble I have is when there ain't enough of it," he said.

We talked for a few minutes, and it became apparent he wasn't going to quit without a little motivation.

"I got me a new wife to support," I said.

He didn't congratulate me or wish me luck or anything. I'd finally had enough of the one-sided banter.

"I need your job," I said.

I raised up and plugged him one with the Side-hammer, right in his right ear. One was all it took. His life came blowing out the other side and splattered the wall next to him. I placed the gun in his hand, wrapped his dirt-stained fingers around it and rested it against the ear that was not there anymore. His mouth opened, but only a stream exited. His other ear heard nothing.

The next day, I came back to see Mr. Morrow about that job, and he had two different holes that needed digging. One was for an old woman who died of something he called "rising of the lights," a thing that sounded so scary, I had to will my feet to stay in position. Rising of what lights? Where exactly were they rising from? Did we all have them in us? How had I never heard of this? The other, he was pained to say, was for a young man by the name of Joe Mack Jolly. Seemed Joe Mack had grown despondent over putting so much death into the ground, took a pistola and wrote himself out of the script.

"I'm sure vexed to hear it," I said.

I was a little vexed to lose that Sidehammer, but it had to be done. That gun had got me through a little thick and a lot of thin. But I'd grown fond of the new Colt Peacemaker, and it represented a new beginning, same way Mobeetie did. I wasn't about to let Jolly get in the way of that. My first job for Grover Morrow was to dig a hole for the previous gravedigger. It was hard work, but I liked the fact that I didn't have anyone looking over my shoulder. I dug for a few hours in the morning, then I dug another one like it in the afternoon for the old lady with the lights and collected a dollar at the end of the day. Mobeetie was looking good enough that I soon put the cattle drive in the back of my mind for a while.

CHAPTER TWENTY-TWO

There was an element in that Fort Worth crowd who, true to Gentleman Jack's words, weren't happy to see a colored man strutting around the stage, trying to convince them that a white boy of seventeen years should be the next person to hang. The gallows was still new, having been built in the spring of '82, and Jack had christened it at the end of May, hanging a man known as Arkansas Pete for stealing three hogs from a farmer on the north side of town. The High Sheriff had given Arkansas Pete the choice between being tried in Fort Worth or being sent back to his hometown of Fort Smith for it. Jack said Pete was horrified at the thought of hanging in front of his mama and sisters, so he chose to die where he was.

I never had a thought toward indulging those elements in the audience on that morning. I didn't hold Jack's color against him any more than I did my own. If I was guilty of the things he said I had done, it wasn't because of my white skin. I had been too young to go off to the war, but if I had gone, I wouldn't have been shooting at those Yankee soldiers because I hated the black skin of the men, women and children in the South. I would've been shooting at them to keep them from shooting at me.

San Antonio had been a colorful city, filled with brown Mexicans and Spaniards and white and colored Texicans. Some of the coloreds were freed slaves, some had never known slavery at all. The colored people, like the Indians, weren't considered citizens. Some didn't even consider them people. But they walked mostly free and unencumbered among us, especially living in the District. I grew up with colored kids who were just one generation away from slavery in the cotton fields of East Texas. One girl named Ginny Hay was my best friend when I was of school age. Afraid to leave the district, Ginny Hay would walk me to the little one room school even though she wasn't allowed in, and sometimes she would be waiting to walk me back home. I thought nothing of it, and, many years later, she would sometimes cross my mind while laying in the arms of someone like Sunny.

"Who gave you the power to try a white boy like this?"

The loudest of a group of men shouted out during a brief pause, and it hung there in front of us. I was as curious as anybody to see if Jack would address it or just act like he hadn't heard it when everyone knew he had. He tried for the second option first.

"This man left Mobeetie with a small band of

men, none of whom could be called experienced cattle drivers," he said. "And it was a small drive, as cattle drives go. Eight hundred head might be a lot for you or me, but we see two, three thousand head drives come through here. Thank God Wilkie John Liquorman wasn't foolish enough, or destructive enough, to take on more than eight hundred."

Reverend Caliber was stepping up to attack this line of thought when the man in the crowd repeated himself. Louder this time, in case anyone thought we hadn't heard.

"Heard you twice the first time, my friend," Gentleman Jack said.

He looked to the Reverend and asked permission to address the question. I was interested in hearing the list of his credentials myself, even if I got an uneasy feeling from the group of men who brought it up. There were plenty of stories of trials breaking out into fisticuffs and then much worse. While such a scene might be good cover for a getaway, I was now perched over a trapdoor with my hands tied in front of me and a noose draped loosely over my head. Not the best place to be if hell did break out.

"I had an agreement with your late High Sheriff to try criminals and execute justice here in this fine city, but I am free to work with or without express consent," Jack said. "I am a bounty hunter, and, as such, I am a full and legal member of United States law enforcement. The Courts have spoken and said so."

I didn't have a clue about courts. It all sounded about as real as castles and kingdoms to me, but it sounded impressive enough. The man in the crowd wasn't ready to let go of his case though.

"I'm not sure the Courts knew they were speaking of a colored man bounty hunter."

The Reverend grinned like a big daddy cat watching a smaller cat play with a baby bird. Gentleman Jack kept his cool. I'm unsure if I would have.

"I was raised by my mother, Babet Delaney, sir. I never knew who my father was. I only know he was a white man. May I ask where your father was and what he was doing in the months before I was born?"

There was a divide between the people who got what he was saying and the ones who were standing there scratching their heads, and it wasn't hard to see. I was happy to see the idiot who posed the question scratching his head and trying to make out whether half the crowd was laughing at him. I was less happy to see Reverend Caliber with a similar expression.

I liked the way Delaney handled the guy, because, when you peeled it back and looked, he wasn't really even attacking the man. He was suggesting that they could be related. And I could appreciate that. It was what had attracted me to the Jackrabbit in the first place, when I followed him through these same streets on his daily rounds. Maybe I had been the idiot then, not seeing that this same man would quite possibly be my end. Then again, maybe I was the idiot now, standing on this trapdoor to the great void and laughing with this colored man as he gently thumped his white brother on the chest.

CHAPTER TWENTY-THREE

The carnival came to Mobeetie in 1881, if only because it was close enough to Amarillo to make the stopover worth it. We didn't attend on the first night. The next day, everyone was talking about it. Even Grover Morrow who never did anything said it was the best time he'd had since he buried his ex-wife.

"Greer, let's go out to the carnival tonight," I said.

Big crowds made Greer nervous, and she wasn't sold on the idea.

Second night was one I'd have to live a thousand years to forget. There was a sky full of stars over Mobeetie, and they all seemed to shine on Greer. I paid out two cents to have a go at some wooden chickens on the arcade and sent them flying in all directions. The prize was a book of paper dolls and costumes, but the boy working the booth let us trade for a gold coin that at least looked to be of some value. Greer liked American coins, so I told her she could keep it.

Horse racing and bicycle racing were both featured at the carnival and eagerly taken to heart by the people of Mobeetie, who found them to be great opportunities for gambling. For three nights, money changed hands like a burning coal, good luck and bad wrestling this way and then that, until the fun and games had to pack up and move on to bigger places. That's when the powers in Mobeetie decided to keep the horse racing going.

It took a little time and a lot of convincing by my friend Polidore, but on a cold autumn night when Greer couldn't be bothered with going out, we set Roman and me up in one of the races. For once, lack of size was to my benefit. We won our first race by seven lengths. There was no stopping then. We won the second race by ten lengths, and suddenly everyone was lining up to have a chance against us. The next night they brought in what everyone claimed to be the fastest horse in all the surrounding territory, and we won by half a length. I felt bad after that, like I'd pushed Roman far enough. I pocketed more money than I made in a month of grave digging and walked away.

My good luck on the horse track meant I was able to relax when grave digging jobs slowed down for a spell. I took a small job selling farming and ranching equipment in a store connected to the livery stable as well. Convenient, of course, because it was right beneath our home. I proved to be ill-fitted for such employment though. On the second day there, an old rancher came into the store and walked up to me.

"I need to buy a calf weaner," he said.

I did a double-take, thinking he was trying to make sport of me. He looked completely serious.

"What was that?"

He hitched up his trousers and stood his ground.

"It was a calf weaner. I need a calf weaner."

Well, I didn't know any better than to laugh at the old man. I couldn't see any way clear on his odd request, so I gave him my best shot in return.

"We don't sell calves, either with or without their weiners," I said.

He looked at me like I was crazy. There wasn't a trace of humor anywhere on his person.

"Son, where in the hell did they find you at?" he said. "A calf weaner is a contraption that weans the calf from suckling on the mama cow's tit."

I don't know what it was that struck me so funny, but the more I laughed, the harder it was to stop. If I looked away, I laughed to be rid of him in my sight, and if I glanced back, I laughed all the harder. I heed and I hawed at the man until I was leaning over with my hands on my knees, trying to think of things sorry enough to make me regain some sense of solemnity.

"You keep right on laughing all you want, but I don't much care for the joke," he said. "I expect your boss won't like knowing it either."

My boss was out for the afternoon, tackling chores that needed doing. It was the main reason he'd given me the job in the first place. I opened a door in the back of the counter and looked into it, making out like I was looking for something that might be a calf weaner. As if I had the faintest idea what such a contraption might look like. I shut the door and moved to the side, opening the one next to it. I took a deep breath.

"I really don't like it when people call me son," I said.

I moved to the third door. From the expression on the old man's face, he didn't seem to care what I liked or didn't like. The Peacemaker was waiting for me inside that third door, and by that time, it was itching to be used. I pulled it up and stuck it right in the rancher's unlaughing face.

"Here's what I think about your calf weaner," I said.

I shot him one time. That's all it took. I stood there for a minute to make sure, but he died so quick and easy, it made me think he must have already been close and ready for it. I pulled him through the back of the store and out the back, where the staircase climbed to our little home above. I didn't take anything off of him except a little .41 caliber derringer I thought Greer might be fond of. She said later that she heard the gunshot and stopped and listened, but, when there wasn't another following, decided it must have been something less foreboding. I never did give her the derringer.

I quit the job there in the farming equipment store soon after, explaining that the grave digging job had gotten busier and I just didn't know enough about the ins and outs of farming and ranching. That was no lie. I had to bury the rancher two days later, and soon enough, all manner of folks were dying again in Mobeetie. The farming equipment business rises and falls with the seasons and with the quirks of nature. Death doesn't get eaten up by swarms of locusts, and it never goes out of season. I decided I had a lot more to offer in that line of business, and I went to work proving it.

Not to say death was my only line of business. Greer and I lived not a quarter mile from the sawmill. Even though I'd never done a stitch of work at the mill at Fort Griffin, it was enough to get me on a shift with the big saw. I ran that thing for half a day and dreamed of it half the night. On several mornings, I woke up for work and counted my fingers and toes. When it wasn't them getting chewed to pieces under that rusty blade, it was an unfortunate co-worker or a boss who had pushed me too far. Alas, they were only dreams, although they did their best to warn me of what lay ahead. On a cold but unremarkable Wednesday morning, the governor on the steam engine broke and the thing overheated, spewing pieces high into the sky, punching through metal and drilling deep into wood and narrowly missing my head. One metal rod punched straight into the head of a worker named Gus, who sat there for half an hour talking to us and then fell limp.

He lived not only to tell the tale but to report back to work the next Monday, but his head of black hair turned white as snow almost overnight. I took it for a warning and quit the next morning. I never even took my final pay.

Things were good for us there for a while, and we might have made a boring little couple there in Mobeetie. She learned to make brooms, which were then sold in the store downstairs, and I continued

with my gravedigging. On a cool spring morning,
she took me aside with promises of good news. I
remember hoping she'd found a new place for us
to live.

"We have a new member of the family joining us."

I stood there and waited for the rest of the news.
A brother of Bricky or a long lost uncle following
the mad trail across the south into oblivion.

"We don't really have the room here for more,"
I said.

She didn't get cross at my lack of insight.

"I don't think they'll take up much room, Wilkie,"
she said.

She had to look down at her slim belly and
make a few faces.

"Oh," I said.

I tried to think of more, but a silent stillness
seemed preferable to anything I knew how to say. I
felt unlike I'd ever felt before or since, which is as
it should be.

"You're happy?" Greer said.

I nodded my head against hers. It was all I dared
to do. You didn't dare say you were happy. That
was challenging the fates. It was enough to feel the
way we felt in that moment and contemplate what
the future might be bringing.

CHAPTER TWENTY-FOUR

Gentleman Jack wanted to take everybody back to the beginning of the cattle drive, so we all convened in the big muddy middle of Mobeetie. This was all a mental exercise, of course, so I'm not sure if everyone else pictured Mobeetie the way it was on that July morning when Ira Lee came to town with Simeon Payne, Leon Thaw, and William Gee, looking for a couple more people to move eight hundred head of cattle to Fort Worth and then north to Kansas City.

"There's a straight shoot from here to Dodge," I said. "Why would you go all the way down to Fort Worth?"

It seemed like a harebrained idea to begin with. Almost all cattle drives took what they called the Jones and Plummer trail to Dodge City. They could sell their cattle there for a good profit. It was easy. It was a straight shot.

"We're meeting up with a bunch of other boys down there. They got almost two thousand more. They said if we could join them and do most of the work between there and Kansas City, they'd split the money."

I could see the attraction in it. I also knew twenty-eight hundred head of cattle was going to be a handful for five of us, if we were pulling most of the weight.

"You really think five of us can pull it off?" I said.

I didn't know any of the other guys from Adam, and I didn't hardly know Ira Lee. He was taller and skinnier than when I'd last seen him, and he moved like a marionette come to life. No strings attached. I didn't much like the looks of the Leon Thaw character. He was driving the coach and didn't show any aspiration for climbing down off of it. He seemed to like looking down on us.

"We expect we'll need one or two more," Ira Lee said. "Unless you know your way around a bowl of beans, a good cook would come in mighty handy."

I immediately thought of my old friend Jacobo. If he was available, I might be talked into it.

"I know a good cook named Jacobo."

I didn't have high hopes for seeing him again. Last I'd seen him, he was peeling potatoes at Fort Griffin and looking pretty happy about it.

"Jacobo Robles?" Leon Thaw said.

I'd forgotten he was even a part of the conversation. And I had no idea if he was Jacobo Robles. I knew him as Jacobo.

"He cook beans for the king and queen of Mexico?" I said.

Leon said he didn't reckon that he did and resumed his silence.

"Cooked beans for the king, and the king let

him go," Simeon Payne said. "I've crossed paths with him."

The Army, trying to push cattle ranchers farther across Texas and the Indians into the territory to the north, had moved Jacobo and about half the Fort Griffin soldiers to Fort Eliot just outside Mobeetie. As a result, Jacobo, who was indeed Jacobo Robles, was peeling potatoes less than five miles from where we were standing.

Ira Lee and his boys camped out at Mobeetie for three days. Ira Lee lost half of his money betting on horse races, and Leon Thaw slept all three nights on the coach, never climbing down to do anything other than visit the latrine and get food from Old Vick's restaurant.

On the third day, the boy named William Gee showed up at the undertaker's office. He had somebody in tow, and I recognized him before I could even identify his face.

"Jacobo," I said. "They talked you into going on this fool's errand?"

He seemed happy to see me. Maybe even excited to be hitting the trail. It was good to see him, and it was good to see Ira Lee too. Good enough that it made me feel alright about casting my lot with them.

"But you've got a good job with Mr. Morrow," Greer said later that night.

What she didn't know was, I was running out of people to bury. I needed some new blood in town. New blood that wasn't my older brother or Jacobo. And, more important, with a child on the way, we would need good money. Money to buy a home of our own.

"It won't take long," I said. "I'll go as far as Fort Worth, and if it ain't going well, I'll collect my pay and come back. If everything's going okay, I'll go on to Kansas. I come back, we'll have enough to buy a piece of land and build a place."

Part of me really wanted to do that. Get some land and some horses, maybe do some black-smithing. Make an honest living and maybe raise up a handful of little buckaroos. Another part of me wanted to shin out and not look back. I liked Greer Liquorish too much to hang around and mess up her life, I sometimes told myself. What kind of father would I be? I had never known one.

At the same time, I needed what she gave me too much to ride away for good. Did I love her? I know I loved being around her. At least most of the time. There were times she got moody and spilled out a terrible hurt on me. First by insinuation and then, as days went by, more directly and more often. She sometimes seemed to blame me for the deaths of her family, as if I had sent them all out into Indian country with insufficient protection. As if, had I been there, things would have turned out differently. I liked to think there might have been some truth in that, but I didn't dare put voice to it.

Two nights before we headed out, I gave Greer my Peacemaker. I thought there might be some-thing poetic in that. I kept the little .41 derringer. It was deadly enough when it needed to be—one like it had been used to kill Lincoln—but it was a single shot. As backup, I had the Whitworth. I wasn't entirely happy with what I had, but me and Roman would surely luck into something better down the trail. Maybe in Fort Worth, maybe in Kansas City.

When we left out at first light, Leon Thaw was cold and silent as his name. Will Gee and Simeon Payne were laughing like two explorers off to discover a Great Unknown. Jacobo was in the back, pulling a wagon with enough meat, beans, corn, and potatoes to get us all the way across Texas. And me and Ira Lee were as miserable as a rainy fourth of July, for reasons neither of us were able to vocalize. I felt like I was leaving something important behind in Mobeetie. Like I was giving up on something. It wasn't Greer. For all I knew, we would soon be back together and buying that plot of land on the edge of town. It was more like an idea of something. Something in my gut. I was trying my best not to listen to it, but it was there, gnawing away at me all the same. This is a part of the story that I hadn't told. Now I will tell it as it happened.

CHAPTER TWENTY-FIVE

Something happened to me and Ira Lee on the night before we left Mobeetie on the cattle drive. We didn't talk about it the next day. We never spoke about it again. I never discussed it with anyone else either until I told Sunny, the night before my hanging.

We'd started the night in a bar called the Owl's Nest. Named that for good cause, it had been converted from an old barn and came with a free family of owls in the rafters. They had since moved on, but the regulars there could all remember when you had to drink your whiskey with one hand over the glass, just to make sure there wasn't anything added from above. The Owl's Nest served only whiskey, but their lack of menu didn't hurt business. They were so packed in that we soon moved on to Gin Lee. I was old enough to drink in any bar in Mobeetie, long as it was kept inside the walls, but Gin Lee pushed the point. They had a kid who was always sipping a beer at the table next to the kitchen, and he couldn't have been any

more than ten. Some said he was the kitchen help's
boy. Some said he came to town by himself and
lived in the bar. Whatever the case, he enjoyed his
drink considerably more than I did, which was the
cause of some consternation with me.

Ira Lee was playing fifteen ball with some galoot
who'd just come to town from back east, and I was
raising my beer to my lip and blowing softly across
the suds, hoping nobody noticed that the level in
my glass wasn't changing. A sheriff came slamming
into the bar, almost knocking the door off its hinges
and commanding everybody's immediate attention.
He wasn't the Mobeetie sheriff. He'd come all the
way from Amarillo to see us.

"Anybody in here know a man by the name of
Henry John Liquorish?"

It was a name I had seldom heard, except in
hushed tones around the house. If I had been
drinking, I would have doubted my own ears.

"Ira Lee," I said.

Ira was standing at full attention, his cue at his
side.

"Henry John Liquorish?" he said.

"From New Orleans, maybe," the sheriff said.
"Least that's what his papers would indicate. If
anyone here knows this man, I would like to hand
him over into your care, so I can be about my
business."

There was a moment that hung in time there
in Gin Lee where I was, for the first time in my life,
a father's son. All of history was rewritten. I felt
drunk.

"I'll take him," Ira Lee said, and the next thing I
know, we were pouring ourselves out into the night

to take Henry John Liquorish of New Orleans off the hands of the Amarillo Sheriff's Department. The sheriff pulled an envelope from his pocket and pushed it into my hands. On it was printed the name Henry John Liquorish—spelled just the way it should have been—and a New Orleans address. The envelope was empty.

"He's right down yonder," the sheriff said.

He pointed at a body lying on the ground about fifty yards away. He wasn't moving.

"He dead?" I said.

Had the sheriff come to ask us to take a dead man off his hands? It was a fact that Henry John's body had never been recovered. It was always assumed by Ira Lee and me that the Comanches had taken care of that. They were known for burning and generally laying waste to whatever and whoever they encountered.

"No, but he sure may wish he was when he wakes up in the morning," the sheriff said.

He said the man had been found lying in the middle of the road halfway between Mobeetie and Wheeler and seemed to be crawling in this direction. The sheriff had been on his way back from Wheeler, where he'd chased down a bank robber trying to sneak away into Indian Territory. He hadn't caught the robber, but he'd found our guy instead. He seemed happy to get rid of him.

We walked down the way to where the man lay face up. He didn't look like anything I was expecting or hoping to see. He was relatively young. Not much older than Ira Lee.

"Well, that ain't daddy," Ira Lee said.

I kicked at him to see if he'd respond. You could

see he was breathing, but, other than that, he didn't look too lively.

"Reckon this belonged to dad?" I said.

I held the envelope out.

This strange new Henry John Liquorish began to squirm there on the ground, and I leaned down over him. He didn't appear to have been attacked or injured in any way. You could smell the liquor radiating from him though. If it was giving me a sick feeling, I could imagine what it was doing to him.

"Your name is Henry John Liquorish?" Ira Lee said.

He groaned something unintelligible and rolled sideways in the dirt. He didn't seem to hear Ira Lee or even know that he was there.

"Maybe we should go get the doc," I said.

I knew Doc Pacheco through Grover Morrow of course. When Doc wasn't successful at his job, Grover moved in with his. It was a team effort, and everyone pitched in. We knew where the good doctor was because we had seen him just an hour or so earlier, propping up the bar in the Owl's Nest. Ira Lee said he wasn't sure what Pacheco could do for our inanimate friend that a few hours' sleep wouldn't do as well.

I wasn't too eager to send him off with anybody else anyway. I wanted him close by, so I could keep my eye on him. By that time, I was convinced that this man had come looking for us. What other reason for him to be crawling from Wheeler in the night? How had he known we were in Mobeetie? If so, who told him? What was his connection to us? What did he want?

"Think he's really Henry John Liquorish?" I said.

It wasn't another way of asking if he was dad. Anyone could see he wasn't. Still, he either had an envelope with dad's name—and a long-ago New Orleans address—scribbled on it, or the two of them shared a name, spelling and all.

"Well, he damn sure ain't daddy," Ira Lee said. "Reckon he could be a cousin."

We were circling around him, trying to find a place to light.

"Could be he's our brother," I said.

I picked him up by the boots and Ira Lee got him under each arm, and we toted him to the livery stable. I knew better than to bring him up the stairs to Greer. We pulled his boots off and put him to bed against a hay bale, with a horse blanket draped over him for warmth.

"We'll check on him in the morning," Ira Lee said to him.

He was in a hurry to get back to his glass of whiskey, and I was equally anxious to get upstairs to bed. It would be my last night with Greer for quite a spell, and I knew where I needed to be. I didn't mention him to Greer, as she wasn't fond of drunks passing out downstairs in the livery stable, but, try as I might, Henry John, or whoever he was, stayed pretty close in my mind that last night in Mobeetie.

My bet was that dad had come into some kind of money from the government or something, and this man had been sent to find us and give us our reward. That seemed the most logical explanation for everything. Then, I wondered if he might be some long lost brother, come to hunt down family. Maybe he would even join us on the cattle drive.

Greer didn't know what I was thinking, but she could tell my mind was elsewhere. She wasn't happy.

"All you can think about is your God-forsaken cattle drive," she said.

I tried to convince her otherwise.

"No, dear, I'm just preoccupied with thoughts of leaving you here with the baby." There was a lot of truth in that, but she didn't buy it. She almost kicked me out of our little upstairs apartment. In a way, I almost wish she had. She was mad, and so we slept back to back when I might have gone down and shared a blanket with the man downstairs. I almost wish I had because in the morning, when I slipped down the stairs to check on him, he was gone. Horse blanket and all. Ira Lee blamed me for letting him escape, but I reminded him that the man wasn't a prisoner. If he had been that concerned with it, he'd have tied him to a post on the night before instead of rushing back to the Gin Lee.

We checked at Doc Pacheco's on our way out of town, and we even stopped by the jail, but young Henry John Liquorish was nowhere to be found. Another ghost along the way, in and out of my life too soon. Me and Ira Lee never discussed him again. Over time, he mostly slipped from my mind, making an appearance only on occasions when I would stop to wonder where he might have gone off to and if he was still crawling around out there somewhere, looking for me.

CHAPTER TWENTY-SIX

It was a seven-day trip from Mobeetie to Wichita Falls, and then another four or five to get into Fort Worth. That's if you're pushing along eight hundred head of cattle, which ends up looking like a lot more than you might think. I'd been told of enough two- and three-thousand-head cattle drives that I'd convinced myself eight hundred head of cattle would go relatively smooth. There might be trouble when we took on the other two thousand in Fort Worth, but we'd be good as gold until then.

It didn't take long to rob me of that notion.

The first two days were fairly uneventful, even if we were running behind schedule by the third. We were all falling into our roles. Thankfully, it didn't matter how we got along. The biggest part of the day, we were far enough apart that we had to shout to be heard. Ira Lee was the trail boss. He had put the whole thing together, knew both ranchers whose stock we were moving. He also put the team together and gave each of us our assignment. Simeon Payne was one of the points. I was the other. My main job was keeping the bell cow going in the right direction. Simeon made sure the others didn't straggle too far off the path. William Gee and Ira were riding left and right flank, Ira back behind me a ways and keeping the herd moving along. Last, Leon Thaw was riding drag. While it was unusual to have a coach driver riding drag, it served a dual purpose in our case. First, Thaw was able to bring Jacobo's supplies, which would come in handy when we made the turn for Kansas. It would be a long stretch, and to have Thaw there gave us an advantage with both food and any other supplies we picked up in Fort Worth. As important, as I found out, Thaw knew the way. He had been born and bred in Kansas City and knew the trail in addition to knowing the market-place once we arrived. So Jacobo rode alongside Thaw most of the time, although he didn't like the way Thaw would look at him and so sometimes moved up and rode between me and Simeon.

Jacobo purchased most of his supplies in Mobeetie after talking with Ira Lee and Simeon. Ira Lee, being the trail boss, negotiated pay for his services, and I never knew what it was. I did know he was paying me more than he paid Simeon, because he told me the first night in Mobeetie.

"Little brother, I'll pay you thirty dollars," he said. "You're gonna have to keep it under your hat, because Payne is only getting twenty-six."

He wasn't making the offer out of generosity or blood bonds. He'd made an initial offer of twenty five, and I'd turned him down. I had made fifteen riding Roman around a mud track a few times. Twenty five seemed lacking.

"You paying that other joker twenty-six and all you can cut your brother in for is twenty-five?" I said.

I might have been able to get thirty-one or two out of him, but I knew the going rate. I was fine with thirty on a couple conditions. One, I wanted the first payment when we reached Fort Worth. It wasn't me wanting money to blow on booze and hookers in Hell's Half Acre. The reasoning was simple. If I wasn't feeling good about things, if any of the guys were causing doubts or frustrations, I was taking my pay and heading back home. I told Ira Lee as much, and the second condition was that I would be able to walk away with no hard feelings. Now, what I didn't tell Ira Lee, but what I thought was eating at me, was this. If I was missing Greer, I was gone when we got to Fort Worth. I believed that was more than a little possible, hookers and all.

What I feared more than anything was Simeon Payne. Not that I feared him in any kind of real sense. I could just see that he had a problem keeping his big bazoo shut, and I didn't tolerate a lot of talk. I would get along fine with Leon Thaw, who still hadn't uttered a complete sentence to me.

It was that third day, with us already dragging behind and having issues keeping some of the cows from straggling behind, that Simeon Payne started getting on my nerves.

"Need to keep that bell cow moving along," he said. "Your left flank is about to run her over."

Of course, he was talking to me, even if he never called me by name. I don't think he knew my name or cared to learn it. But he was convinced that I was slowing us down, no matter that the right flank had been falling back and we were having trouble with stragglers, whose responsibility fell on either Thaw or Ira Lee, since he was trail boss.

"Take it up with Ira Lee," I said.

What I was trying to get across was, there was a boss and it wasn't Simeon Payne. I dismissed him and thought no more of it. When we broke for dinner that evening, just as the sun was starting to touch the western horizon, Ira Lee came to me.

"I'm going to switch out with you, little brother, at least until we get to Fort Worth."

Besides being a few years older, he was also a head taller, but I outweighed him and could take him in any fair fight. I almost got to prove it. Funny enough, it was Leon Thaw was stepped in.

"Payne's trying to get there tomorrow. It's still three or four days off."

Ira Lee looked at him like even he had never heard him put two sentences together before.

"We let 'em go at their own speed, the herd ain't no longer a herd. It's just a bunch of cows walking in the general direction of Fort Worth."

I had to admit, Ira Lee could sound smart. Jacobo laughed at what he was hearing. I figured it might be a good time to bring up my issue with the way things were going.

"Payne's trying to tell me the bell cow's moving too slow," I said. "If I speed up, I won't even have Jacobo's wagon in my sights."

I was hoping Ira Lee would have forgotten about his decision to switch me over to the right flank. My hopes were dashed.

"We're like a damn accordion, pulling apart and pushing back together across the trail. I'll run point and keep the bell moving. Wilkie John, you pull back and ride swing on the right side. Help Simeon keep everything running and, if you need to, pull back and help Willie."

After a plate or two of beef jerky and beans, there came a fitful night of sleep and staring up at a skyful of far away promises, us taking turns to keep the fire burning and the coyotes at bay. In the morning, we got up and went to work. Ira Lee had the final say, and that's the way we done it. Unfortunately, for all Ira Lee's bossing, that's where it all started going to hell.

CHAPTER TWENTY-SEVEN

Gentleman Jack looked good on the stage, even from a distance, in his dark blue frock coat and red hat, but I noticed it was missing its feather. I had a work shirt and a sack coat, no hat and little of Jack's way with a crowd. Reverend Caliber wasn't half bad. He certainly knew how to work a congregation up, but this was no normal congregation he was facing on this not-so-good Friday. Most of them weren't churchgoers. Most weren't believers in anything except their own hard work. I may not have been as book smart as Jack and Elijah were, but I think I grasped that one truth a long time before they did. The folks out there in the street were a lot more like me than either of them.

"So when you look at this young man," Jack said, "you may not believe what you're seeing, but hear me out. This is the face of a murderer, because he did rise up against the very men he was working with, and then he proceeded to visit his death and destruction on the innocent people of Wichita Falls."

The Reverend had his arms folded and was shaking his head side to side. Several people in the street were watching him with some amusement. Maybe it was the heat, but I felt like my knees were going to buckle and kept trying to reposition myself against falling flat out on the stage between them.

"But let me back up a bit," Jack continued. "This all started when the cook on the cattle drive, a Mexican named Jacobo Robles, came down with a bad case of food poisoning. Halfway through the trip into our fair city, he got extremely ill. From what I can tell from Simeon Payne, who luckily managed to survive this horrific ordeal, the cattle drive was already in deep peril. Our young murderer here had already been reprimanded for slowing the drive down. Had even been taken from his post at the head of the drive and put in a less crucial one. It seems the men in charge were already trying to keep this murderer in check. All their foresight was to be of no avail."

Now it was me who was shaking his head. And me who was thinking I should have killed Simeon Payne, if I was half the murderer they claimed me for.

"I don't think the facts bear out this little flight of fancy at all," Reverend Caliber said.

I'm not sure half the people even understood what either one of them was saying.

"According to Simeon Payne, a man who has no bad history following him, the cattle drive's cook got sick very quickly outside Wichita Falls," Gentleman Jack said. "The drive continued, he says, but it was forced to stop at several points to contend

with this illness. Finally, both Ira Lee Liquorish and
Mr. Payne suggested that you and the cook take
some cattle into town, sell them, and call for a
doctor to attend to Mr. Robles."

He then walked over to me.

"The rest of them would wait outside of town,
settle in for the night, and move on toward Fort
Worth in the morning.

"Is this fairly close to the way you recall it, Wilkie
John Liquorman?"

He knew what he was doing. Unfortunately, I
didn't quite catch on.

"Liquorish," I said. "And Jacobo had already
died by the time I went into town."

He cupped his ear and leaned in.

"What was that?"

"Jacobo was dead," I said. "And my name is
Liquorish, not Liquorman."

I knew I had fallen into a trap before I ever
heard it close around me.

"But Liquorman—isn't that the name you used
when you were jailed in Mobeetie just a few years
ago," he said.

The snap was quick and clean, and, like that of
any good trap, mostly of my own making. I looked
down into the crowd, and they were still looking
back, but they were seeing me different now. I
could see it. I was trouble visited upon Fort Worth.

CHAPTER TWENTY-EIGHT

On that fourth day, Jacobo woke up with the chills. That might have put Leon Thaw in a bad mood if there had been a way to tell. But even mornings in July were a long way from cold, so everyone knew it was something serious. And where usually you would point the finger at the cook, we all felt bad about blaming him for his own sufferings, so we played it off.

"It'll pass by noon," Ira Lee said.

"Lie down inside the coach and try to sleep it off," I said.

"Those beans are too good to do you that way," said William Gee.

All of our expert opinions were for naught as we lurched to stop after stop along the north Texas landscape, looking for a tree or at least a cactus for Jacobo to crawl behind. And then William Gee started to feel it.

"Your mind is playing tricks on you, because of Jacobo," Ira Lee said.

"Just make it to Fort Worth and we can stop for a day or two," I said.

"I'm telling you, it can't be those beans," said William Gee.

Jacobo thought it was a case of bad chili, and he had me and William dig a hole to bury it in halfway between Mobeetie and Wichita Falls. We held onto the beans and the meat. It was still enough to get us to Fort Worth. Through it all, Leon Thaw didn't say anything, but his expression said plenty. Finally, I started suggesting that, if we could make it to Wichita Falls, we would look for a doctor. By the time we were getting close, the first few cows were starting to get sick. It moved swift and silent like a wolf through the herd. The first of the livestock went down before noon that day. By noon, there were half a dozen.

"We've got to separate the herd," Ira Lee said. "We know the bunch up front and to the right of the bell cow have all the symptoms. I need a couple of us to break off and pull the infected ones as far from the rest as possible."

I drew the short straw and took William with me. For all the trouble we'd had keeping the drive together, once we started culling the sick ones, we found it difficult to keep them separated. For the most part, cattle like staying together, and they weren't inclined to separate from the main part of the drive.

"It's like they know what's coming," I said.

William Gee reminded me of myself, maybe because he'd done most of his growing in San Antone, and I found him easy to talk to, even if he was a little green.

He laughed, and I could tell by the way it came out that they knew more about what was coming than he did.

"I don't have a whole lot of shells," I said, "but I can get more once we get to Fort Worth."

My gun was better for the job than his. I was better for the job than he. So William Gee wrestled the already-dying cows and the sick cows and the seems-like-they're-getting-sick cows and the they've-been-hanging-around-close-to-the-sick cows into an area between a bend in the Wichita River and a patch of undergrowth that narrowed into a piece of bottomland about an acre across, and I loaded the rifle and went to work.

I don't have much compunction with shooting livestock. They're raised for food or for hide anyway. But when you have to put that many down, and you aren't able to use the meat, it's not a satisfactory feeling. The buzzards were already circling, waiting for us to clear the area, by the time I worked my way through. When I finished, I looked around to find Gee upchucking into the undergrowth.

"I must have a touch of whatever's going around," he said.

He looked a little peaked.

"You'd best hope not," I said, "or I might have to put you down next."

I was only half joking. Maybe not that much. I was beginning to suspect we had something bigger on our hands. Something that had stricken the herd and the drovers alike. I knew it happened. The only positive I could see in it, it probably meant Jacobo hadn't poisoned himself. The negatives were too enormous to contemplate.

I rejoined the main part of the drive within a couple hours, and things hadn't gotten better there. Ira Lee had stopped just a couple miles outside of town, downstream along the Wichita River, and was trying to replenish our stock of water.

"We've been drinking water, trying to clean whatever it is out of our system," he said. "I was watching the cattle drinking right down from us, and it hit me."

Ira Lee didn't look good, but I didn't dare mention it. I was trying to make it be the pressure of the drive or maybe the lack of sleep the previous night.

"I've heard of cow-pox," Simeon Payne said. "Ain't never seen it."

The best part of taking the sick cows off from the drive had been having a few hours without Payne. I wanted to tell him that never in my life had I met a man so of a piece with his own name.

"It's not cow-pox," I said.

I had no way of knowing such a thing, but I had already seen Ira Lee shaking his head no, and so felt fairly secure in shooting the idea down.

"No, it ain't cow-pox, and it ain't bad chili," Ira Lee said. "I'm fairly sure we've got red water disease. And the worst thing I can tell you, I'm seeing it in a few of the head here."

Red water disease didn't sound all that mean and menacing. The red part sounded a little bloody though, which was a bit unsettling.

"How bad is that?" I said.

Usually, when a disease struck animals and man in the same swipe, it wasn't anything to laugh at. Still, at that point, my concern wasn't for myself or

anyone else as much as it was for my friend Jacobo.
Jacobo was wrapped up in two quilts and sweating
like a pig on a spit, but Ira Lee said if I came to his
rescue, he would stop sweating the poison out of
himself and would quickly make a die of it.

From time to time, he would come to himself
and talk perfect sense, even if it was uncomfortable
to listen to. He said he could hear a mariachi band
playing in the sky at one point, which even spooked
Leon Thaw, who climbed down from his perch on
the wagon and took a long walk to stretch his legs.
Later, Jacobo started talking to me in Spanish, and
I couldn't be sure of what he was saying, but the
words *familia* and *Méjico* came up a lot, so I knew
he was wanting to go home.

During this time, Ira Lee and Simeon came up
with a plan. We would push on for Wichita Falls.
If Jacobo wasn't better by the time we reached
town, I would take him and ride in with a small se-
lection of our best cattle and try to sell them for
medicine and clean food. That might have been a
workable plan. I've wondered what might have
happened if I had been able to fulfill it. Instead, in
the hour between coming up with it and getting
the cattle together, Jacobo fell into a deep sleep.
When it came time to move out, I couldn't stir
him. He died there in the dirt, peaceful but maybe
too peaceful. No one there to know that he had
once cooked for kings and queens, that his cooking had once saved his life. Nothing we did could
save it this time, and I buried him in a shallow
grave next to Wichita River. It wasn't the Rio
Grande. He would never see his Mexico again, and

I wondered if his *familia* would ever hear of the manner or location of his death.

I didn't have time for much contemplation. I had to get into town and see if I could do something to keep the rest of us from following in Jacobo Robles's dying footsteps. I still had enough hope to think maybe we would find help, that we would find an end to our troubles in Wichita Falls.

CHAPTER TWENTY-NINE

Reverend Caliber didn't believe in hanging anybody. His reasons were complicated, but they centered on an undying belief in the ability of God to turn any man around and to use him, even if the man didn't believe in God or himself or anything else.

"Wilkie John," he said, "I believe God will use a fool to teach a wise man. You understand what I'm saying?"

He already knew I didn't put any stock in what he was yacking about, and I'd made it clear it was only my neck that needed saving and not my soul.

"I think you're calling me a fool," I said.

This conversation was being had on the gallows, during a five minute break to allow Gentleman Jack, the Reverend and I to empty our bladders and take a drink of our preferred beverage. I'd just knocked back a beer. I didn't much care for it, but I hoped it might take the edge off my nerves. The Reverend had surreptitiously been delivered a vodka that appeared as water to anyone who didn't know better.

"I'm saying one man's fool is another man's sage. And that you are here to accomplish something that nobody sees coming, that nobody has ever seen.

It still seemed like he was calling me a fool, but I knew what he was trying to say. That we were going to turn this thing around on Jack Delaney in a way he wouldn't see coming. Not until it was right on top of him and running him over. I wanted to believe. I truly did.

Five minutes came and then six and seven, all with no sight of Gentleman Jack.

"The Gentleman Mr. Delaney seems to have gotten himself trapped inside the earth closet," Reverend Caliber said.

I wasn't sure what an earth closet was, and the look on my face must have said so.

"The privy," he said.

A few men close to the stage got plum tickled over our conversation and began to roll off all their favorite names for doing one's business in the latrine. One old cowboy said his father had always called it cutting off a monkey's tail. His friend answered that his father had referred to it as lengthening your spine. It provided a few moments of levity while we waited and, in spite of and maybe because of the gravity of the situation, gave us all a good laugh at Gentleman Jack's expense when someone said they saw him coming. Before that happened, though, Reverend Caliber did pull me aside and whisper in my ear.

"Jack's gone. What you say, we kind of just mosey on outta here?"

Now the good Reverend said what he said, but I saw him look around and check out the stairs for a back exit first.

"I was thinking about it," I said. "This crowd would probably string both of us up."

There was a slow murmur through the crowd, and then the sound of feet climbing the thirteen steps to meet us. The way the footfalls fell around one another, you knew it wasn't just Gentleman Jack. It sounded like a band climbing up—a drunken band—and they were carrying horns and drums along.

"God rot it!" the Reverend said.

I was still laughing in spite of myself. Seconds later, my laughter got caught in my throat. There, filing up the stairs ahead of Gentleman Jack was a man I recognized as Pete from Wichita Falls. Ahead of him and clutching onto the dirty paw of Simeon Payne, in a blue cotton dress I couldn't recall ever seeing before, was Greer Lusk Liquorish. My Greer, her belly now noticeably full of our child. She was looking down at the stairs as if she was afraid she might miss one, and, when she finally topped out, skillfully managed to scan her surroundings without ever looking me directly in the eye.

"Greer."

I'd had dreams before where I was calling out to somebody. Maybe they were in a burning house or about to ride into a snake pit, and I was trying to get their attention.

"Greer!"

What came out of my lungs as something of a

holler withered in the air and hung there, never getting to the ears of its intended subject. Reverend Caliber elbowed me in the ribs.

"Jack's trying to rattle you, son," he said. "You go off and do something stupid, you'll look exactly like the hothead he says you are."

It's a damn good thing I didn't have any gun on me, because I would have drawn it, and I would have killed, starting with the bastard Jack Delaney.

Standing there doing nothing did something interesting to me. I could feel something break inside like a rope between my head and my stomach. It reminded me of the time I'd been beaten by a group of soldiers in the District for taking their money in a game of billiards. I could almost hear it untangling and pulling apart, and I could sure enough feel every inch of it. I had never had to stand and face the music as a grown man, yet here I was, being asked to face it and dance and try to keep a smile on my face.

Funny enough, it set me free. Not free like Reverend Caliber's bible talked about getting set free. Not free like Texas was a free state, and not like Jack Delaney had been born a slave but now he was free. I mean I was finally free to see myself as I really was, and that made me free to see Jack and Simeon Payne and all those faces in the street as they were too.

I just couldn't see Greer.

"Ladies and gentlemen, I have three different witnesses here who will tell you in their own words about the man on trial today. The first is Mr. Simeon Payne, who was the only person who survived to tell the story of what happened on the cattle drive from Mobeetie to Fort Worth. He will tell you what happened when the drive pulled into Wichita Falls. He will tell you what happened when the drive finally fell apart in the desert between that city and this one."

Simeon Payne stepped up next to Jack like he was about to take a bow for the role he was playing. He was dressed to the nines, and I could tell he hadn't ridden into town in that getup. It was a little too clean. It made me wonder if Jack hadn't taken him, Pete and Greer all shopping.

"This next young man is Pete Doon from Wichita Falls, who will tell you what happened when the man standing on trial came riding into town and made a devil's bargain with the townspeople."

Pete looked me square in the eye, and, even when I looked away, I could feel his gaze. I didn't know this man well enough for him to be saying anything about me. I had never even known his whole name until that moment. Doon? I think that was what he said.

"And this beautiful young lady is the unfortunate wife of Wilkie John Liquorman or Liquorwhateverhisnameis," Jack said. "She is also, as you can plainly see, the expectant mother of this man's offspring. Although I can assure you that, if justice is truly served here today, which I believe it shall be, we will also be giving this lady the new beginning she so richly deserves."

And with that, the trial recommenced. I didn't care what happened at that point. I was ready to get it all over with. If that was the way Gentleman Jack wanted to play, he was indeed about to see something that nobody saw coming.

CHAPTER THIRTY

I lost all spirit to keep going when Jacobo died on the outskirts of Wichita Falls. Nonetheless, I agreed to take a small herd of cattle into town and sell it for supplies that would keep us going and maybe allow us to reform the drive. If we could get to Fort Worth and regroup, adding a few more experienced men to the team, we could still make Kansas City and leave with enough money to make it worth the trip. I would still have enough to return to Mobeetie and buy a ranch. Then I could raise horses and maybe some cattle, and, if there was another drive, I could hire someone else to do that work while I stayed home with Greer and the baby.

I wound up taking fifty-eight head of cattle into Wichita Falls that afternoon. I say into. I never actually got past the entrance to the town. A welcome wagon was parked there waiting for me, and they didn't exactly have their arms open.

"We're not allowing no outside cattle in," said a man who introduced himself only as Pete. "We've had some of 'em come down with Spanish fever, and, to tell the truth, we really don't need anybody coming in unless you're an animal doctor."

I told him that I wasn't a doctor of any kind, but that we had some sick people just a few miles northwest, and we could use a doctor ourselves.

"I have fifty-eight head of cattle here," I said. "If I could trade them on some supplies and some medicine, we won't cause you any grief. We'd sure be obliged."

Pete wasn't having none of it and was about to turn me away, cattle and all, but one of his companions stopped it.

"Those cattle ain't got no fever?" he said.

I told him they didn't. I didn't mention the other thirty head we'd put down. All I wanted was to get some solid food and something for stomach problems and push on toward Fort Worth. I had no yearning to see any more of Wichita Falls.

The men discussed the fact that, due to them losing so much of their cattle to the Spanish Fever, they could sure use some new ones to replace them, and, after some mully grubbing back and forth, they offered to take them off my hands for thirty dollars, a supply of water, two bottles of quinine and a little laudanum. I didn't have any room to negotiate. I took the deal and rode out, wishing them well. I was thankful for the quinine, as I was beginning to feel less than outstanding myself, and I stopped halfway back to camp to take a swig, just to make sure I got me a taste before the bottles went around. A little farther on, I stopped and took an equal nip from the laudanum, just to even things out.

We decided to move on around the town and stop for the night on the south side. That way, when we woke up the next morning, we would have maybe three days ahead of us before arriving in Fort Worth. Even then, that distance was beginning to look like a sea, and when I lay down to sleep that night, the ship was rolling on wave after wave of sand. I would grab the dirt in both hands trying to keep myself steady and keep both eyes fixed on the moon.

It was a long night filled with staring at the sky and then dreaming of staring at the sky. I kept hearing Jacobo calling me, but when I looked around, it would end up being William Gee or Ira Lee. That seemed even worse. As far away as the ship full of sand seemed to take me, I still knew, somewhere inside, that Ira Lee was getting worse and worse. I finally vomited over the side of the boat and passed out. Waking up to Ira Lee splashing my face with water, I discovered that William Gee had died in the night. Leon Thaw looked at me strangely all that morning, and I started to ask what was on his mind, but, when I looked around as we were breaking camp, I had a dim recollection of the waves that had tossed me about the sand, and of the ship that was now just a memory, a wreck along the trail. I decided to say nothing.

We buried William Gee along with about twenty more head of cattle that had either perished or were too far gone to be of any value to anyone. On the other hand, I felt better than I had in a day or two. I looked for the quinine and found it bone dry, but there was still some laudanum, so I took a dose and gave a taste to Roman. I'd heard of people giving it to their animals, and something from the night's dreams had concerned me for his health. Had he been on the ship with me? I couldn't remember, and I didn't like the thought of him not being there. I'd purposefully kept him as far as I could from any of the cows that seemed to have the fever, but it seemed to be spreading. I made up my mind to split from whatever was left of the drive as soon as we got to Fort Worth. I wanted to see Greer.

"Wilkie John, I'm not sure I'm gonna make it to Fort Worth," Ira Lee said.

We had never been close, but I couldn't envision a world without him out there somewhere, calling me to come and join him. I didn't like the notion of him calling me from the grave.

"I don't wanna hear that, Ira Lee."

Simeon Payne was pulling the livestock together for another long day under the summer sun. He didn't seem to be showing any effects from the fever. He was too mean to die, I decided.

"I want you to take me back to San Antonio," he said. "I want mama to know I died on my feet, trying to get somewhere and not laying in a bed waiting for the end."

I wasn't so sure it would make mama any difference. I couldn't understand why he cared what she thought anyway. He hadn't been home in years. And either way, he would be dead. I suggested I tell her he went to Dodge City instead. Seemed to me like maybe the nearest thing to a real heaven for folks like me and Ira Lee.

"Maybe you're right, little brother," he said.

Later that day, when we'd gone maybe fifteen

miles, he stopped, climbed down from his horse and took a long drink of water. That time he told me just to shoot his horse and bury them together wherever he fell. And that's what I promised I'd do.

We rode on for a couple more days. We rode so long that we slipped past Fort Worth to the west and wound up in Comanche. Ira Lee was riding up front with the bell cow, all the way to the end, and for the last few miles, I watched him teeter to one side and then the other. I had given him the last of the laudanum that morning, and I was concerned that he might fall asleep on the trail. I called out to him a time or two, and he righted himself, only to start tottering to the other side a mile later. The second time, he fell right over. I watched him go in slow motion, but there was nothing I could do but call out his name. It seemed to die there in the air along with him.

Ira Lee fell and hit his head. I don't know for sure if he died on his horse and fell off or if he fell asleep and then died when he hit his head. There was a lot of blood, but he never blinked or flinched or said another word.

His last words had been about an hour before when he looked back at me and said, "You still following, little brother?"

I hadn't answered. I had only followed along. Now, it seemed like it was up to me to lead the bell cow. When I looked at her, I wasn't sure how much farther any of us could go.

"I think we're going in the wrong direction," Leon Thaw said.

This was after we'd shot Ira Lee's mustang and buried them in the sand. I wanted to put up some kind of marker to tell anybody else who followed that a decent man had gone down there. I had no supplies to do such a thing, and I quickly discovered I lacked the energy as well.

"We've been going in the wrong direction ever since we left Mobeetie," I said.

It had become a quest to stay alive, a matter of survival, finding our way out of that ocean-sized death trap. From there on, it was every man for himself. Just as it had always been, just as it was meant to be.

CHAPTER THIRTY-ONE

"What we see is not always reality," Gentleman Jack said. "One day I saw a magician at work right here in this town, in a small theater. I was maybe as far from him as I am from you people right down front. He took a pack of normal playing cards. I know they were normal playing cards because he let me shuffle them."

I felt a raindrop on my arm. I looked up to make sure it wasn't a bird flying over and saw a scattering of rainclouds moving in from the west.

"This magician placed that pack of cards into a hat," he said. "The hat wasn't all that different from the one I'm wearing now."

I'd never seen him in any other hat. It was seldom that I saw him take it off.

"Well, he waved his hand around over that hat, and, lo and behold, when he stuck his hand back into it, he pulled out a rope. He pulled and pulled and that little stage began to be filled with rope. A hundred yards of it. Maybe two hundred. Now the key to the whole thing, if I can believe what I'm being led to believe, lies in that moment when he was waving his hand. Not because waving your hand causes a perfectly good pack of cards to turn into more rope than you could ever use."

He stopped and let his words sink in for a moment.

"When the magician is waving his hand, you've got to look close at what his other hand is doing."

At that point, a cowboy off to the left of the stage decided he'd heard enough of this line of thinking.

"If you want to ruin the magic trick!"

Gentleman Jack wasn't pleased.

"The difference between you and me, my friend, I know there's no such thing as magic," he said. "Now that might not seem like such a big difference. Maybe you truly want to believe this magician turned that deck of cards into half a mile of rope. That right?"

The men standing with the fellow in question liked his sudden importance.

"Damn straight he does," one of them said.

I had to admit, Jack was a wonder to behold, especially while he was focused on someone other than myself for a few minutes.

"There's where I have total control over him," he said. "If your friend chooses to believe in a magic that doesn't exist, he's handed control of the situation over to me."

He turned back to the man.

"I can use your belief in something that doesn't exist to manipulate you."

I'm not sure any of them had any idea what Jack

was saying. I didn't know what his point was either, but it soon became clear enough.

"This man—John Liquorman, Wilkie John Liquorish—wants you to look at him and see something other than reality. You see a kid, somebody too young and innocent to have left such a bloody trail behind him, you've fallen for the trick."

Reverend Caliber was ready this time, and he found enough of a pause to jump into the conversation.

"Mr. Delaney brings up an excellent point," he said. "But let me ask you to consider this. The magician has one objective: to make you think he's doing one thing, while he's doing another. Now, look here. My client, Wilkie John, is standing here and telling you what happened. He's told you about the Indian friend who was scalped by his own people for being a servant and helping to bring people together. He's told you about this young Scottish lass who stole his heart and, from the looks of things, broke it into pieces. He's not trying to fool anybody. I would suggest that every time Mr. Delaney waves his hand at my client, it's Mr. Delaney who's trying to produce a rope where there isn't one. Keep an eye on him and don't be fooled by what he's doing."

I thought the line about the rope was particularly good, and so did a few people out in the street. Fort Worth had a mix of Confederate sympathizers who were angry about the way things had shaken out and settlers who hadn't ever thought slavery belonged in Texas, and both audiences responded equally to any mention of justice and a rope. Before Gentleman Jack had come to town and, with the High Sheriff's assistance, built the great contraption we were standing on, there had been several trees and more rope than you could measure out. Hangings had been a weekly occurrence, often with less of a trial than I was being afforded. Now, there was the lure of the new, of the proper, but, from where I stood, it didn't look much different. Reverend Caliber had just put any vigilantes in the crowd on notice.

"I don't just have rope," Jack said. "I also have the law on my side."

He walked right up to the lip of the stage.

"If I took a poll right now, how many of you fine citizens would vote that this young man has killed enough? How many of you think he should pay with his life, this very day?"

Not everybody raised their hand. I can tell you that. I tried to take some solace there, but there wasn't much to be found. A good sixty percent had their hands in the air. I looked at the Reverend, who seemed, at the moment, like a preacher in danger of losing his flock.

"Let's hear the rest of the story," he said. "Great people of history have often been killed due to their juries and their judges not knowing the full story. Think of Joan of Arc."

It's doubtful many people there had any idea who Joan of Arc was.

"Think of our lord and savior, Jesus Christ."

The same man who had spoken out earlier about believing in magic raised an objection.

"This little pipsqueak ain't our lord and savior, preacher man."

I could feel the people becoming more hostile,

and it wasn't the preacher they were taking issue with. There would be no ropes for his pious neck on this day.

"Oh, but have you not read, my brother," Caliber said, "for the lord said, 'Inasmuch as ye have done it unto one of the least of these my brethren, ye have done it unto me.'"

Never before or since have I loved the Lord so much. There was such a ruckus through the crowd—and then a groundswell of applause—that the preacher, in his excitement, shouted "Hallelujah!" and I thought we might just be victorious.

CHAPTER THIRTY-TWO

I left Meridian with nothing but Roman and Ira Lee's .44 Colt. Simeon watched silently as I dug a grave for Ira Lee and his horse, then announced to me and Leon Thaw that he was turning back.

"Y'all can keep going if you want to," he said. "I got just enough learning to turn around when I see the gates of hell itself."

I scanned the horizon for a sign. If I was looking at hell, I also had a sense that our salvation lay ahead of us, in Fort Worth, and not all the way back in Mobeetie. As much as I missed Greer, I don't think I would have survived the trip back. And, if I did, I didn't want her to see the kind of shape I'd be in.

The ranchers back in Mobeetie had drawn us out a map to Fort Worth. None of us had ever been, and now Ira Lee never would. It was one more reason that pushed me on, even though the rancher had said if we got all the way to Meridian, we'd gone too far. I would turn and go northeast and leave Simeon Payne behind. There was no sweet sorrow in the parting. I hadn't liked him from the get-go.

That left me and Leon Thaw. I made the turn for Fort Worth, and Leon came right along with me, never saying a word about it. I was glad to have him back there over my shoulder. We had thrown out most of the remaining food after it became obvious that we were all either sick or dying, and then we'd eaten what little jerky remained. The water was gone as well. I had given too much of it to Ira Lee as he lay dead in the dirt, soaking it up but needing none of it. That had been the last straw for Simeon. Now, I regretted it as well.

"Don't waste effects on the dying."

I had heard Granville Hanley say it. Back at Fort Griffin, it had been drilled into all the soldiers. Medicine, food, water. All limited resources. You had to know when someone was dying and accept it. There was time for a goodbye, maybe a last message for a mother or a sweetheart, but you didn't pour out rations on a dying man. I started to wonder what Hanley would do if he were in my position.

Roman was suffering too, so I walked alongside him as much as possible, stopping to ride only for short intervals. I thought I was a day and a half outside Fort Worth. Just close enough to keep me moving, it was the carrot on the horizon, the mirage on the stick. That switching of images in my by-now fevered brain set me off in a fit of laughter that came periodically as I pulled myself across more sand than I had ever imagined. I tried looking down at my feet, thinking progress would come faster if I wasn't watching it. After almost stepping on a rattlesnake, I nixed that idea. Looking up, it didn't seem I had come any perceptible stretch anyhow.

Somewhere on that first day, around sunset, I looked back to see a cloud of dust moving northward across the skyline. With the sun filtering through it, it almost looked like a ball of fire. I sat on a nearby rock and watched it grow smaller and smaller, its tail burning away in the orange-pink light. My first thought was it was Indians. Probably Cherokee, maybe Blackfoot. Later, I thought it might have been a meteor. I'd seen one of those follow the horizon before out in the empty spaces south of Fort Griffin, and it had taken my breath away.

I didn't sleep much that first night. I had nothing to make camp with. Nothing to make a fire and nothing to cook on one. I could tell Roman was jittery too. He was tired, but he wouldn't lay down. He wanted to be ready to go at a moment's notice if we were approached. Nothing approached us all night long except for the cattle. We were leaving a trail of them behind us, some just giving up and dying. Worse were the ones who fell and lay there blinking away dust, lowing and waiting for death to steal them away.

Leon Thaw had fallen away to leave me alone in a hard country full of danger. If I didn't exactly notice when he disappeared, it couldn't be surprising. He had followed behind and to my left most of the way, often falling almost out of sight and saying little during the times we were together. I waited for him to show up for a while, thinking he'd likely stopped sick at one end or the other. Hadn't we all, some more than others?

Ira Lee, I hated thinking on. I would sometimes momentarily forget, thinking I was still to meet him in Fort Worth. Or was it Amarillo? The next morning, after finally getting a little sleep, I was awakened by a rustling and a voice. Long Gun. I heard him, but not clearly; saw him, but not well. Still, he was there, standing right in front of me.

"We need to get a move on."

And then, "stand yourself up, Wilkie John."

I didn't know where I was, and it was a confusion that stuck with me on and off through the day. At times, it seemed I was walking to Amarillo to find Ira Lee, and I believed it would come into sight at any moment. I told Sunny about it later, and she said I should tell her friend Reverend Caliber. That was actually how I first heard his name. I never told him. He would feel a need to find meaning in it. I went the opposite direction.

It was just me and Roman, still alive and somehow wandering on in the general direction of Fort Worth. Of course, I yakked my jaw off to Roman. I always had, especially when we were out on long stretches of the trail. I had known him longer than anyone except Ira Lee, and he was now gone. So it wasn't unusual that I would talk as we went along. I felt like we had passed through some kind of gauntlet, that we had passed a test of some sort, and it brought us even closer together.

"I don't think Long Gun was real," I said.

I had pretty much convinced myself of that. How else could he have disappeared like he had? Even a Blackfoot Indian couldn't have gone anywhere but into the ground or into the sky. Blackfoot Indian. Was he a Blackfoot? What was he? I couldn't remember. I walked on, and I might have walked him back out of my mind if I hadn't looked down to see his rifle in my hand.

"You are Long Gun."

Maybe the words were just bouncing around in my fevered head, but I heard them as loud as the ones that had awakened me. Once I chased the rabbit that far, I naturally went a step farther. It's the same thing I had that kept me moving.

"If Long Gun was never real, maybe Greer wasn't real. Maybe Fort Griffin. Ira Lee. Mobeetie . . ."

San Antonio was real. Mama. After that, it got questionable. Maybe I hadn't been jailed for refusing to hand over my *Encyclopedia Britannica*, sixth edition. Had that been real? Had I shot those Indians in that hotel in Mobeetie? Had I even been a gravedigger?

I still don't know what part of that second day was real. Dreams and reality arm wrestled over me until I finally fell face-forward into the dirt and passed out. I wouldn't even know any of it happened if I hadn't opened my eyes under a night sky that was raining down on me. I instinctively opened my mouth and drank it in for as long as it lasted. Then I fell back asleep. When I awoke again, the Milky Way had stretched out above my head and the clouds had passed to the east.

I studied my map, unsure of where I was, and decided to continue northeast.

CHAPTER THIRTY-THREE

"Leon Thaw arrived in the coach a day after Wilkie Lee," Gentleman Jack said. "Unfortunately, poor Mr. Thaw had taken a gunshot to the head, and arrived too late for any medical help."

Jack held up a photograph of Thaw stretched out on the slab in the photographer's studio, the top of his head noticeably missing and no noticeable brain at all. The men in the crowd all shielded the eyes of their women and children, and the children fought to see through and around their fathers' hands. I had seen enough that it didn't bother me much, but I looked away anyway. It seemed like bad luck to gaze upon a dead man from my perch on the gallows.

"Mr. Simeon Payne is here to confirm that Leon Thaw was alive and fairly healthy at the time that he left the drive," Jack said. "Would you step forward, Mr. Payne?"

Simeon took three steps forward, his knees locked in a soldierly fashion. I caught the eye of Greer, but she quickly looked away and repositioned her hat to block me out of her line of view. I didn't recognize the hat either.

"The cattle were all dying," Simeon Payne said. "Ira Lee, my co-leader of the drive, had fallen ill and died. As had the cook. As had William. The only two who were in good shape when I left were Leon Thaw, who was driving the wagon, and him."

He pointed at me.

"What do you think happened after you left?" Gentleman Jack said.

The Reverend jumped in.

"What does it matter, what this man 'thinks' happened? I don't care what any of you 'thinks' happened. That has nothing to do with why we're here. Maybe I 'think' Jack Delaney is no gentleman at all. Maybe I 'think' he murdered this coach driver whose photograph he waves around. If I can't prove it, I probably shouldn't even bring it up. It's all about what he can prove. Remember, don't let him fool you."

Gentleman Jack waited for Caliber to make his point and then picked up where he left off.

"Mr. Payne, could you kindly tell these people what you think happened after you left and returned to Wichita Falls?"

Payne's answer seemed well practiced.

"I knew one of them, either Thaw or Liquorish here, had poisoned the crew. Everyone was falling ill except for them. I couldn't figure out which was the guilty party, but I didn't aim to stick around and find out. I knew one of them would show his hand."

I found myself getting interested in his thinking, even though I knew it to be flawed at best and completely hell-bent on railroading me at worst. I was no great admirer of Thaw, but why in blazes would either of us want to poison the crew?

"Why would I do such a thing?" I said.

I had almost forgotten I could speak up, and so had some of those watching. One of them being Simeon Payne. He looked at Jack as if asking for permission to speak.

"Maybe you wanted all the dinero for yourself," Payne said.

The only dinero I received had been taken out of the Tubbs's General Store till. It hadn't covered expenses.

"Here's what I propose," Gentleman Jack said. "We know the cook, Jacobo Robles, knew Wilkie John previous to the cattle drive. I believe Mr. Robles and Wilkie John conspired. I believe they planned to poison the crew, mostly likely after reaching Wichita Falls. Most likely with the plan of bringing in these eight hundred head of cattle themselves, collecting all of the money, and moving on."

The Reverend said, "Mr. Delaney, I believe, if you check the facts, it was Jacobo Robles who died first."

Gentleman Jack had sprung yet another trap.

"Simeon Payne will tell you fine people he is the reason for that most unfortunate turn of events," he said. "Mr. Payne, can you enlighten us please?"

Simeon Payne had remained in position, still on the front line and awaiting further orders.

"The cook was making beans that afternoon," he said. "I saw him dipping out of two separate bowls and approached him about it. I didn't trust him, him being a Mexican. He stammered around and said one beans was made with one recipe and the other beans was made with another. I made him switch with me. If he wasn't willing to eat from my beans, I didn't want no part of it."

There was another collective gasp from the crowd. I raised my hand like a school child waiting to solve a problem. Jack ignored me. The Reverend came to my rescue. I told them everything I could recall about Jacobo being the official cook of the king of Mexico, and how his beans had been good enough to set him free and keep him alive during the final days of the king's reign. I think I got most of the important details right.

"What the blazes are you trying to say, son?" Gentleman Jack said.

He knew how much I hated being called son.

"I'm saying that his special beans were in one pot and the not-special beans were in the other," I said.

I didn't know this to be true, but it certainly made more sense to me than what they were claiming. Jacobo was new to the drive, as I was, and I'm sure he was anxious to impress. What better way than to make a pot of his most acclaimed dish.

"If Wilkie John's right, and there's no proof that he isn't," Reverend Caliber said, "you're accusing this cook, Robles, of acting to poison himself."

Gentleman Jack pushed on, undeterred. I'm not sure he'd heard a thing we had said.

"Woefully, I also have Wilkie John's most unfortunate wife, Greer Lusk from Scotland," he said. "When we think about Simeon Payne's account, that this cook and Wilkie John had connived to kill off the crew and split the money, we can turn to this lady for her accounting."

Greer took a step forward where Simeon had taken three and kept her eyes fast on the floor. Looking at the face I knew so well, I saw every sorrow she'd ever had to face and then some. She seemed older but not wiser in the ways you would hope.

"Mrs. Liquorish, could you please state, for the record, what you told me about this matter?"

She never raised her head, and her words spilled onto the floor as if she was bleeding them out. Caliber caught me by the shoulder to keep me in my place.

"He said he would bring back enough money to buy us a piece of land and set up a ranch."

The crowd was quiet, trying to piece the words together. Slowly, they understood what she was saying.

"I would suggest that the pay for a drover, on one very small cattle drive, would hardly cover such an expense," Jack said.

Simeon Payne knew we were planning to meet another drive and move on to Kansas. He didn't seem in any great hurry to mention that part of the story.

CHAPTER THIRTY-FOUR

Walking to Fort Worth for those final thirty miles took the most of two days, and they were two days filled with sand and death. I found one of the cows wandering far from the trail and shot it. Partly to put it out of its own suffering but mostly for food. If I hadn't done so, I'm not sure I would have survived, as my energy was quickly wasting away.

The sand was everywhere. In my shoes, in my clothes, my eyes, my hair. I had been wearing a hat at least as far as Wichita Falls, but it had mysteriously disappeared. Mostly, the sand was in my mouth. I could feel it on my tongue, between my teeth. If I breathed through my nose, it filled my nostrils. Breathing through my mouth, I could feel it all the way to my lungs. At times, I had so much trouble breathing, I believed I would drown. And die of sand.

The cow was more of a job than it should have been. It was scrawny and as near to death as I was. Either I needed to eat it or it me. I had the upper hand there, but just barely. I shot it with Ira Lee's

.44 but quickly discovered I lacked the strength or the tools to properly do anything with it. I certainly couldn't hang it and butcher it. I was finally able to get it to bleed out enough to take a little meat from its shoulder. Tried eating it raw, right there where I'd shot it. Not successful at all.

I took a short nap and got back up as the sun was setting. Afraid that if I didn't do something soon, the meat would spoil, I worked on lighting a fire and was able, with greater work than usual, to raise a little blaze against the approaching dark. There I cooked enough of the meat cut from the shoulder to fill me and Roman and have extra for later.

The combination of the rainy night and then the small meal saved me. Almost immediately, I had more energy. As we broke camp and began a search for the trail leading into Fort Worth, we happened on a bridled but unsaddled mule on wobbly legs. I didn't recognize it, but I thought it might have been William Gee's. He'd had a mule named Bird, strangely enough, and I wasn't sure what had happened to it.

I fed Bird a handful of our meat then tied her to us and pressed on. I found that my mind was in constant turmoil, spinning from one subject to another, none of them calming or satisfactory, and so I searched through my bags and found a worn copy of *Journey to the Center of the Earth* by Jules Verne and was thus able to focus my mind on Hans and Axel who had nothing to do with sand, Indians, and dying cattle. Or maybe they did. I could relate to Alex who seemed sure he was seeing things.

Seeing things. What a peculiar way of talking, saying one thing and meaning the opposite. If you were seeing things, and they weren't there, how were you to believe anything? All reality became suspect. Again, I was circling back around to a world in which nothing could be taken for granted except for me. I was on my own journey, and, with the heat edging higher and higher, I wouldn't have been at all shocked to see the sand open up and turn to a river of lava.

Even so, riding across the sand reading from the book, sometimes aloud to Roman and sometimes, when he appeared disinterested, silently to myself, was more agreeable than thinking of Ira Lee or Greer. It passed much of the second day and, when we unexpectedly reached darkness before we reached the town, I lay next to a small fire and kept reading until I could barely make out the letters.

I was concerned that I had fallen off course and missed Fort Worth all together. I'd seen neither hide nor hair of anything resembling humanity since Simeon Payne and Leon Thaw left, and they were a close call. The only map I had was drawn by memory from a man I couldn't even name. I looked at it again, tucked away in the back of the Jules Verne, and decided I'd veered too far south.

The last page of the book. Oh yes. They had been going southeast, same as me, hadn't they? They had been hit by a white and azure blue ball of fire that nearly wiped them out and set them off course. I thought of the light I had watched moving across the horizon. What were the chances? Had I been dreaming it? Was I dreaming now? I couldn't be sure, but I couldn't dismiss it.

I decided to tack northwest for a while and see if I lucked up on something. There wasn't any other option really, except for laying down and dying. The closer that got, the more frightening it seemed. Dying. We all ran from it our whole lives, even as we ran right into its arms. I tried to remember the psalm from my childhood, at the Catholic church just across the way from the District. There was a nun there—Sister Mary Constance—who repeated it all the time. Sister Mary Constance. How could I recall her name and not the prayer?

I walk through the valley of death and fear no evil.

I hoped that was enough. That seemed like the important part. The gist of it. I repeated it, over and over, that one line, trying to summon more from the darkness of my memory. It was no use. I was there, and if it wasn't the same valley of death Sister Mary Constance had been praying about, it was damn well close enough. The fear wasn't of shadows or monsters in the dark. It was the dark itself.

"Roman, you remember what things were like before you was born?"

I waited, out of respect, for him to think on it, even if he wasn't inclined to answer.

"I can't remember anything at all."

The three of us might have walked for a quarter mile. The darkness seemed unending, so distance hardly seemed to matter. This wasn't the kind of darkness I could ride out of. I was going to have to think my way out.

"What if, when we die, death is like that?" I said.

I wondered if a horse might want to be a man in the afterlife. Why would he want to? Roman had seen enough to not make that mistake.

"Are horses afraid of dying?" I said.

Trouble with that, I knew if you were truly afraid of dying, you were afraid of living too. I rode on through the night, talking to Roman, talking to myself, thinking my way along, until I awoke there by the remains of the fire, my book still in my hand. My journey was still unfinished.

CHAPTER THIRTY-FIVE

Gentleman Jack was beside himself.

He was playing his best card, and it wasn't the ace he had imagined. In fact, it appeared to be nothing but a big old blank. He was telling everybody it was a royal flush, but they weren't lining up to buy it.

"Mrs. Liqourish said it herself," he said. "Wilkie John was scheming to do something much bigger than riding point and following a bell cow halfway across Texas. It was his scheming, and his recklessness that endangered not only his crew but the eight hundred cattle."

The Reverend was trying his best, but it was like swatting at a bunch of flies coming at him from all directions. "The cattle drive was supposed to extend to Kansas City. They were trying to do their jobs. There was no scheming. The cattle were infected with Red Water Disease before they even left Mobeetie. Before the crew ever saw them. How can you call that scheming?"

He smiled at the crowd, confident he'd made his point.

"Mrs. Liquorish," Jack said, "you tell me, and I remind you that lying could put you in a fair amount of harm as well. Was your husband, Wilkie John here, a good, upstanding, law abiding young man? Yes or no."

Greer never raised her eyes, never raised her voice.

"I'm sorry," Jack said, "I didn't quite catch that."

I saw her lips move, but no words could be heard. I felt Caliber squeeze my upper arm and realized he was still holding me. I could have wrestled free. I came close to trying.

"The answer would be no, wouldn't it, Mrs. Liquorish?" Jack said. "The true answer to that question would be that your husband had killed many a man just in the short time that you knew him. Would you agree?"

She didn't say anything. Simeon Payne, who had been holding her hand as they came up the steps onto the platform, whom I thought must have designs on my wife, attached to her as he was, right in front of me, put the squeeze on her just as Caliber had done with me. I knew, at that moment, that she was being forced to testify against me. And, if she was doing so, I wondered what else she'd been forced into.

"Let her go free and I'll tell you everything you want to know," I said.

I didn't talk it over with the Reverend. I didn't need to. I didn't feel like I'd ever been responsible for the death of an innocent person, and especially not a lady. If I had got her into this situation, it was up to me to get her out. Short of shooting our way out, this seemed like my best move. Gentleman Jack wasn't so sure.

"What makes you think I would give my ace up so readily?"

I knew what she knew and what she didn't know. At least I was pretty sure I did.

"She doesn't know," I said. "Only I do."

You could see Jack thinking. He looked at Simeon Payne, as if Simeon could tell him anything.

"I won't let her get away so easy, Wilkie John," Jack said. "But I might be persuaded to keep her from hanging with you today, depending on how much you talk."

Now you might think I would be inclined to push my luck and see if the deck cut my way. And you would be right in most situations. But I didn't play loose with other people's lives, and certainly not with Greer's. I might have been the only one, but, when I looked at her, I still saw the same girl who came wandering into Fort Griffin with her family, who sat across the fire from me on a night when her eyes shone brighter than the flame or the starlight. Who charmed me with the soft singsong in her voice when I could scarcely make out a word she said.

"Take her down from here, and I'll hang alone for everything I done."

I meant that. I still thought Reverend Caliber was capable of winning my freedom. I thought I had the crowd on my side. I hadn't given up the fight. But I was more than ready to negotiate the prize. I wanted her off the table.

Gentleman Jack took a pause to think it over, looking over a page of notes as if this very option and its riposte was copied down there. He murmured something and, looking across the stage at Greer, shook his head no. The Reverend sensed an opening and took it.

"Jack Delaney has long called himself a gentleman," he said. "Gentleman Jack Delaney, he says. Let's see if he can live up to that name and let an innocent young lady walk free today."

Another great cheer grew from across the way, like a wave of kindness crashing up against our pier of death. It put Jack on the spot. Jack didn't like being put on the spot.

"I'll effect a compromise with you," he said. "I'll take her down from the gallows, if you'll do as you say. But she will remain secured at the back and, if I later determine you haven't lived up to your word, she will be brought back up to answer for her own crimes."

I don't believe, at that point, there was any admiration left for the son of a bitch. I wanted nothing more than to scalp him the way I'd seen the Blackfoot Indians do to so many Anglos. Maybe it was only then that I began to understand the hate those Indians must have felt for the people who were bringing war against them and taking over their land.

"And what crimes might those be?" I said.

I could think of nothing legitimate to hold her for. If she was to account for anything, it seemed only fair that it be spelled out publicly and specifically.

"The crime of living with and giving refuge to a

murderer," Jack said. "Of knowing the repulsiveness of the man whose name she took, and yet doing nothing about it. Look at her. The crime of bringing the child of such a depraved man into this world. Of not attempting in any way to stop the dreadful plan that he embarked upon, the plan that led us to this very day, this very moment."

If I hadn't accepted Gentleman Jack's deal, Greer would have stayed on the gallows, just feet away from me. The reason I shook on it and agreed? In the event I hung, I didn't want her up there. It's as simple as that. A minute later, she was being led back down the stairs by Simeon Payne, a vision I couldn't gaze on. In case I swung, I refused to let that be my final memory of her. She might have misunderstood, watching me stand there with my back to her. It was all I could do at that moment, and I hoped she understood.

CHAPTER THIRTY-SIX

Moving on in the pale light of that third morning out of Meridian, my muscles burned and my mind was bruised by too much sand, too much sun, too much struggle. What I remembered mama calling "too much too much." We had seen tough times. She saw tougher than Ira Lee or me. Back in the days right after Henry was killed, when we bounced around from place to place, losing more and more with each move until we were left with nothing but each other, mama couldn't have found much beyond us two boys to live for.

Walking along with Roman, I eyed Bird a time or two, but I didn't trust her, as far as riding went, and she looked at me like she didn't trust me either. My shoes had come apart, and I was now walking barefoot, leaving small drops of blood as a marker. I could make out a path in front of me, even if it had no signs to tell me where it was leading. The sand managed to hide it for long stretches, but it would eventually show itself again, and, if I had gone astray, it was never quite so far that I couldn't correct myself.

I told Roman stories I'd told before, thinking maybe their familiarity would be comforting to him. If Bird paid any attention at all, she didn't show it. I told the one about the day I caught a young soldier coming out of mama's bedroom in our little crib in the District.

"What was that man doing in there with you, mama?" I'd said.

I can still remember just how she looked. Sad but strong, and beautiful beyond words.

"Sometimes men come to me and I'm able to talk to them and help them out," she said.

I felt like I had a clear understanding there. Mama had certainly helped me and Ira Lee and even the other girls up and down the row.

"Like when you help me do my work for the church school?"

Ira Lee and me both went to the Catholic school for a few years. It didn't take with Ira Lee, and he was soon skipping off for more adventurous diversions than math and reading. I stuck with the reading, even if math failed to hold my interest.

"In a way, it's like that," mama said, "except they pay me money for it, and I use that money for our food and clothing and school books."

I thought that was spectacular news. The next day, with my love for mama guiding my way, I went down to the area where the Sporting District met up with the Army base. There I would meet up with men on their way to the gambling halls and saloons and tell them about my mama. The men would laugh and ask me to tell them again, or they would bring their friends around and get me to tell them again. Most of them went on their way. A couple even gave me coins from their pocket. But a few asked me to walk them to our crib and knock on the door for them.

It was another year or two before I had any idea what kind of help was really going on in that tiny little bedroom. As for mama, she told me never to do it again, but she never brought it up again, and, a few years later, when I said something about it, she denied that it had ever happened.

Once again, a denial. A question. I could still recall small but specific details. The uniforms of the soldiers. The way they smelled. But mama said no. I dreamed a lot, she said. It had been a dream.

In an effort to comfort Roman, I took the saddle-bag from him and draped it over Bird. Bird was a young mule, and I hoped she would withstand the conditions better. She fussed for a while and managed to shake herself out from under it once but finally resigned herself to the situation and walked right alongside Roman.

We had been on the move for several hours when, just as the sun was beginning to climb toward its loftiest height, I saw a storm cloud rising up on the northern horizon. I at first thought it to be a dust storm and maneuvered to take a north-western tack around it. Roman sensed it too and seemed skittish. He was weak from too much of the too much, and so I looked for a way to get far enough away from the coming winds and stop for a while.

I believed that I was making a big mistake even as I did it. If we were caught inside a true Texas dust storm, it could come at us for hours. We wouldn't stand a chance of making it. The best thing that could be said, it would kill us and bury us all in one swoop. A model of efficiency. We moved to a high place that seemed to have once followed along a creek. The creek, long since gone and forgotten, as we might soon be. I only hoped our altitude would keep us above the worst of things.

Looking back now, it was fortune and not fate that stopped us so close to the approaching trail of dust. From higher above the desert floor, I was quickly able to see that it was no storm. It was a wagon coming toward us. Maybe it was Leon Thaw, I thought.

I tied cloths over the nostrils of both horses and waited. I could make out a single horse pulling the coach, and it looked like it would pass to the south of us. I thought about moving back in that direction, but Roman didn't want to. He seemed to think we stood a better chance of being seen if we were up high. It made sense, so I agreed. I tied a leftover piece of cloth—the one I'd saved to hold over my own face as the dust grew nearer—to the end of Long Gun's rifle and held it as high as I could manage. The gun, not light to begin with, seemed to have tripled in weight. I could scarcely keep it high. I brought it down and waited for the coach to draw closer before trying again.

The horse and rider had kicked up enough earth on their trip into our field of vision that the cloud arrived a good minute before they did. By the time they pulled up, I could only see a dim outline of them, like a ghost truly returned to dust.

"Leon Thaw?"

I didn't know it was him, but I didn't know who else it might be. If it had been him, I'd have been happier to see him than I would have thought possible. There was no answer from the coach. Roman stood strong. Bird kicked at the dust and tried to pull away.

"Leon Thaw, that you there?" I said.

And waited.

Slowly, I saw a figure come from the coach and make its way toward us.

CHAPTER THIRTY-SEVEN

"Wilkie John Liquorish, I need a simple yes or no answer. And I would like to remind you that, like your Mrs., you are under oath to tell the truth. Yes or no, have you ever killed a man?"

Gentleman Jack seemed to lose a bit of his gentleness with the removal of the only woman from the stage. I wasn't concerned. I knew if I kept my composure, it would make him look desperate by comparison.

"Lots of 'em," I said.

Reverend Caliber wiped his brow. Jack jumped back, surprised at my answer.

"I'm sorry," I added. "The answer would be yes."

You might think the women in the crowd all blushed and gasped while the men laughed. Truth is, the women laughed louder than the men, who seemed unsure of what to do.

"You are aware that you are being charged with murder and sentenced to hang for your crimes?" Gentleman Jack said.

In my mind, I was standing in front of Sister

Mary Constance and the class in downtown San Antonio. My hands were in my pockets, and everyone's eyes were on me.

"You do know that you were supposed to have your homework done before you came to class today, right, Wilkie?"

I lived to make the Sister throw her hands up in defeat. Or cry. Or laugh.

"I did it, Sister Mary Constance. I swear I did."

She walked across the room to my desk and looked down at my hands. I knew the drill better than she did. I laid my hands across the desk and held my breath. She came down across the knuckles on my right hand. I sucked in air and closed my eyes. The left hand always came second. Always hurt more that the right. Because it was the weaker.

"You know you're not to swear," the Sister said.

Then I would take my homework out of my back pocket and unfold it on my desk. I always did my homework. I made good grades. When it got boring, I made it more interesting.

"I was a soldier," I said.

With one exception, any killing I had done was after being sworn in to the Army at Fort Griffin.

"Wilkie John was a private in the United States Army, sworn to serve and protect the very lives of you people here today," Reverend Caliber said. "And this man here gets hemp fever and wants to hang him on evidence that's flimsier than a floozy's nightdress."

He pointed his finger into the chest of Gentleman Jack, who recoiled like he'd been hit with holy water. I was standing there thinking this all boiled down to a verbal fighting match between two egos who cared less about my immediate future than their own reputations.

"Why don't the three of us just arm wrestle. Loser swings," I said.

The reverend looked horrified, like I'd double crossed him. I'm not sure either of them got my point.

"Before we get into that, I think it's time to call my third witness up," Gentleman Jack said. "Pete Doon has come from Wichita Falls to tell us what happened when Wilkie John brought his destruction into town. He was there when Wilkie John showed up and he saw firsthand what followed."

Pete Doon stepped forward, took off his hat and held it over his heart. He exhibited a solemnity that had, up till that point, been lacking. I appreciated his serious-mindedness, even if it did give off the air of being at a funeral.

"Mr. Doon, do you reside in Wichita Falls, and did you reside there on the day that Wilkie John Liquorman visited the town?" Gentleman Jack said.

Doon looked at me close before answering. I guess he was running my face through his head and comparing it with whatever was in there. He deliberated on it for a spell and seemed satisfied.

"I live there," he said. "And yes, I recognize this man."

I resisted the urge to smile at him. I was still a little mad he'd offered me such a paltry amount for those cows. Even madder I'd taken it. I didn't think they were sick. They never looked sick to me.

"Mr. Doon, you are, in fact, the one who met

Mr. Liquorman on his way into Wichita Falls, are you not?"

I was getting more and more annoyed at Jack getting my name wrong, but I knew he was poking me. I refused to react.

"No, I am," Pete Doon said. "I mean, yes. Yes, I was. I was there."

Pete Doon as star witness didn't seem to have the sense God gave a chicken, but he had indeed been there. I hadn't known his name, but I never forget a face. And he had a face that perfectly matched the name Pete Doon.

"Did you hear or see Wilkie John kill anybody, try to kill anybody, or even talk about killing anybody?" Reverend Caliber said.

Doon shuffled his feet like he was about to launch into a song and dance.

"No sir," he said. "No sir, I can't say that I did. That he did, rather."

This guy was a puzzle, and he hadn't quite solved himself.

"Can you tell us, in your own words, what happened on the day you met Wilkie John Liquorman there in Wichita Falls?" Gentleman Jack said.

The Reverend looked to an empty sky.

"Heaven help us," he said.

"We wasn't actually in Wichita Falls," Pete Doon said. "We was a ways up the other side, as we'd heard tell there was a big drive coming. It didn't turn out to be much of anything after all, just a few cows."

I guess he thought we were driving fifty-eight head of cattle across the land.

"But you turned him away and wouldn't let him

enter," Reverend Caliber said. "Why did you take it upon yourself to turn this man away?"

You could see Doon trembling from where I was standing, I guess just from being that close to the rope. Maybe he had a guilty conscience. Maybe he just shook by habit. I hadn't gotten to know him that well in Wichita Falls.

"Well, sir, it wasn't so much a turning him away. I mean it wasn't nothing to do with the fella. This fella here," he said. "Leastways, not right at the first. We'd had a outbreak of what they call Nervous Fever. That's what I always heard it called. The doctors call it Typhoid. Something like that."

He looked like he was still suffering the effects of Nervous Fever to me. And he was standing so close, he was beginning to contaminate me.

"So you were merely trying to warn him," Jack said. "How did he respond?"

I didn't remember any mention of typhoid when I was there that day. Just a few men telling me I wasn't welcome.

"He was in a hurry to sell off a bunch of cows he had," Doon said. "I didn't want them cows. A man who was there with me, now he's a rancher. He took a look and said okay. I was uneasy about it, I guess you could say. Way I seen it, anybody take twenty-five, thirty dollars for, I guess it must've been seventy, eighty head of cattle or so, you can just about go tell it on the mountain. You understand what I'm saying? I knowed there was something going on."

I remembered most of what he was saying, even if I didn't remember it exactly the same. It was a way of looking at it.

"And what then happened?" Jack said.

The puzzle got harder.

"What you mean?" Pete Doon said. "My friend Rafe paid that man right there and took his cows back to his pasture."

I wanted to mention that there was only fifty-eight of them, but I waited until the right moment had passed, so I kept that detail to myself. I couldn't remember if I'd already gone on the record about that or not.

"This is getting a little ridiculous," the Reverend said. "It's utterly obvious. This man, United States Army Private Liquorish, didn't murder or do anything to purposefully take the life of anybody in Wichita Falls. He didn't even set foot in Wichita Falls. What he did was swap a herd of cows for a fair price, plus a few bottles of needed medicine, which he was bringing back to his crew. That, my friends, is hardly criminal."

I liked the way the Reverend sounded. It reminded me of Ira Lee after he'd had several beers and started expounding on why slavery hadn't ever been needed in Texas and why John Booth hadn't really been killed in Virginia like they said. Sometimes it doesn't matter if a thing is true. It's just whether it's said right and heard right.

CHAPTER THIRTY-EIGHT

It wasn't Leon Thaw. It wasn't anybody I'd ever seen before.

He walked into my field of vision like he was walking into a bank and I just happened to be the teller on duty. I thought he was going to rob me. One of us would have died right there if he had.

"Stranger."

I figured him to be a fur trader due to the pelts lining the top of his wagon. I'd seen wagons like it in San Antonio, usually parked in the market. As a child, I had wanted one of the beaver pelt hats I'd seen a fur trader wearing there. Of course, it was priced out of our reach. If I'd got one, I likely wouldn't have remembered it nearly so well. Hunger provokes many actions, good and bad. Eating provokes a siesta at best. Poisoning and death at worst.

"Takes one to know one, don't it?" I said.

He stepped down from his wagon, his hands in front of him. He knew I could see the Colt Dragoon on his hip. He'd already scoped me out.

"That's a mighty fine looking animal you got there," he said. "What are you doing way out here in the middle of nothing?"

What threatened to loom large perched on top of the wagon was, at ground level, not so much taller than me. He didn't look like a local. With his beaver hat and fur, he certainly wasn't dressed for the weather.

"What I hear, somebody hid Fort Worth around here somewhere," I said.

I ignored the part about Bird. I wasn't interested in selling her.

"Five, six miles maybe," he said. He looked me up and down like I was the one dressed funny. "What kind of business you got in Fort Worth?"

I wasn't sure I had any business at all there, but I was bound and determined to get there and have a look around. I also had the name of the man we were to meet up with when we got there. Any pay for delivering the eight hundred head of cattle had burned up in the summer heat, but I wanted some kind of satisfaction for all the trouble we'd been through.

"I aim to see a man," I said. "Personal business."

The stranger pulled his hat off, wiped his brow and replaced the hat. His hair fell down around his shoulders, but he was smooth as a baby's ass on top and damn near as pasty.

"Don't ever make your business too personal," he said. "Who is it you're looking for?"

I scraped the map out of my bag and unfolded the name written across the back.

"William Henry Tubb," I said.

He spit at the ground and stared at the pattern he made.

"Don't reckon I know him. Heck of a lot of people I don't know though."

It was like he'd seen something in that design on the ground, because when he looked back up at me, he was looking different. I thought he might have it in mind to rob me, even though I had nothing of any value.

He laughed. "Don't worry, friend. I like the looks of your horse, but I'm not gonna hold you up or nothing. I can be a handful of trouble, don't get me wrong, but I don't mete it out on the undeserving."

He gave the appearance of reading my mind. I didn't much care for it. Didn't like him talking about my horse either.

"I have five more miles, I'd best be on my way," I said.

I'd hoped he would climb back up that wagon and git, but he didn't do that. He stood there like he aimed to watch me walk away, unable to kick up any proportionate amount of dust as I slowly made my way across the expanse before me.

"Watch yourself," he said. "There's more crows than true sparrows on the road ahead."

He had a way with words. It reminded me of Bricky Lusk, except for being easier to understand.

"You a fur trader?" I said.

I was trying to get a move on and be friendly all at the same time. I was feeling a little bad for thinking he was going to rob me, but I was mostly still trying to keep him from wanting to. Why didn't I just draw iron and shoot? Believe me, I considered it. The fact I didn't may give you some inkling how petered out I was.

"I prefer the word *furrier*," he said.

I couldn't help laughing. It wasn't a deep, belly laugh. I didn't have the lungs for that. It was just a small chuckle really, mostly from hearing this fella, dressed to the hilt in animals, trying to sport such verbosity. He didn't take kindly to it.

"Get your hands in the air, friend!"

He had that Dragoon steady between my eyes before I even heard the first word. My reflexes were off. My instincts were shot. I didn't have a move, and we both knew it.

"I'm taking your horse," he said. "I don't want anything else. I'm not gonna hurt you. I'm going to keep this leveled right at your brain, and, assuming you don't do anything foolish, I'll just ride away. I'm going toward Nacogdoches. You're going to Fort Worth. Got it?"

I was fine with it. It wouldn't have been worth making a move. Not if he'd taken Bird. When he reached over and grabbed Roman's bridle, that changed things. I couldn't stand by and watch him ride off to Nacogdoches on Roman. I'd have rather died right there, five miles from my destination.

I pulled Ira Lee's Colt just as he was swinging his leg over Roman and caught him in the side. Roman reared up, not liking this stranger any more than I did. He fell off backward just as I shot again. The second shot hit Roman. He fell sideways. It took all of five seconds.

There's not a lot I can say about what happened there on the outskirts just south of Fort Worth. No way of describing what it felt like to see Roman lying there, bleeding into the dirt. I could have just as easily put a gun to my own mama's head. I shot twice, and I made them count, because I was saving bullets. The only thing that pushed me through it, watching my closest friend—maybe my only friend—dying at my own hand, was the hatred of this furrier who'd brought this all upon me.

"Don't shoot me. Please don't do it."

Those are some lousy last words to cap off anybody's life. They didn't do much for me.

"You should've taken the mule," I said.

I shot him once right in the gut. Then I shot him in the knees, just to make sure he wasn't going anywhere. When he hit the dirt, coins spilled out of his clothes like a pinata. I gathered up a handful. I didn't kill him. The crows would do that soon enough.

CHAPTER THIRTY-NINE

"I never killed nobody," I said, "but there was some people who died of their wounds."

The people in the street loved that line. Most of the people on the stage with me didn't. Reverend Caliber was intent on wrapping things up. There wasn't a case to be made, far as he could see, and it seemed he'd done a decent job of making those in the crowd see it too.

"Indians and the like," the Reverend said.

He was going back through my history, or, at least my history since it had been set down in writing. That meant more or less everything from Fort Griffin until the present day.

"Mostly Indians," I said. "Not so much the like."

Gentleman Jack had heard enough. He was pacing back and forth like a tiger who was scared of looking like a housecat. He pulled his watch from his jacket pocket and flipped it open.

"I think we've afforded this man more of a defense than he deserved," he said. "Is there anyone here who has anything else useful to add, either to his credit or his detriment?"

Nobody wanted to be the first to speak. I looked to the side of the gallows and saw Sunny coming through the throng of people, Madam Pearlie right behind her and pushing.

"I want to say something," Madam Pearlie said.

People turned to take in the sight. Most everyone in Hell's Half Acre, if not all of Fort Worth, knew Madam Pearlie on sight, knew her as the owner of the Black Elephant. More had graced its interior than would have admitted it there in broad daylight.

"Madam Pearlie, step forward," Gentleman Jack said.

As if she wasn't already doing so.

"I have a few things I want to get off my chest, Jack Delaney," she said.

I was hoping she would climb the steps to the top of the platform. Partly because it would make me feel better, but mostly because I knew it would make Jack feel worse. She was a big woman, and she wasn't intimidated by his fancy clothes and slick act.

"I can hear you just fine where you're at, Madam Pearlie," he said.

She walked all the way up to the front of the crowd. Refusing to look up to Jack, she spun around and addressed the people in the street.

"I'm a businesswoman here in Hell's Half Acre, and I have gotten to know this young man, Wilkie John Liquorish, over the past few days," she said. "Wilkie John Liquorish arrived in our town weak and hungry and needing a place to stay. We took him in at The Black Elephant, because that is what we do. That's what Fort Worth does. At least, that's what we always did."

The Reverend leaned over to me.

"That's a good woman."

I knew he'd found a place to stay there more often than I had.

"When people come into my place, we don't ask what they're leaving behind them," Madam Pearlie said. "They're all the same to me. Colored, Anglo, slave or free, they come to The Black Elephant to get away from whatever they're leaving outside. Same as Jack Delaney here did."

Jack had been standing to my side, biting off his fingernails and spitting them at me. Finally, he'd heard enough.

"Careful, Pearlie," he said. "I've seen you doing some questionable things. Why, I could just as easily snatch you up here and put you on the stand."

I'd seen her throw men out of the saloon herself for less. She looked smaller than usual but no less fierce down there among the rank and file.

"If I've violated a law, I'd like for you to name it right now, Mr. Delaney," she said.

Jack looked bewildered, like things were starting to get out of his control.

"I seem to recall you celebrating the High Sheriff's death a few days ago," he said. "Surely that's not the type of thing we would expect from a businessperson in the Acre."

There was an immediate swell of shouts toward the sky. Celebrations were still going on from one end of Hell's Half Acre to the other, even if Jack was somehow unaware. I had watched them in amazement, not quite sure what to think. The Black Elephant and the White Elephant, never adversaries to begin with, had both slashed prices upstairs and downstairs. The same with the Red Light Saloon. And the Emerald Saloon. The Nance Hotel. The Cigar Factory was handing out free cigars.

I had almost come clean to Sunny on two different occasions. The only reason I kept mum? I didn't want to put her in a position later where Jack was pressing her for details and she had to make a decision.

But there on the corner of Main and Houston, with the crowd egging me on, and the rope hanging loosely around my neck, with Gentleman Jack acting like some Southern preacher and the Reverend looking unsure if even he would see tomorrow, I made a decision.

Truthfully, I don't think there was enough of a mental process to call it a decision. I didn't use my heart either, for I knew it couldn't be trusted. Something came back to me that mama had said one day when we were standing at the front door of the Alamo mission. Every year around Christmas, mama would get sentimental, and we would make the journey to the place. There we would stand quietly and stare until mama was satisfied that respects had been paid. I thought for years that Henry had died within the walls.

"Great men laid down their lives for a cause," mama said.

I tried to imagine them shooting from the doorway or pouring out into the dirt lot with bayonets. It all seemed too quiet.

"Who killed them?" Ira Lee said.

I can still remember this all, clear as a bell.

"The Mexicans did."

We looked around us in astonishment. Mexicans lived all around us. They ran the shops, made the food, some of them walked the streets in U.S. Army battledress. Mama saw our faces and quickly added, "*Different* Mexicans."

Before we left that sacred spot, mama bent down and huddled us together.

"Sometimes we have to do things we don't wish to do. Sometimes adults have to do terrible things so that people, their children, can have a chance to live a better life."

I always thought she was talking about Henry. Later, I realized who she was really talking about.

"When things are going bad, when you're surrounded and you don't feel like you have a satisfactory exit," she said, "remember that you'll always be okay if you go with your gut."

I looked up and saw Madam Pearlie looking at me. It was like she was hearing my thoughts. I don't know exactly what Gentleman Jack was saying. Something about the price of killing. I raised up my hand. I had something to say.

It seemed like the whole town fell silent. Maybe it was the blood rushing to my ears.

Chapter Forty

The carpet of sand laid out between the spot where I buried the best horse a man ever saw and where I rode into Fort Worth on a mule named Bird was more dangerous than quicksand. Comanches didn't call the area home, but they were known to cross in and out of it, sometimes at battle with the Tonkawa. It was known to be Tonkawa land, and more than one unsuspecting Anglo had found himself caught between two warring parties. In that case, you could be forgiven for wishing there was a little quicksand or a mud bog to hide in.

I wasn't in the best of shape, and my spirits were even lower. Bird was a little shaky and seemed to be watching close for snakes. She wasn't dumb to do so. Stories had been traded way back along the trail of giant nests of rattlers.

"You could hear them things buzzing for a quarter mile," Leon Thaw said.

That had seemed something to marvel at, a saving grace, at the time, but now there seemed to be a constant buzzing inside my head, and if I would turn it one way or another, it might strike and fool me into near hysterics, jumping no less than if it had been a snake.

I might very well have died out there in that desert. Truly, something inside must have. If so, it wasn't the distance between me and Greer that did it, although it probably could have been. It wasn't the death of my brother Ira Lee that did it, although it might well have been that too. If part of my heart was left on that deadly stretch, it was the part that beat inside the skin of that faithful Saddlebred, and I had been the one that stilled it. To say it killed me to ride away was closer to truth than anyone might have suspected.

Sometime in the night, a man on a black mare pulled alongside Bird and me and traveled with us clear through till daylight. I didn't recognize him, and he never uttered his own name or asked for mine. He claimed to have come from Acorn, Arkansas, where he worked on the section gang of the Texarkana–Fort Smith Railway line.

"You a long way from home, mister," I said.

I didn't know where Acorn, Arkansas, was, but I knew it wasn't anywhere south of Fort Worth.

"I been gone two whole months," he said. "A man can see a lot of country in two months."

We would travel for a while in silence, which was fine by me as I had no urge to talk and not much of one to listen either. He didn't seem to mind that any. Sooner or later, something seemed to nudge something in his mind, and he would go to talking. Sometimes I would act like I was asleep in the saddle, and sometimes I might have even fooled myself. But he kept on talking, all the same.

"They got word to us in Acorn that the bridge had washed out down on Chances Creek," he said. "The train was coming down, and there weren't no way to get word out. This was middle of the night, mind you."

It had to have been middle of the night out there in the desert too, an ironical fact that seemed to slip by our new companion. I hadn't had any intention to stop and camp, due to the travel being easier at night and me wanting to get on into Fort Worth as soon as possible. He was beginning to make me reconsider though.

"I got out of bed and went down to the tracks wearing nothing but my nightshirt and slippers," he continued. "It was wet as a beast in the rain. Ain't that what Chaucer said?"

I looked at him like maybe he was a ghost and I was hearing things. What man from Acorn, Arkansas, riding along the Texas desert in the middle of the night, starts quoting Chaucer? He didn't give any room for an answer, maybe thinking what kind of man riding alongside him in the Texas desert would know enough to give one.

"I got there not five minutes before I saw the headlamp on that engine come shining through the trees. I straddled the track just like you straddling that mule of yours and swung my lantern for all it was worth, just hoping it had the might to show itself to the engineer."

By this point, I was trying not to care but was casually curious what would happen next, if only to get it over with and get some peace and quiet.

"I realized too late that I should've stood farther up the track," he said. "The bridge was washed out not twenty foot behind me, which didn't give me no room for error. When that engine came grinding toward me, sparks flying like July fourth, I thought I was a goner and the crew on the train did too. I kid you not, that damn thing come to a screeching halt no farther from me than you and your mule are right now."

Considering I could have reached out my foot and given his horse a kick, I found that somewhat doubtful, but, like the impulse to follow through with that kick, I let it go.

"You rebuild the bridge in your long johns?" I said.

If part of me still doubted he was an actual physical being, his bark of a laugh made him all too real.

"Much to my chagrin, I was not suited up in long johns," he said, "but yes, with the help of the engineer and his assistant, I did rebuild that bridge. I did something else while I was at it. I got myself a job with the railroad. I went back home for breakfast and told the wife, I was now the lead member of the section gang south of Acorn, Arkansas."

For such a stroke of good fortune, he didn't seem happy at all in the telling of it.

"Railroad's a good job," I said.

I had thought from time to time about a railroad job. What kid hadn't?

"Far as I'm concerned, only good railroad job is me holding a six-shooter and the engineer throwing down bags of gold and bank notes."

I turned to look at the fellow, trying to judge

whether he was serious or what. He was dim enough to blend into the night. I wondered if I had fallen asleep and dreamed up the whole thing.

"You funning me?" I said.

He barked, and I knew again, he was real.

"I married a girl from Philadelphia who came west to be a teacher," he said. "She lived in that house in Acorn with me for several months, but her daddy came and took her away. I know for a fact they come down this way, but I lost their track around Fort Worth. I'm starting to think they discovered me and changed course to throw me off. I been riding in circles out here ever since."

I hawed Bird, and away she went. People don't realize how fast a mule can run when it's nudged along. The man rode along next to us, sometimes close enough to hear him talking, even though I couldn't make out the words and didn't try, and sometimes far enough out there that I thought maybe we'd lost him.

Soon enough, the sky began to lighten up to our right, which was where he'd been riding, and I couldn't see any trace of him. Maybe he didn't want to be seen. Maybe he had no interest in Fort Worth. I dozed off and on, and Bird kept about her business and didn't tarry. Not long after, the whole incident had grown questionable in my mind, and I struck it up to lack of sleep or lack of food or maybe just a lack of anyone to talk to.

Had the man been the furrier? The mere thought made me seem crazy. Surely I had seen him shot down by my own hand. Only thing I was absolutely certain of, I missed Roman dreadfully.

CHAPTER FORTY-ONE

Me and Bird entered Fort Worth from due south. That route brought me into the Texas & Pennsylvania Railway yard. Just over the tracks lay a small tent city. The only place I'd ever seen anything like it was in war photographs in the shop back in San Antonio. In those, army tents dotted the landscape as battalions gathered prior to battle. My background gave the sight there on the south side of Fort Worth an ominous feel.

"You dying, mister?"

The first words uttered to me upon arrival might have been an omen if I'd been paying more attention. I wasn't thinking of how I must appear to the small boy standing just outside one of the first tents I rode up on. For an answer, I pulled the Colt .44 from its holster, silently poked it in the kid's face and then shushed him with my finger. He turned tail and disappeared as I made my way down a long row of campsites, temporary homes of families who had come in on the train and were waiting to find jobs and more permanent lodging inside the city proper. Coming into town from that direction, I missed the route the coaches took into town. Because of this, the town rolled out slowly, block after block, until it seemed bigger than San Antonio, though it wasn't. Third Street took me in a northeast direction, past a scatter of small clapboard houses, all either painted white or else left natural. Each block, the houses got bigger and closer together. Now and then, there was a hotel. I crossed Jones, which seemed to be a street of some significance, but decided to keep moving. I was intrigued. How long would the town continue to unfold? How much bigger would the buildings get? I could see three and four story ones ahead as I approached Calhoun.

"Climb down off that animule and let us pour you a drink, there, feller."

I looked to the left to find a doorman standing out in front of a two story building called the Panther Saloon. He didn't look any older than I was.

"I'm looking to find a man named William Henry Tubb," I said.

He motioned for me to tie Bird at one of several hitching posts in front of the building. I thanked him but declined the offer. Another voice followed, attached to a lanky cowboy just freeing himself from the Panther's grasp.

"Tubb you say?"

His long legs got him over to me before I had the sense to depart, so I told him what little I knew.

"I believe his name is William Henry Tubb," I said. "Works cattle."

He looked up Calhoun to the west and then up

Third, like he thought he might see Bill Tubb walking down one of them.

"He own a store?" the man said.

I told him I had no idea. All I knew was, he was expecting a big herd of cattle to come wandering in from Mobeetie soon. I didn't figure this fellow needed to know any more than that, unless he was in fact William Henry Tubb.

"Tubbs," he said. "Bill Tubbs. He owns Tubbs's General Store back over in the Acre."

I was laying about fifty-fifty odds this guy knew what he was talking about. I was pretty sure from what I'd heard Ira Lee say that our guy made his living in Hell's Half Acre or else they wouldn't have been anywhere near that high.

"Bill Tubbs, you say."

He started telling me how to get to Tubbs's General Store, and I tried to keep all the turns in order, but I guess the look on my face must have given him some doubt. He started rummaging through his coat pockets, and I hoped he was going to pull out a map. Instead, I got a small card.

"Let me jot the street down for you," he said. "It's on Main and Sixth, but the best way to find it is go to Sixth and Main."

He handed me the card and sent me on my way, which was down Calhoun to the west, in search of Sixth Street. I spent the next few blocks wondering if I'd been foolish to put stock in this total stranger. He might have been the biggest drunk in Fort Worth as far as I knew, and here I was riding away from the big, new buildings I'd seen farther north and into the wildest, most lawless place in all of wild, lawless Texas.

CHAPTER FORTY-TWO

Tubbs's General Store was right where it was supposed to be. I sat inside Frank's Saloon, on the opposite side of Main, and watched it for an hour or two, drinking down a couple sarsaparillas and paying extra for a Garfield Headache Powder that promised to make me feel like a new man. Maybe it worked too, because I did feel like a new man. Fort Worth represented the new life, and all that had come before was like a story leading up to it.

I had seen a fortyish looking man come out onto the front porch of the general store a time or two and decided it must be Tubbs himself I was looking at. I thought about crossing the street to pay him a visit, but by then, the sarsaparilla ran round my head and trickled down into my digits and appendages, and I was beginning to feel a little heavy in the eyes and light in the head.

I flipped the little card over in my hand and noticed for the first time that it was an advertisement

for a local establishment called The Black Elephant
Saloon.

THE BLACK ELEPHANT SALOON
Pearlie Tutt & Frederick Washington, *Prop'rs*

Main at Fourth Street

~ LIQUORS, WINES, BRANDIES & CIGARS ~
The most beautiful ladys west of the Mississippi

I wasn't nearly as interested in the liquors and
cigars as I was the beautiful ladies, but, three hundred miles from home and feeling newly reborn,
I was most interested in finding a bed to lay down
and sleep in. I paid for the sarsaparillas with one of
the furrier's coins and mosied on out of Frank's,
letting William Henry Tubbs wait for another day.
I was in no all-fired hurry to return to Mobeetie.

The Black Elephant wasn't difficult to find. Two
stories high with a full length porch across the
front and a matching veranda above for the girls
to stand on and wave down from, the name was
spelled out in ornate black letters that took up half
a block on Fourth and another half on Main. Coming
up on it from Fourth Street, the sign seemed to read
The Black El. Then from Main, *ephant Saloon.* As a
result, as I would soon discover, many local folks
referred to the place as The Black El.

The first time I saw Sunny, she was standing on
the veranda, right above the main entrance. With
her golden skin and red hair, she seemed to
shimmer in the afternoon light, a strange but al-
luring new presence. If I was only there out of a

mild curiosity, the sight of this girl was enough to bring me through the swinging doors.

"How do you close up shop?" I said.

I had already ordered a ginger cola, and, because the barkeep, a big colored man with one eye, hadn't poked fun at me, I tried to maintain a conversation.

"Close up shop?" he said.

I motioned to the swinging doors. I hadn't seen any like them in Mobeetie, or, far as I could recall, in San Antone.

"Fort Worth don't close up," he said.

I had yet to learn that, in those types of establishments, most all the money is made between sundown and sunup. Nobody slept those hours. Even so, or because it was so, an empty bed was hard to find. As much as I wanted sleep, I wouldn't find it until the kitchen cook was making breakfast. Before then, I would see Sunny once again. And I would meet Madam Pearlie, whom I felt like I knew already from the card.

"Where you come from, little one?"

I don't like being told I'm little. It's not clever. I've never been tall, so it's nothing I've somehow overlooked or never contemplated before. I never liked Ira Lee mentioning it, in fact, the only time I'd ever whooped him was one time when he'd called me Puny John in front of Ginny Hay. Still, the one person who could call me "little one" and get away with it was mama, and, right at that moment, Madam Pearlie was about as close to a mama as I'd seen since the woods burned over, so I let it lie.

"I come here from Mobeetie," I said, "but in general, I guess I come from San Antone."

She thought that was such a magnificent answer, she repeated it to the one-eyed barkeep and a man on his way out the swinging doors. They all seemed to agree I was okay, even if I didn't order up any of the liquors or brandies or cigars.

"You looking for a place to stay at?" Madam Pearlie said.

I sure was. At that point, I didn't know there was a White Elephant Saloon just a few blocks down Main, but I'm glad. I felt at home there in the black one, and I felt even better about it when Sunny came gliding down the staircase and into the room.

"Come meet Mr. Liquorish who comes from San Antone," Madam Pearlie said.

Sunny sat down at my table and welcomed me to town in a most hospitable way. She even offered to take me upstairs and give me a look at her room. I took her up on the offer and didn't leave the room for twenty-four hours. By the time the night was over, Sunny and me had done a whole lot of talking, and I fell hard asleep. It was a dark, dreamless sleep but not restless. I slept better than I'd ever slept in my life and woke up to Sunny sponging me off and patching me up in places that needed it. It was already night time again, and the doors were still swinging.

CHAPTER FORTY-THREE

"I'm the one killed the High Sheriff of Hell's Half Acre," I said.

Gentleman Jack looked offended. Not offended that I might have done such a thing. More like offended that he hadn't thought to accuse me of it first. The crowd hooted and hollered, and a few hats were thrown into the air. Then, just as quick, it fell silent, waiting for Jack's next retort. He mulled it over like a cow chewing its cud then spit between the slats. I wondered if anyone was unfortunate enough to be standing in that particular space beneath the platform.

"I seriously doubt that, young Wilkie John."

He'd been trying fairly hard not to make me look too small, too young, thinking the crowd might not have the stomach to watch a youngster dangle at the end of a rope. Now, suddenly, I wasn't big enough to have done what I said I done. That didn't please me.

"I shot him right betwixt the eyes," I said.

I thought about the halo of flour that rose over

him as he lay there on the floor of Tubb's store with his blood and water leaking out. I could tell them about it, but so what? If they weren't there, what would it prove?

"This little fella says he walked up to the High Sheriff and shot him right between the eyes," Gentleman Jack said. "Does he really expect us to believe our High Sheriff would let a pipsqueak like this shoot him right between the eyes?"

Some guys down close to the front were laughing at the thought of it. I'd shot plenty of people like them before. I tried to study their silly faces in case I lived to run into them again. Other folks in the crowd were looking at each other and wondering aloud if such a thing could have happened, and how happy they were that it had been done, however it had been done, and whoever had done it.

It seemed to me Gentleman Jack was in real danger of losing the crowd. He'd spent most of the afternoon trying to convince them how dangerous I was. Now, faced with the possibility that his friend the High Sheriff had been beaten by someone half his size, he was tacking in a new direction.

"You really expect them to believe I killed anybody?" I said.

I thought Jack was going to have to take another break. He hiked over to the back of the gallows and took a long look down the stairs. I thought maybe he would bring Greer up the steps again. Part of me wanted to gaze on her one more time like I had around the campfire at Fort Griffin.

Reverend Caliber wasn't sure what to do at that point. He felt like he had to do something. He stepped up into the space vacated by Gentleman Jack Delaney.

"Wilkie John Liquorish," he said, "do you have any means by which you can authentically lay claim to killing the High Sheriff of Hell's Half Acre?"

I was trying to formulate an answer.

"By that," the reverend said, "I mean, do you have a way to prove your claim?"

I thought for a minute, during which, Jack reappeared.

"I think I do," I said. "When I was in the store where it happened. . . ."

"Stop right there," Reverend Caliber said. "Hold on tight to the rest of that thought."

He turned to Jack who had turned to Madam Pearlie, who was still right where she was, at the front of the platform. Sunny had told me a story about Pearlie, back on that first night. Pearlie, she said, had once married a preacher from St. Louis. She had gone to church with the man. Some great big church in St. Louis or somewhere. She had been just fine with it until one day her husband preached on the relationship of Jesus and his mother Mary, and he'd told how Mary sat and watched her son be crucified.

"Pearlie got up and walked out of the church and never looked back," Sunny said. "She said she couldn't put no stock in someone who was supposed to be this ideal woman but was really a passive damn mother who would sit and watch her son suffer and die and never jump up there and say something or beat seven shades of you-know-what out of them Roman soldiers who were doing the cross building."

Turns out, getting away from the church wasn't even enough for Madam Pearlie. She also got away from that preacher husband of hers and even managed to escape from St. Louis in whatever state it was in. All the story, as related by Sunny, had been offered as an explanation of Pearlie's fondness for Reverend Caliber. Not that he rekindled any passion for the preacher in St. Louis, but he served to remind her what a doubting, despicable old sinner he had been and how fortunate she was to be shut of him.

Now, here I was on the stand, and she wasn't going to sit silently by any longer.

"Wilkie, you tell this man, you give him the information he wants, he gonna have to give you something in return. You hear me?"

As inconvenient as it was, Gentleman Jack had a soft spot in his heart for Madam Pearlie too, and this new offer tossed up at his feet intrigued him. Jack walked over between the Reverend and me.

"Okay, so what kind of deal is it you want to make?"

My first thought was to ask them to let Greer loose. To maybe give her coach fare back to Mobeetie or wherever she wanted. I was feeling for Arkansas Pete who had chosen to die in a town far from family, to spare them having to sit and watch it. Which meant I was feeling pretty sorry for myself.

Ira Lee had taught me, back in San Antone, to never settle for a little bit until you know you can't get a lot. When you were playing billiards in a game room or poker in a saloon and you had the

Army boys by the thingumbobs, you didn't tickle. You squeezed.

"If I can prove I done it, I want you to set me loose and let me go free," I said.

Jack looked at the Reverend and then at Madam Pearlie. His lips were moving in a way to suggest he was counting up numbers in his head. No discernible sound was coming out.

"If it turns out he killed the High Sheriff," Reverend Caliber said, "you'll have solved the biggest unsolved crime in all Fort Worth."

"And the killer goes free?" Jack said.

The Reverend pointed out into the crowd.

"If it turns out he really did it, these people gonna have themselves a new hero. You really wanna go and make him a martyr too?"

Jack looked out into the crowd. It seemed to still be growing. Not only that, it was getting impatient.

CHAPTER FORTY-FOUR

There was a deputy sheriff of Fort Worth who never set foot in Hell's Half Acre. Some said it was out of fear. Others said he was getting paid by the saloons and bawdy houses to stay away. Both were probably right. His name was Shadrack Parnell, and he was standing at the bottom of the thirteen steps, too close to Greer Lusk and Simeon Payne and too far from where Gentleman Jack had spit between the slats.

Jack stood at the top of the thirteen steps, mouthing words down to the deputy while everyone else stood around and switched their weight from one leg to the other and then back. If someone had been renting chairs, he'd have retired a rich man by suppertime. Soon enough, Jack rejoined the festivities, this time bringing his sidekick Shadrack along. Shadrack looked like he wanted to be a thousand other places.

"Ladies and gentlemen of Fort Worth, this young man has, in a last ditch effort to spare himself from his fate, tried to strike a deal with justice," Jack said. "It seems that, in a move to curry favor with y'all, he's trying to take claim for the cold blooded murder of the High Sheriff of Hell's Half Acre. I would assume, since William Henry Tubbs was also found dead in the same location, he's going to plead guilty to that death as well."

Jack looked at me with a crocodile grin.

"I shot 'em both," I said, "and I dumped 'em in the broom closet."

Everybody there knew the bodies of the High Sheriff and the General Store owner had been discovered in the broom closet. That had been old news by the time it made it into the next day's newspaper. Everybody knew how Deputy Parnell brought in the Texas Rangers, and how they'd turned the General Store upside down looking for clues left by the killer. Most had also heard that Parnell didn't want the job of High Sheriff of Hell's Half Acre. Some said he was thinking of turning it over to one of the Texas Rangers. Others said an infamous lawman and killer of men had been offered the job.

"It true Bat Masterson's coming to town to take the High Sheriff's position?" I said.

If Gentleman Jack talked like a man who was being paid by the word, Parnell acted like he was being paid to keep his mouth shut.

"No," he said.

"If he is, you won't live to see it," Jack said.

I'd read Masterson had killed twenty-six people. That put him several ahead of me, and he was being called a hero for what he'd done in Dodge. He was being offered jobs. It was enough to make me vexatious as the Reverend called it.

"We have your word that Mr. Liquorish will be allowed to go free if he can prove that he was the man who killed the High Sheriff," Reverend Caliber said. "Are you reneging on that deal?"

Parnell and Gentleman Jack shrugged at each other and shook their heads no. They weren't reneging.

"Deputy Parnell led the investigation into the killing at Tubbs's General Store," Jack said. "He knows details that no one else but the killer would know. I will look to his word as the final word when it comes to any evidence."

He turned to the people in the street, his words as much for them as me.

"If you have evidence, present it at once."

I took one step forward and felt the rope tighten against my neck.

"There was but one thing missing from the store after the killing," I said. "I have that thing in a box under a bed in the upper quarters of The Black Elephant Saloon. May I have somebody go to retrieve it?"

I looked at Sunny. She was the only other person who knew three boxes of bullets lay inside a small box under the bed in her room. I had never even mentioned them to Madam Pearlie, out of fear that it would come out that three such boxes were missing from the store. Pearlie treated me like her son, and I wasn't sure if that would change things or not.

Sunny disappeared into the crowd and thus began the longest fifteen minutes of my life. There were times I thought Jack was going to lose all patience and open the trapdoor beneath me. What if

Sunny never came back? I learned much later that she had indeed been stopped several times in her journey to the Black El and then back again.

"Do you think he really killed the High Sheriff?"

"You don't think they'll hang him for it, do you?"

"If I visit The Black Elephant, may I ask for you by name?"

"Yes."

"And what name might I call?"

And away she ran, the box tucked tightly against her side.

I knew she was coming before I saw her. The cue came from the crowd, which began to murmur and then pull apart as she rounded the corner onto Main. Fifty yards from the platform, she held the box over her head like a prize, so that everyone could see. Jack was too busy watching his watch.

Why did Gentleman Jack agree to the deal that, if I could prove my guilt, he would let me go? There are multiple theories. One was simply that, having been one of the few to see the crime scene inside the General Store, he didn't think I was capable of it. That is the simplest theory, the most obvious one, and maybe the best. It also had one of the craziest notions I'd ever heard of going for it, and it may have been just crazy enough to amuse Jack. If I proved decisively that I had killed the High Sheriff, I would be free. If my self-prosecution fell short, I would hang.

Some thought he didn't support the High Sheriff and was secretly happy for his demise. Reverend Caliber was among that group. He'd heard stories about the two of them duking it out over the

future of Hell's Half Acre. The High Sheriff was
bound and determined to clean up the whole ca-
boodle. Also a deacon in the Baptist Church, he
didn't cotton to any kind of natural sin, especially
drunkenness and fornication, two of the Acre's
specialties. On the other hand, Gentleman Jack
made his living off drinkers and fornicators, so
closing down the Acre was akin to pulling down his
own shingle.

Whatever the reason, Jack seemed fully prepared to go along with our scheme, even to the
point of applauding the return of Sunny with her
wooden box. As she made her way to the front of
the stage, I held out my hand to stop her.

"I don't want you to hand the box over," I said.
"I want you to hold it closed, so that everyone can
see it."

I was now the magician putting the pack of
cards into the hat, with the hat being Sunny's box
and my very fate being the deck of cards. I had the
crowd's attention. Gentleman Jack and Reverend
Caliber were both leaning in. Deputy Purnell
looked uninterested.

"Now," I said, "does Deputy Purnell know what
single item was missing from Tubbs's General Store
after the High Sheriff and Mr. Tubbs were gunned
down there?"

Deputy Purnell looked at Gentleman Jack, and,
seeing Jack's quizzical expression coming back at
him, answered as only he could.

"Yep."

I could feel the sweet breath of freedom on
my face.

"And do tell, what might that item be, Deputy?"

Deputy Purnell cleared his throat and took a long step toward the people.

"It was four cans of beans."

The crowd got a hoot out of that. Purcell smiled in appreciation. I was beginning to see crows circling overhead.

CHAPTER FORTY-FIVE

Deputy Purnell got close enough, I could feel his breath on my neck.

"You really think I was going to be put on the spot like that?"

I had been made a fool, and I'd never seen it coming. I cursed him, and I cursed myself, and I wanted to go back and do it over. I didn't know how I would've done it, but I knew how I wouldn't.

Two men quickly joined him on the stage, and I first suspected them of being the Texas Rangers we'd heard about. They didn't have the famous peso badges though. In fact, they didn't have any badges or uniforms at all. One had Greer by the arm, having marched her back up the thirteen steps and into the blazing sun, which had slid just far enough to the west that it now glared straight at us. The other man had Simeon Payne in an arm-and-leg shackle. Payne should've been hopping mad. Instead, he looked beat. Like he'd just been told some dire piece of news that took the life right out of him. The mood of the proceedings, along with the crowd, had changed as suddenly as a dark cloud rolling over the sun. I could've used that cloud. It was nowhere to be found.

"This is unlawful as all git-out," Madam Pearlie said. "You can't be doing this."

Gentleman Jim had given control of things to Deputy Parnell and his boys. He raised his palms and shrugged. It was out of his hands. He had done his job. Reverend Caliber was asked to lead everyone in a prayer, and he delivered in his own unique way.

"Lord, I am weary of my crying."

He stopped and waited so long, those who had closed their eyes were peeking, and we who didn't were thinking he might have fallen asleep or else died and went to heaven right there on the spot.

"My throat is dried. Mine eyes fail while I wait for you," he continued. "They that hate me without a cause are more than the hairs of mine head, and they that would destroy me, being mine enemies wrongfully, are mighty."

I wasn't a praying man, and I didn't want to be one of those men who suddenly become one when they're facing down their end. All the same, there was something pretty in the words that reminded me of mama and also a little of Sister Mary Constance. Maybe I could see Jesus clearer up there on that deadly contraption, because I even found some reason there, some comfort in the thought that maybe mama could just sit quietly, respectfully and be present while I made my exit from the stage. She had been there when I made my entrance, after all.

"Lord, I pray for those of us who hate without

cause," the Reverend went on. "I pray like you taught us in the Bible, saying Oh God, rise up against those who would cause us harm. Let their table become a snare before them, and that which should have been for their welfare, let it become a trap. Let their eyes be darkened, that they see not; and let them be blotted out of the book of the living forever and ever.

Amen."

Gentleman Jack shook his head.

"Preacher, the Lord's Prayer would've worked just fine."

The rest happened so fast, it didn't seem real. I don't know how to write something that was so real and make it seem like it wasn't, but it seemed like everything hastened and railroaded on, so that you either went with it or got left behind. Me, pushed aside and into the arms of the preacher, while Greer was fitted for the rope. Part of me got left there in those moments while the sun blotted out the sins of the guilty and lay them at the feet of the innocent.

"Greer Lusk Liquorish, for the sin of conspiring with your husband, a known and admitted murderer and thief, for keeping knowledge of his deeds in your heart, for being one in the spirit with a moral degenerate, you are committed into the hands of God Almighty. Do you have any final words?"

Greer shone like a tent with a light inside it, so thin you could almost see through the membranes and into her insides. I couldn't see her eyes, couldn't make out her face. She appeared already an angel.

"God save Wilkie John," she said. Not loud. Soft. To herself.

She, like the preacher, might have eventually come up with a few more words. She wasn't given that convenience. Deputy Parnell pulled the lever, the door opened up and my Greer vanished from the stage, her dress billowing up as she went like she was hanging onto a racing thoroughbred. She made no noise except for the rope stretching and then popping with her on the end of it.

Simeon Payne went even easier, already so dead to the world that one of Parnell's men had to hold him up. Payne made no last statement, or, if he did, only he could hear it. Deputy Parnell said some words over him, none of them fitting, about being part of a cattle drive that brought death and suffering to its own as well as others. His tall, lanky frame needed less rope, and still, his boots touched dirt before the rope caught him and dangled him like a dead fish on the end of a line. He coughed up a sound or two but, thankfully, went quiet soon after. They cut him down and unceremoniously laid him next to Greer, a thing that never would have happened in life.

I thought I would put up a fight. When my time came, I thought I would go kicking and clawing to stay on this side of the dirt. If I had no belief in an afterlife, it stands to reason I would clutch that much tighter to what life I had. Maybe the fact I had no particular belief was working for me. I couldn't even muster up any belief I was going to die.

"Mr. Liquorman, your time of reckoning has

come at long last. Do you have any last words before you're cast into the long suffering arms of justice?"

I could see no light left in Gentleman Jack. He was already dead as his stone of a heart and angry that I had something he did not.

"I do," I said.

And I began a tale, the tale which you are reading now. A short tale. A tall tale. A true tale of a life of lies. Whatever you want it to be. When I began it, the street was full. The sun was in my face. When it was over, the sun was gone and so were most of the witnesses. Who wants to see a man's unnatural and ungrounded death when they know him so intimately?

The good Reverend Caliber stayed by my side, and I mean it when I say he was good. Maybe he had no more belief than I did, but he at least had the grace to listen to my story. Jack filed his fingernails and walked in circles, talking to himself. Was he trying to talk himself out of his actions? If he was, it didn't succeed. That evening, the story of my life having gone full circle, I ended my soliloquy by raising an invisible sword and quoting a line I remembered from King Henry IV:

"Death rock me asleep, abridge my woeful days."

I got part of the line wrong, having substituted *woeful* for Shakespeare's preferred *doleful*. No difference. I followed that with a petition to hang me high, that I might long wave. Parnell's two saps accosted me, one on each side, and maneuvered me to my downfall. There was a scramble as they realized they hadn't a third rope. I would hang on Greer's, a detail I appreciated. It was brought to position and hung on the tree, then put into position around me. I wanted to say more. I wanted to call out to Madam Pearlie, to Sunny. To Gentleman Jack, whom I could no longer see. I tried to fill my lungs with one last breath. I couldn't breathe. I panicked.

"Wilkie John Liquorman, for your transgressions, I commit you into the arms of death," Jack said.

I remember the feeling of falling, not unlike falling in a dream. I saw white, and suddenly I seemed to be flailing as if in a river. Pushing up, trying to catch air. Voices. Screaming. I'm sure one belonged to Pearlie. My lungs felt as if someone had lit a matchstick and dropped it down my throat.

I may have died for a few minutes. I came back alive when they were cutting me down. I thought they were laying me next to Greer and Simeon. I thought I was still dead. That was not the case.

I was splashed with something that burned down into my nerves and brought me roaring back to life. Somebody's whiskey poured in me from a flask. If I was on fire before, I now thought they'd revived me once just to kill me a second time. I passed out. But I didn't pass away.

CHAPTER FORTY-SIX

Two more days passed before I began to come to. In that space and time, I visited places in my past, places I knew where I saw faces familiar to me. Sister Mary Constance. Mama. Ira Lee. Long Gun. Lemuel Yost. Bricky Lusk. Greer. I was always looking over my shoulder for Jack, but I don't remember ever seeing him. Each of the people knew me. Received me warmly. Talked to me. Assured me my life wasn't over.

Sunny watched over me during those long nights when my breathing grew labored by the injuries to my windpipe. She poured buttermilk and Vapor-Ol into me to coat it and give me relief. Slowly, I became myself again.

"You was left dangling there for ten minutes, like a puppet on a string," she said on the third day. "First off, you turned red in the face, and you wheezed and whistled and gasped and fought something awful. If you weren't going to die, I wanted to. Just to put an end to watching you. Then you turned white and got real quiet-like.

That was no better. Still we kept watch for each small twitch of the leg or eye and lamented loudly to your punishers. They wouldn't let us cut you down for ages."

In her own way, Greer had saved me, by stretching the rope out just far enough that my toes could stretch and find earth. I was near strangled to death but survived with severely bruised neck muscles and a belief I had been spared for a reason. Because I had no religion to pin it on, I believed I was reborn because I had experienced a rebirth. It was, to borrow a term I'd heard Reverend Caliber use, a most simple faith.

I was nursed back to health inside Sunny's old room in the Black Elephant. She moved just down the hall, though she was often found reading to me—the newspaper and a copy of *Around the World in Eighty Days*, left in one of the rooms. So potent were the readings of the book, I would sometimes misremember that I had been the one racing around the world while I was actually recuperating inside that room.

Sunny read and re-read the newspaper story that came out on the day following my trial. On the first page, it fit under the headline "Texas Cattle Driver Unofficially Credited with Killing of High Sheriff and Store Owner. Hell's Half Acre Has Been Saved." The headline was as long as the story, but the truth had been revealed. Along the way, I had somehow survived my own hanging. I was famous.

There was an article on page two in which the editor complained of two botched hangings in as many months. He was calling for both the end of capital punishment in the city and an investigation of Jack Delaney himself. As a result, Gentleman Jack had disappeared. Madam Pearlie said he went high-tailing it back to New Orleans, but Sunny heard a different story altogether.

"You keep making progress, Wilkie John, you up for entertaining visitors, I'm gonna bring somebody up here to see you. I think he'll really open up those green eyes of yours."

By then, my eyes were awake most of the time, and the buttermilk had given way to chicken broth and ginger ale. I was already having visitors, truth be known, as a steady stream of people—most of whom I didn't recognize—came by to get a peek at the man who cheated the hangman's noose. Even more, I was the man who fired the fatal bullet into the High Sheriff's upper story.

Celebrations continued without pause as each new word leaked out that somebody had refused the newly opened position. No one else was fool-hardy enough to take on the Acre when it was running at full power. It was as if the entire place, from Throckmorton to Main, Calhoun to Jones, had survived the noose. And now, I was being visited upon by an authentic Texas Ranger.

David Hubbard Hubbards came from a place called Birdville. He dressed like a drab sketching of Gentleman Jack, and the peso star gleamed on the colorless collar of his long coat. He wore his hair like an Indian; that is to say, it was thick and long over his shoulders like a woman.

"I don't care how many people you've shot," he said. "Whatever the number is, I've shot one more."

I liked him immediately. I'm not sure the feeling was mutual.

"That really your name, sir?" I said.

He looked at me with eyes that said he'd seen plenty of my kind, had heard everything I could say, and failed to see any humor in any of it.

"I'm a little surprised that someone with a name like Wilkie John Liquorish would find amusement in someone else's name," he said.

It was a fair point, and I said as much.

He was there with Deputy Parnell to impart news about our friend Jack Delaney, and also to seek an answer or two. According to Ranger Hubbards, Gentleman Jack was a first-rate con man, and had a twenty-five-year path of swindling and sweet talking behind him.

"I've been on this guy's trail for the better part of two years," he said. "We had him in Wichita Falls and let him get away. But he's a bad penny."

It might go a long ways toward betraying my state of mind that I first wanted to defend him. Surely he hadn't been such a scoundrel. What it meant was surely I hadn't been so hornswoggled.

"You certainly weren't the only one," Ranger Hubbards said. "He's had sheriffs and deputies in his employ from Tennessee to Texas. He seems especially savvy at fooling law folks. He's good at making big promises. He's gonna come in and clean up the town, and they're all gonna pay him to do it. Meanwhile, he's taking pay from the saloons and bordellos, saying he'll protect them when the storm comes."

I could tell enough by the gloom setting in on Sunny's face. The countless hours Jack had whiled away in the Black El's bar, hobnobbing with the barkeep and slapping the girls on the backside. His quick trips in and out of the White El on Main Street. Where it once seemed peculiar, it now just criminated. How could I have not seen it?

"So he was taking pay from the High Sheriff with one hand and Madam Pearlie with the other," I said.

Deputy Parnell, every bit as dour as he'd been on the gallows, chimed in.

"Store owner was in on it too," he said. "They was in cahoots."

The Texas Ranger was standing at the foot of my bed. I was sitting straight up and trying to remember the details of an old story Sister Mary Constance had told. There was a man in a bed and an angel standing at the foot. The angel was saying something.

"Mr. Liquorish, I need you to know one thing. You have my word of honor, I have no interest in prosecuting you for anything. Now, in return, I need to know one thing. When you shot the sheriff and Mr. Tubbs—and based on the three boxes of bullets in your possession, I have no reason to doubt your testimony—did you overhear or see something that you felt put your life in jeopardy?"

He had blue eyes that looked like Ira Lee's blue eyes. When we had been young, people would stop him just to marvel at those blue eyes. My gray-green eyes, unspectacular, would hide my jealousy. And later, unobserved, I would look intently into those same eyes and wonder what I was missing.

There in the little room in the Black Elephant, I didn't miss anything.

"Yes."

I said a silent thank you to Ira Lee.

"We found your brother's name on a ledger in William Tubbs's office," Ranger Hubbards said. "It didn't take much at that point to start putting things together."

They only had one loose string that needed tying off, they said. And it would lead us to Gentleman Jack.

David Hubbard Hubbards had good enough reason to think Gentleman Jack was in Wichita Falls. Seems Delaney Blacksmith Shop was located right smack in the heart of town and, according to the Texas Rangers, got enough business that Jack could've eked out a fine living making horseshoes, nails, hinges, and hammer heads.

CHAPTER FORTY-SEVEN

I don't kill people who don't ask for it. There was a Dallas businessman who made a habit of visiting Fort Worth to do a certain kind of business he couldn't be seen doing at home. There were actually enough of that sort that, if you put them all on a train and sent them our way, they would fill a good number of cars. This one fellow, though, was named Hampton Balfour, and he had an eye for Sunny. An understandable thing, except for him being forty years past her in years and already having a house full of family thirty miles east.

It had gotten to the point where, whenever Mr. Balfour would present himself in the drawing room of the Black Elephant, Madam Pearlie would sometimes hold Sunny back from the line-up and tell him that she had taken ill. This had the effect of raising his concern, and he would bring flowers for her room. If she told him that Sunny was otherwise engaged, he would become irritated and even paranoid, suggesting that we were conspiring against him. This wasn't far from the truth.

On an early morning, I was walking down the block to purchase a copy of the daily news, with a coin donated by Pearlie. She liked to have a copy of the *Fort Worth Chief* laying around in the front room, just to make us look more worldly. I was aware that I was being followed right away. I have a nose for that kind of thing. It was easier to sneak up on Long Gun, the Indian, than it was me. I figured, in this instance, that it was Gentleman Jack, as he customarily kept me in his sights. Soon enough, I knew better. The footfalls were all wrong, timid instead of quiet, unsure where Jack was steady. I stopped and admired a hat in John Barbon's Men's Clothing store. Hampton Balfour appeared in the glass.

"What you following me for, Hamp?" I said.

He moved right up next to me and talked to my reflection in the glass.

"I need to have a discussion with you, boy."

I hadn't retrieved my gun for this short ramble, and for that I was sorry. He had me in a tight spot, and he knew it.

"Right here?" I said.

If he would follow me back to the Black El, I would be a little happier to sit down and talk with him. I didn't see why whatever he had to say couldn't wait.

"Not right here, but right now," he said.

He patted his gun for added emphasis. I couldn't tell what he was carrying. It was holstered inside his coat. I knew it beat what I had.

"Okay. Where?"

Hampton Balfour led me down a narrow alley between the corner store with its paper rack and the dressmaker that all the whores went to for clothing. People said she was the best paid dressmaker west of the Mississippi, and I have no doubt it was true. Most of the whores had money to spend, and they all tried to look better than the rest.

At the end of the alley was a bunch of tables and chairs. I recognized it as the backside of Frank's Saloon, even if it was a side I'd never seen before.

"Marguerite," Balfour said.

A good-looking Mexican girl came out as if this was something Balfour did on a daily basis. He ordered two beers, which I thought hospitable, and motioned for me to take a chair. I didn't put up a fight. He lit up a cigarette and offered me one of those too, but I passed. Not that I won't smoke a cigarette on occasion, but I didn't want to be any more indebted than I had to be. Plus, far as I was concerned, this was no occasion.

"What do you want?"

He smoked the cigarette halfway down before he found his words.

"I'm a successful man," he said. "I operate a land office in Dallas County. I make enough money to blow a good portion on frivolities here in your town."

I didn't consider Fort Worth to be my town, but I said nothing.

"Sometimes, what appears as a frivolity might not, in fact, be a frivolity," he said. "Do you understand what I'm telling you, boy?"

I tried my best to say it back to him in my own words.

"You're a rich son of a bitch who thinks he can buy his way to happiness."

He didn't agree with that assessment. By this time, Marguerite had returned with drinks in hand. Balfour pawed his glass, sucking off the foam and lapping at the brown liquid. I pushed mine away.

"You little lick-spittle, I could blow a hole through you right now and leave the mess for that little Mexican girl to clean up. You understand me?"

He could count himself lucky I was unarmed. He was old enough that I could probably have taken him in a fair fight, but the gun beneath his coat made that impossible.

"So you've got money," I said.

It was my attempt to get the train back on the track, even if I didn't like where it was going.

"I'm willing to pay you a generous amount if you'll help me to achieve a goal," Balfour said. "I have a proposal."

I thought of Greer back in Mobeetie. I thought of the baby. Money was the reason I left town in the first place. After everything that decision wreaked, I was still chasing it.

"How much?" I said.

"How much would you have to do?"

"No," I said. "How much money?"

The whole Tubbs's General Store debacle hadn't convinced me that there weren't a couple of banks in town that needed robbing, but if the bank was coming to me instead, I would at least listen to what it was saying.

"What was Bill Tubbs supposed to pay you for those cattle you were driving?" Balfour said.

It took me a minute to process. There was a heck of a lot of information in that question, and I wasn't expecting it.

"What makes you think I have anything to do with Bill Tubbs?" I said.

I knew I had made a series of mistakes. I was at the end of a narrow alley. Without a gun. With someone who seemed to know more information than was good for him.

"Bill was paying off cattle drives for whatever amount and then sending them on to Kansas and making big money. Everybody knew it."

He paused.

"Probably what got him killed."

I pulled my drink over and took a sip. I still didn't care for beer, unless it was root beer.

"I was supposed to get paid thirty dollars when I got here," I said.

Enough said and all true.

"I'll pay you twice that amount if you'll get Sunny to be my macushla. I'll buy her a house right here in the Acre. I'll buy her one on Main Street if that's where she wants it. I'll give her a monthly allowance. Enough to buy perfume and dresses from Chicago. I'll buy her a piano. Piano lessons. Whatever she likes."

What did macushla mean? I'd never heard it before.

"She likes reading about places like New Orleans and New York," I said.

He looked delighted.

"I'll buy her books."

It was a start.

"And . . ." I said.

He looked confused. "Anything she likes," he said.

"Trips to places outside of Texas," I said.

Part of me felt like I was selling someone back into captivity. I didn't have any right to speak for Sunny, much less on a matter of such importance. I told him as much. I think it must have come as a sock on the jaw, as he'd mistaken my banter as something more than it was.

"So we have an agreement?" he said.

No, we didn't. Seemed to me, the only thing me and Hampton Balfour had in common was a sincere like of Sunny. Not that I was jealous or anything.

"If you're paying me to deliver Sunny to you, that sounds like slavery," I said, "and that's illegal even here in Fort Worth."

He began to get real restless. I could tell he was about to lose his composure. I didn't expect it to end in tears.

"I don't want to purchase her," he said. "I want to take care of her. I love her very much."

I heard a lot more than that, some of which doesn't bear repeating. It's enough to say Mrs. Balfour no longer gave her husband much cause to come home, and she never looked at him anymore in the way Sunny did. I didn't think it was a good time to mention that Sunny looked at him that way because that's the way Sunny looked. She looked at me and Black Price Hardwick and Kitch Howard the exact same way. She looked at her breakfast that way too, far as that goes.

On the other hand, as much as I hated to, I empathized. If I'd had that kind of money, I might have wanted to do the same thing. And who was I to say anything about Mrs. Balfour? At times like that, I thought about my Greer back at home and grew flat out melancholy. I thought about killing Balfour a few times. Even dreamed about it and woke up sure I'd done it, a kind of reversal of what had happened years before when I killed Gallo and then halfway-convinced myself I had dreamed it up. I might have killed Hampton Balfour for calling me boy, for calling me a lick-spittle. I didn't really know what a lick-spittle was, but I was pretty sure he was calling me little or something equally disagreeable. I could have shot him for crying or just for claiming to love Sunny. But I didn't. I just didn't have the heart. Of course, I didn't go running back to tell Sunny about our conversation either, although maybe I should have. I never collected a penny from Hampton Balfour either.

CHAPTER FORTY-EIGHT

Bird and me left Fort Worth on a balmy morning, pointed in the one direction I was least interested in going. I might have lived a thousand more years without a hankering to visit Wichita Falls if I didn't have business there. And if that business hadn't been solicited by a Texas Ranger.

I tried to talk Hubbards into making the trip back with me. He didn't see any upside in it. It would double the chances of us being spotted, he said. I tried to argue back that it would only double the number of people being spotted. That wasn't the same thing at all.

We left with Sunny and Madam Pearlie standing in front of the Main Street side of the Black Elephant and waving handkerchiefs, Ranger Hubbards having left in the opposite direction an hour previous. Wichita Falls would be a stop along the way and nothing more. I was contemplating Indian Territory. I hadn't ventured up that far before, and it seemed like a change of scenery was in order. I didn't want to go South. I was sure of that much.

The trail to Wichita Falls was made up of untold layers of earth and history, generations buried away and built over one at a time until you could feel the ghosts under your feet. It had been Indian land—mostly Cherokee—maybe as long as there was land. I felt like an intruder. The only thing that broke up the landscape, besides the occasional bald eagle or wild animal, was Decatur. A little less than halfway, the town gave me a short relief from the heat and a chance to check Bird's hooves. She was in need of new shoes. Maybe I should've seen a smith there in Decatur, but I had the smallest scrap of a plan, and I wasn't ready to give it away. I knew I could make Wichita Falls in two days, so I pressed on.

According to the Texas Rangers, Jack Delaney was married to a woman named Rachel who still lived in the town. She and Jack had a girl named Tennie who stayed in the home. Jack had returned there on a regular basis up until the last ten or twelve months, during which his visits had become shorter and more erratic.

"He had a son," Ranger Hubbards said. "If you go back to Wichita Falls, you need to know what happened. Just to understand what you're getting into."

I rode along for those two days, going over what Hubbards had said to me. I wanted to learn it so well that I didn't have to remember it. I wanted it to become a part of me.

"We were there working with the sheriff, old fella named Ples Thatcher, and we were there to serve a warrant for cattle thieving. We knew Delaney was working with someone in Fort Worth.

At that particular time, we weren't sure who. We were planning to go easy on him, work to get him a short sentence if he would turn over a few names."

I saw where Hubbards was going in time to head him off at the pass.

"Jack was rustling cattle and selling them? To who, William Tubbs?"

"Oh hell, they even had the ranchers on the other end involved," the Texas Ranger said. "They were rustling small numbers, less than a thousand head, sometimes less than five hundred, mostly so Delaney and a couple of his boys could manage them, get them into Fort Worth and either sell them off to meat-packing plants or mix them in with bigger drives headed up north."

Delaney would get a cut, the High Sheriff would get a cut, and they would start all over again. When Delaney needed a suitable day job to keep him around town, Gentleman Jack the bounty hunter was born.

So Jack never gave a damn about Wichita Falls. Probably didn't shed any tears over the High Sheriff and William Henry Tubbs either. What he did care about was the end of his con game. His final con had come up just short.

Not short enough to make any difference to Greer. That's why I was traveling northwest toward Wichita Falls instead of north into Indian Territory. I had a pain in my neck that wouldn't quit and a chest that still felt like raw beef, but it wasn't about me. Or maybe it was. Greer was dead and buried in a shallow grave behind Reverend Caliber's Baptist Church, but I would have to either go home to a house in Mobeetie that wasn't home anymore or decide to never go back. Either way, Jack Delaney was the cause of it, and he would have to deal with me.

One man at a saloon in Decatur said he'd seen Gentleman Jack just two days before.

"He wear one of them Lincoln hats," he said, "only it was red?"

I don't know why he wore that thing. Well, I knew why he wore it. Because it made him stand out in a crowd. His vanity would be his undoing.

"With a feather," I said.

We were sitting in the Number Nine on First Street in Wichita Falls, and I was drinking whiskey. They were permanently out of ginger ale, and it seemed like time for me to grow a little hair on my chest.

"Fella bought me a drink," the man said. "Seemed like a pretty decent man."

By appearances. In actuality, he was a Bunce's Ten Cent Novel inside an original William Blake cover. Only a Bunce's Ten Cent Novel would have more entertainment value.

"For a cattle rustler," I said. "And a cheat. And he killed my wife."

He was eyeing me with some suspicion by that point. I could understand why. I pulled my coat out of the way, just enough to show the peso badge pinned to my shirt collar. He sat up straight in his chair, suddenly sober as a Quaker.

"Oh, you a Texas Ranger," he said.

I had it pinned on upside down. Partly so I could look down at it and see it right. Mostly because I'd heard a Ranger say you weren't supposed to turn it over until you got your first kill.

I put down two bits and started to go. Then I stopped and dug two more bits from my pocket.

"See him around these parts again, you tell him he's gonna regret not ending me."

If I'd really been able to deliver a message, I'd have told him to kiss Rachel goodbye. There were times I wanted to kill her, just to put him through the same thing he put me through. I wasn't sure she deserved it though. I wasn't sure I should leave the girl without a mother. I wasn't sure about a lot of things, but telling Jack to say his goodbyes wasn't one of them. He wouldn't know whether it was him or Rachel I was coming after, but he would damn sure know I was coming.

If I had been able to deliver a message.

CHAPTER FORTY-NINE

"One of our men got into a shootout in Wichita Falls and thought they had Gentleman Jack himself. Turned out to be his son, Jack the second."

I had the details committed to memory, but it was the first time I had spoken it aloud. The part about Jack Delaney getting shot up at the Delaney Blacksmith Shop in Wichita Falls the year before. The loss of his legs, his livelihood. Then the loss of his dad.

I wasn't talking to a man in a bar. I wasn't talking to a woman in a bedroom. I was talking to Bird, and we were trying to get to know each other. I was missing Roman something awful. I had come to the realization, somewhere between Fort Worth and Decatur, that the dream where I'd been searching through all those lit up tents back on that field where the Lusk family had been killed, had been about Roman. He's who I had been searching for. Don't ask me how I figured that out. Once I did, it didn't matter how.

Bird was limping pretty bad by the time we made

the outskirts of Wichita Falls, and, in a fanciful way, so was I. What had been designed as my undoing— my ending—had turned out to be my beginning. I wasn't following Ira Lee. I wasn't chasing Greer Lusk. I wasn't running from the U.S. Army. I was making my own way.

I was a deputy Texas Ranger.

Delaney Blacksmith Shop was on Fifth and Burnett in Wichita Falls. From Ranger Hubbards's report, Jack wasn't likely to be there. It had been run by Jack number two, and when he was shot, they brought in outside help. As a business, it paid the bills and put food on the table for Rachel and the girl. Jack Junior lived in a hospital bed. No legs to run off on. No hope of getting anything but closer to death. A constant reminder of how one man's fate was visited upon the son.

Gentleman Jack wasn't in. The Blacksmith was working on hinges for a barn door but said he'd be happy to fix Bird up if I could leave her for an hour or two. As a kid, I'd spent hours with Ginny Hay watching clouds form shapes then break up and reform again over Central Texas. As an adult, I could recognize an opportunity when I saw one.

"Got a horse I can borrow for collateral?" I said.

He nodded at a mule out in a field behind the shop.

"A mule for a mule," he said.

There was a nice little mustang running down the fence line.

"How about that one?" I said.

He laughed and shook his head.

"That one's mine. She don't let nobody ride her but me."

I stood there and watched him pound a hinge into shape on a piece of railroad track, the fire blowing so hot I could feel the hairs on my arm curling up in response. I looked at Bird and then at the mustang in the field. He was coming toward us at a brisk pace. It seemed like he knew what was about to go down.

"You know where I might find Jack Delaney?" I said.

The man continued his work, bending the glowing hinge to his will.

"Old man or the son?" he said.

I had Ira Lee's .44 Colt in hand and was sliding its nose up and forward.

"The father," I said.

As the mustang got closer, the mule seemed to turn and watch him approach. The dust was kicking up a trail behind him.

"They're out at the Clara house, far as I know," he said.

I raised the gun up and pulled the trigger twice. The fire in the forge seemed to leap with each blow, and his body fell against its side and slumped to the ground. I pulled him up by his collar, dragged him onto the forge and stoked the flames as they ate away at the evidence.

Clara was a small community just outside town. I'd ridden through it once before on a dark night with a pale moon that barely beamed through the cloud cover. It was one of those nights when shadowy hoofbeats seemed to give chase and the trail hissed and moved around me like a snake.

I knew if I made good time and everything fell just right, I could be out of Clara and on my way into Indian Territory by sundown. If I took the mustang. And if anyone saw me along the way, they would think I was the blacksmith on his way to pay the boss a visit. I took his hat and duster to further the effect, being careful to pin the deputy Texas Ranger onto the inside breast of the coat. I still pinned it upside down.

I left Bird with the other mule there at the shop. I felt real bad about that, especially because I hadn't let the blacksmith fix her up before I shot him. Still, it was all in service of the greater good, as I had heard Reverend Caliber once say. That was a concept I understood well. I had seen how things, often terrible things, worked for good many times in my life. Enough times that I'd begun to consider it a pattern. And once I looked for the pattern, I was surprised how often I found it.

On the way to Clara, I asked the mustang about himself. I didn't have a clue about his name or the blacksmith's either. I still remembered naming Roman after the Roman literature I was hearing during Sister Mary Constance's lessons.

"I could name you Vulcan after the Roman god of fire," I said.

The mustang didn't seem impressed.

Clara looked almost as ghostly by day as it did by night. There was only one trail running through it, and aside from a small church and a handful of houses, it appeared most of the residents lived on the other side of the ground. I found a man sitting outside the church with a shovel in his hand, and I wondered if he'd buried the whole town and was just waiting around the join them. He reminded me of my old friend Grover Morrow.

"Howdy, Stranger," I said.

He face looked like too little skin stretched over too much face. His mouth pulled open into a frozen silence. Maybe he thought I was the ghost.

"You know where a Jack Delaney lives around here?" I said.

The man moved the shovel into a vaguely defensive position. He cleared his throat, which seemed to rattle all the way down into his lungs.

"You kill that Texas Ranger?"

I didn't like the way he looked at me, didn't like the way he talked.

"Beg your pardon?" I said.

He used the shovel to pull himself to his feet then leaned unsteadily on it.

"You killed that Texas Ranger in Decatur, like Jack said."

He was staring off into the distance, or, at least, I thought he was. Turns out, it wasn't that great a distance. Maybe twenty, thirty yards at the most. For it was there that Gentleman Jack himself stood, tall and silent as a steeple. He didn't have his fancy duds on. He wasn't wearing the Abe Lincoln hat with the feather in it. I wouldn't have recognized him in any other situation. I knew there was nobody else it could be.

"Hi Jack," I said.

He had a rifle pointed right at my head, something I'd never seen a church steeple do. If I moved for the .44, crows would be picking at my brains for supper.

"Why in the hell are you riding Lee Otis's horse?" he said.

I looked at the horse and tried to think. For a

few moments, the only thought my brain seemed to have in it was the one about not wanting to die in Clara, Texas. Then it slowly yawned back to life.

"You know this horse's name?" I said.

When it came right down to it, and it looked like I was going to cash in, I didn't want to get that close and then die not knowing that damn horse's name. It seemed that important.

CHAPTER FIFTY

David Hubbard Hubbards had been going south when he rode out of Fort Worth. Why he was laying dead on a slab in Decatur, Texas, forty miles north of town, I couldn't tell you. Gentleman Jack seemed to have a few things to say on the subject.

"He's dead in Decatur, and you show up here two days later wearing his badge," he said. "You don't seem to learn, do you?"

Jack, the old man, and me were standing inside the church building in Clara, Texas. The old man, who turned out to have the keys to the place in his pocket, had used the shovel to wedge the front door shut. It wouldn't have kept me inside for more than a few seconds, if I had a few seconds with it, but it seemed to be there more to keep folks out. A thought that disturbed me just a little. Gentleman Jack was pacing back and forth in much the way I'd seen him do on the gallows in Fort Worth, only now, he was walking the aisle of the church, up to the altar and then retreating back into the pews. The rifle was still pointed at my head, and now he had Ira Lee's .44 Colt for backup. I had a few bits in my pocket and the peso badge. After accusing me of killing Ranger Hubbards and taking the Colt, he hadn't searched me further. Not inclined to give it up, I was trying to decide whether I could use the pin side of it as a deadly weapon.

"If he's dead, I'm pretty sure I know who killed him," I said.

The truth was plain as the nose on Gentleman Jack's face. He knew Hubbards deputized me. That must have put some kind of fright into him. The Texas Rangers were onto him, and now I was one of them. His final, desperate play: Kill Hubbards and, like the peso badge, pin it on me.

"I'm pretty sure I know who killed Lee Otis, too," Gentleman Jack said. "What you say, let's take our stories to Sheriff Thatcher and see which one he believes."

I knew that, according to David Hubbard Hubbards, Thatcher had been cooperating with the Texas Rangers in their pursuit of Jack. Jack didn't seem to have a clue about that. I also knew I couldn't be any less safe in the sheriff's office than I was in a secluded church house in Clara, Texas.

"I'll take you up on that," I said. "Let's do it."

I could tell that didn't make Jack happy at all. He shoved the rifle into my face, close enough that I could smell gunpowder. He pulled it down, cocked it and fired. The blast rattled the whole building, from the vestibule to the choir loft. A board proclaiming twenty-two in attendance on the previous Sunday fell to the floor in panic. A hole in the floor opened up, not nearly wide enough to swallow me up.

"The sheriff sees you today, you're gonna be dead weight on the back of a mule," he said. "You wanna know a secret? You didn't get away with anything in Fort Worth that I didn't let you get away with. You think you cheated the hangman. That's malarkey. If I'd wanted you dead, believe me, you'd be asleep in Jesus right now."

I wondered if that could be true. Of course, it could. I tried to recall the moments of the hanging. It had all happened so fast. I remembered my heart racing. I got tunnel vision. The sounds became a roar in my ear. I remembered the floor opening up and having the sensation that I was being pulled upward instead of down. Then I must have passed out, because I woke up gasping for breath. I remembered being acutely aware that I'd soiled my trousers.

"Greer died to teach me a lesson?" I said.

The old man with the key to the church was watching the proceedings intently. The shovel out of his hands, he was clutching something in his left hand, but I couldn't be sure what it was. He looked nervous. It was understandable.

"It doesn't make her a saint or anything, Wilkie John," Jack said. "Everybody's death teaches somebody a lesson."

That wasn't a lie. I had been taught enough, I was slowly putting things together in my mind. I had been taught that Gentleman Jack didn't want to kill me. He'd said that much himself, hadn't he? If he'd wanted me dead, I would have died in Fort Worth while he had the rope around my neck. That crowd had been hungry for blood. Standing shoulder to shoulder in the streets to watch the rope break the neck and kill a young Scottish girl with no blood on her hands.

There weren't many things Jack could've wanted from me. I didn't own any land yet. I had no business. I was a failed cattle driver.

"I think enough lessons have been learned, Jack," I said.

I looked into the hole at my feet. I guess I was looking for an answer there. I would have expected that hole to open up and start talking before Gentleman Jack did.

"Fear the Lord your God," the old man with the church key said.

The floor itself might as well have said it.

"What in tarnation is that supposed to mean?" Gentleman Jack said. "God is love, preacher. I've heard you say it."

The old preacher pulled a Smith & Wesson out of nowhere and pointed it right at Jack.

"God is love to the lovable."

Shots rang out all over that Baptist church. The first one came from the preacher's Smith & Wesson, and it hit its target. Jack turned, his rifle ready to roar, but the bullet through his right shoulder into his neck had done damage. The first two shots from Gentleman Jack's rifle ripped through the pews and chewed through the pine walls, but didn't come close to the old man.

"Fear," I said.

The answer had come to me. Jack hadn't killed me because he needed me to fear him. If he killed me, his power would be gone. But what had I done to cause the whole thing? Why me?

I didn't get the chance to ask him. The third shot from his rifle hit the old preacher in the upper thigh and knocked his legs out from under him. He hit the floor and started leaking blood that matched the red carpet under him. I thought he was as good as dead. And I would be next. Maybe Gentleman Jack didn't want to keep me alive after all.

"This is the look of fear," Jack said.

He stepped out from behind the pulpit and stepped down three steps to the preacher, who was struggling to get up on all fours.

"Jessie, dammit, you made me do it," Jack said.

The preacher knelt there all pasty, sweating like he knew that, just maybe, all his fancy words and beliefs had been for naught. He could die alone on the floor of his own church, and there might not be any angels coming to carry him off, no Jesus beckoning him to come unto him and find rest. He might just die.

"No," the preacher said. "You caused all of this."

The preacher let out a whoop so loud, it curled the clapboards. It sounded like an old Confederate charge, and maybe that's what it was. It seemed like a whole battalion came through the back side of that church, busting the hinges clean off a door I hadn't taken note of. I don't rightly know how many Texas Rangers bombarded that little church. It's possible there was even more than the twenty-two on the church attendance chart. There were also more gunshots than a man with only two hands and two feet could keep up with. I lay down on one of the pews with my hands over my head

and tried my best to throw a prayer out. I could
hear bullets biting into the wood all around me as
I did. I could also hear the soft thud as they hit
flesh. For half a minute, I just lay there. Oh God,
how I hated church.

CHAPTER FIFTY-ONE

"I seen your dang badge. I was trying to tell you I was with the Rangers," Jessie said. "You gonna keep wearing that thing, you'd best learn to listen. Learn to see. You weren't nothing but a damn hinderance in there. Hiding in the pews like a sinner on Sunday morning."

To be precise, he was Reverend Jessie of First Baptist Church of Clara, Texas. As if there would ever be a second one. He was also, believe it or not, an active member of the Texas Rangers. And he was sitting just outside the front door of the church in his longjohns, showing his new clean-through wound to anyone who asked. I didn't ask. I still didn't like him one bit.

"Can you hang around until everybody's gone?" I said. "I'd sure like to talk to you."

Of course, Sheriff Thatcher was there, walking around and inserting himself into each person's story. Yep, he had seen Jack Delaney in Decatur within the past week. Yep, he had been instrumental in selecting the church as a meeting place, because he knew Jessie could make it work. Even when Jessie was unsure of the plan, the sheriff had encouraged him to push on with it. Yep, he swore, Delaney had been so close to him at a restaurant in Decatur, he could have spit in Delaney's soup as he brushed by.

Thatcher went on and on, scarcely taking a breath. He never referred to Delaney as Gentleman Jack. Just Delaney. Only the newspaper man and me seemed to know who we were dealing with.

"Sheriff Thatcher says Gentleman Jack was coming after you. What you done to cause such a stink?" the newspaper man said.

The *Wichita Falls Times* was a weekly rag. Small and just barely legible. But, if I was lucky, the word might eke out to Fort Worth, Dallas, to Kansas even. Who could tell?

"He killed my wife," I said. "Tried to kill me too, but he underestimated me. Maybe he overestimated himself. Either way, he should've known better."

He was as slow jotting down my response as I figured he would be. I started to ask if it would be easier for me to just interview myself, write it all down, and hand it in next time I was in town.

"I guess you got a pretty good look," the reporter said. "You think he's gonna make it?"

I took my time and thought on that one.

"Make it?" I said. "He'll make it for a little while, but, in the end, he won't. Same as all of us."

He must not have liked that answer much because he didn't even try to get it down. He nodded and walked on, looking for his next good quote. Most of the men pushed him away. They were too busy talking to each other. It was a regular old

Texas Ranger congregation, right there on the church grounds. These were my people. Well, for the most part.

As for Gentleman Jack, he was carried out on a wagon, and he was making as ungodly a noise as I'd heard all night. Sheriff Thatcher said it was a good sign, as it proved he still had the fight in him. He may have, but he also had more bullets in him than anyone could count. He'd somehow managed to keep most of his essential parts intact. There was a bullet hole in his chest that came within an inch or two of blowing his candle out forever.

"Jack, you might not see it this way," Thatcher said, "but today was your lucky day."

I felt a little bad seeing Jack in such shape. I pushed up through the other Rangers until I got to the side of the wagon holding his ripped and torn hulk. They had him wrapped in a blanket, but you could count the spots in the fabric where blood was oozing in and get a good idea of how shot up he was. I looked at his eyes, still open even if they were glassed over, and moved myself accordingly. I wanted to make sure he got a real good look at me as the driver hawed the horses and drove away. Jack didn't say anything, but I could tell he saw me. You could see the light get just a little dimmer as I smiled and waved at him.

The Rangers stood around outside the church, drinking from flasks and smoking cigars, for half an hour after the horse and wagon departed for Wichita Falls. Some were placing bets on whether Jack would last the trip. Money said he wouldn't. I knew better and got in on the action. After a while, Preacher Jessie hobbled around to me. He

was using his shovel for a crutch and still managed
to have a flask in one hand and a cigar in the other,
so it seemed like he might have been my kind of
preacher. I even gave him a small chance at re-
demption.

"So what was it you wanted to say to me, young
man?"

I had been hoping we would be alone. Unfortunately, there were still six or seven other old
Rangers still milling about. They looked like they
were at some kind of strange military dance, the
way they stood together and then stepped away to
the next partner and started the process again.

"I was wondering about something you said earlier," I said, "about me not being Texas Ranger
material."

When he laughed, he sounded like a donkey
braying.

"Well, son," he said, "I respect that you've got
the badge. Obviously, someone must have thought
you had the beans to wear it."

He tossed the soggy end of his cigar on the
ground at his feet and danced it out with his right
foot.

"You hold onto that thing, I expect you might
grow up and into it one of these days," he continued. "Specially if you watch us grown folks and see
the way it's all done."

He didn't talk his way out of my anger. If he'd
kept on with it, he might have done it, although
my suspicions are he'd have just kept talking his
way farther in.

"No," I said," I want to talk to someone about

my soul and dying and heaven and so forth. Could I meet you maybe tomorrow morning, Preacher?"

His look said he didn't really want to do anything tomorrow morning unless of course it was Sunday, which it wasn't. All the same, I needed to get on the road early and didn't care to hang around Clara, Texas, any longer than necessary. The place spooked me, and I wondered if there was anybody who was born and raised there and had warm thoughts of the place. Then it hit me.

"Did Gentleman Jack really come from New Orleans?"

"Hell, no," Preacher Jessie said. "Who told you that? He come from right here in Clara, same as me. I knew his old daddy when Jack wasn't no bigger than a mess of minutes."

"Jack his own self probably told him," one of the other Rangers said.

"Half of everything that man said was a ball-faced lie," the preacher said, "and the other half was just flat-out wrong."

He leaned over to me and whispered.

"Meet me here at the church. Tomorrow, noon. Don't be late."

I nodded, and pretty soon after that, I left them with it. There was a team of Rangers inside the church, scrubbing it down and taking all the blood out of it. The rest were standing around talking about Jack in not-so-gentlemanly terms. One of them looked a lot like Kitch Howard, but I couldn't be sure. It all left me wishing I hadn't been such a coward inside the church, and thinking that Gentleman Jack could have very well stood a few more bullets to send him on his way.

I stopped and asked one of them if he had ever heard of a man named Henry John Liquorish. He acknowledged that the name sounded familiar, but it soon turned out to be me he was thinking of. I started to tell him the story of Henry John who came to Texas with the New Orleans Greys. Who fought the Comanches and died at their hands. Of the man who came crawling toward Mobeetie with that same name on an envelope. But I left it at that.

As I rode off on my new mustang, I told the horse he could count himself lucky too. If he'd been a girl, I might very well have called him Clara, just to remind me of where I never wanted to go again.

"But we're coming back tomorrow at noon," I could almost hear him say.

He still didn't have a name, the little cuss. Or I guess he did, I just didn't know it yet.

CHAPTER FIFTY-TWO

"Word is, Jack Delaney never made it to Wichita Falls," Jessie said.

I had arrived at the First—and only—Baptist Church of Clara a few minutes early, hoping to scope out the surroundings. A lot of times, places that look spooky in the night will look completely different in the light of day. The First Baptist Church of Clara looked the same.

"Really?" I said. "He's dead?"

The mule brayed again, but I was too busy trying to work the idea of a dead Gentleman Jack into my imagination to deal with it.

"Boy, he ain't dead. He managed to get his hand on a gun and shot the fellow carting him into Wichita Falls. Jack's gone. Horses, wagon, and everything, just gone."

The inside of the church showed little evidence of what had happened the night before. Someone had already nailed a cross-shaped piece of wood over the gunshot hole in the floor.

"You think he's coming back this way?" I said.

I'm not saying I was afraid of the thought, but I wasn't in any all-fired hurry to meet back up with him either.

"He won't show his face around these parts for a while," the preacher said. "He knows the Rangers have him in their sights. He's got nerve, but stupid he ain't."

I wasn't so sure about that.

"He's not so smart as he thinks," I said.

Neither was Preacher Jessie, far as that went. He might have been a more spiritual man than my friend Reverend Caliber, but Caliber was the one you'd trust with your life. Which would the Lord Jesus regard most highly? I didn't believe in any of them enough to care. They could take the Lord and his religion and go jump in the lake.

"Careful, my young friend," Jessie said. "Foolishness is bound in the heart of the young."

I was willing to give him that too, at least as a general statement. If he was trying to say something about me, I told him, I would appreciate it if he'd just come on out with it. He said he felt likewise. So I took him up on it.

"You claim to be a Texas Ranger," I said, "but you don't wear the badge."

He stood up and pulled his jacket off, and I thought we were about to launch into fisticuffs.

"You'll find out soon enough," he said. "That badge will bring you more trouble than anything. I wear it, but I wear it right here."

He patted his hand over it, pinned to the inside of his overshirt, against his heart.

"I know it's always right here, and, if I need to flash it, I can do that too."

There was something I almost admired about the guy. He had replaced his shovel with a rifle of his own, which gave me some pause, but he seemed about as likely to pull it on me as to whittle it into a whistle and play a tune about the terrible wickedness of life and love.

"So is that what calls us back here on my squirrel hunting day?" he said.

I'd spent the past few nights taking target practice with my left hand. I liked the idea of keeping my right hand open and free, and now, with my Colt moved to the left side and that hand resting lightly on it, I was fighting the itch to unholster a little foolishness in the preacher's direction.

"What do you think happens when a man dies?" I said.

His face said he was fully aware he could be walking into a trick. He wasn't.

"A Godly man has nothing to fear," he said. "An ungodly man has everything to fear."

I was hoping to hear something I hadn't heard before. Something more meaningful. I had watched enough people die to realize something profound happened. Even Indians. And horses. Especially horses. Something that didn't seem to happen when a fish or a squirrel died.

"You think you're a Godly man?" I said.

He was nervously caressing the stock of his rifle.

"I try to be," he said.

The Colt was pointing right at his guts. He had no idea how close to God he really was.

"See, I tried to believe in God too," I said, "but, it always seemed to me, killing a man who has it coming, well, that's being Godly in its own way. You can see that, can't you, Preacher? Don't that make sense to a man like you?"

His lip made a certain move—a tremble, a nervous betrayal—that reminded me of someone I'd seen before, on a different day, a different stage. It was only then that I saw the truth for what it was.

"Jack Delaney," I said. "I'll be damned. That's your boy, ain't it?"

He sat there and said nothing.

"He didn't come from no New Orleans," I said.

He shook his head no.

"That sly dog," I said. "Never was no slave or blacksmith or a real bounty hunter or a real anything, was he?"

He sat there like he was trying to recall something real about his son.

"Yes, he was a slave," he said. "We was all slaves so long, we didn't know who we were supposed to be or how to be free once we finally got there."

That might have been true. People will put a world of hurt on you, and you carry the scars whether you show them or not. Some got more scars than others.

"You know I'm going to kill him, sooner or later, don't you?" I said.

He nodded.

"He had it coming, I wanted to be the one to do it," Jessie said.

There was something to like in Jessie Delaney. I took a single step back and raised the Colt in his honor.

"When he gets there," I said, "tell him I said good riddance to bad rubbish."

I shot Jessie Delaney five times. I didn't have to

do that, but I wanted to make sure he died good and fast. He probably deserved that. He fell dead in his own church, which should have meant something to the God he served. He wasn't a good man. He said a lot of bad things and did bad things too. But I guess he did try to be Godly, whatever that meant to him.

Jessie Delaney. His death served as a promise. A deposit against a future reckoning.

I pulled the star out from inside his overshirt and pinned it on his jacket lapel, where it belonged. Then I got my horse and rode out.

I've seen my fair share of towns. No two of them are alike. San Antonio could make you feel like you were in the presence of spirits, even when you lived in the filthy streets of the Sporting District. Mobeetie, in spite of outlawing the *Encyclopedia Britannica*, was about as bad as a town can get when it comes to murdering, cheating, and general evil-doing. Still, those towns had hearts that beat crazy, twenty-four hours a day. Clara was the only town that ever made me feel the way that town made me feel. It reached down in you and just strangled your insides. There's not a word in the English language for that feeling. At least, not one I know. And I'm glad for it.

CHAPTER FIFTY-THREE

I liked talking to these men. Real authentic Texas Rangers. I read about them in dime novels, people like Buckskin Sam, chasing down Mexican bandits and American outlaws. I had seen a few growing up in San Antone, but they always seemed like a different breed, like if I spoke words to them, they wouldn't even hear a sound. Now I wished for nothing more than to have Ira Lee to show my peso badge off to. Not that he would have been impressed. Annoyed was more like it. Anyway, I halfway expected some Ranger to come riding up, tear the badge off, strip me of the title and bolt away. If any had ever thought about it, they never said anything or acted on it.

I got word in Decatur that a Ranger named Junior Ellis was hunting me down, and I immediately thought the worst. I didn't wait around to see if he'd appear. I was traveling southwest, in the general direction of The Flat, and I wanted to stay in motion. I was less then ten miles outside Decatur when he showed up. How he tracked me down in the middle of nowhere, I didn't have a clue, but he was, after all, a Ranger.

"Heard tell you was asking round about a man called Henry John Liquorish."

My heart jumped into my throat. Ellis slid off his horse and walked toward me with his hand out. He was built like a beanstalk and wore an oversize hat that called attention to it. I determined not to say anything long as he said nothing of my slightness.

"Well, I'm not sure that's his name," I said. "He was toting around an envelope with that name on it. It was my dad's name."

We shook hands and quickly confirmed that we were each who we thought we were.

"So where'd you run into this fellow?" he said.

I gave him as detailed a rundown of the story as I could recall and then explained where Mobeetie, Texas, was located.

"I'm guessing that's an Indian word," he said.

I told him he guessed right.

"They named the town Mobeetie because they thought it was the Comanche word for Sweetwater," I said. "What I hear, it really means buffalo dung."

I didn't know if that part was true, but I sure hoped it was, and if it was, it fit the town all the better. Not to mention it got a laugh.

"Listen, we've been following a character named Jack Delaney for a good while," Ellis said. "I know you've personally had a run-in or two with him."

That was an understatement.

"Only reason we ever learned about you, Wilkie

John, was because Jack Delaney had you in his sights."

I told him that Gentleman Jack—I still called him that—had come within a whisker of killing me and that I had, at some endeavor, returned the favor. He already knew all of it, but he listened patiently, chuckling in a few appropriate places, shaking his head and whistling in others.

"If you follow the trail backward," he said, "we're pretty sure this Henry John Liquorish is the man that paid Jack Delaney and give him the information needed to bring you down."

I wasn't sure I followed.

"You saying Henry John Liquorish paid to have me killed?"

Ellis nodded.

"You may be in some danger from either one of them, or both of them, considering the circumstances," he said. "Mr. Liquorish seems to have paid Delaney a considerable bounty for your head. He's bound to be somewhat unhappy, Jack Delaney having his money and you still running and gunning."

Believe it or not, it was the first time I'd fully contemplated there being a real bounty on my head.

"So who exactly is this man, Henry John Liquorish?" I said.

Junior Ellis looked surprised.

"We were hoping you could help us with that one."

I told him I was very suspicious. I had never been told of anyone having the name other than my

father who died many years ago. I laid out my
theory that the unknown man had only been carrying an envelope belonging to my father and was
looking to deliver some sort of news to me. Ellis
acted like he had never entertained that thought
at all and didn't think much of it.

"Could be true, I suppose," he said, "but we know
he took lodging in Fort Worth under the name
Henry John Liquorish."

He had been in Fort Worth earlier, on his way
toward Mobeetie, it would seem. He'd met up with
Gentleman Jack there, ordering and paying for my
demise like you would a new suit or a mail order
bride.

"And you have no clue why this is happening?"
I said.

Junior Ellis said what he wanted to do—why he
had come out into the desert to find me—was
follow me at some distance while I made my way
wherever I was going, to make sure I was safe, on
one hand, and to be in a position to act if either
man were to show up, on the other. I didn't like
the idea.

"I don't much like the feeling of being followed,"
I said.

If he was going to do such a thing, I wasn't sure
why he wouldn't just ride alongside me, although
I didn't like that idea any better.

"Not sure how much help you would be to me,
following along," I said. "You damn sure didn't do
anything to stop what happened in Fort Worth.
The man hanged me right in the middle of town."

He had the nerve to laugh again. I was beginning to feel an old familiar twitch in my shooting finger.

"How you supposed we would do that?" he said.

If he hadn't been a Texas Ranger, I might have drawn on him right then and there.

"It's your job to figure that out, partner," I said. "You're the Texas Rangers."

He rode right up next to me and winked.

"Well, if we were anywhere good as you say we are, seems like we might be able to stretch a rope a little bit."

That was what Ira Lee used to call a mouthful of useful information, and I would reflect back on what all it might have contained, what it hinted at and implied, many a time. For the time being, I continued on my way.

"So," I said, a few minutes later, "are you telling me Elijah Caliber is a Texas Ranger?" I said.

He had begun to fall back behind me at that point. I was trying to convince myself he was going to leave me be, but I knew that was highly unlikely. I did still believe in my own ability to change direction and lose him though. It was a natural born talent.

"Why don't you ask Madam Pearlie that question next time you see her," Junior Ellis said.

I contemplated on that a while, and, next time I looked back, he had disappeared. I stopped and looked hard for him, but, like so many people I'd shared the trail with, he was nowhere to be seen.

CHAPTER FIFTY-FOUR

I almost named the mustang Maximilian after the stories Jacobo used to tell about making beans for Emperor Maximilian. It was a good idea, but Jacobo had survived the emperor's overthrow only to die of food poisoning in the Texas desert. It didn't quite fit. I thought about naming him after one of the characters in *Journey to the Center of the Earth* but all the names except Axel were difficult to pronounce. I identified with Axel too much to give that one away. Again, it didn't fit.

I finally decided I'd been calling his name all along. That's how he came to be Little Cuss. After a while, it ceased to have any meaning. It was just his name.

When we left Clara, I didn't have a clear picture of where I wanted to be. I did have a list of places not to go. Those included Mobeetie, Clara, and Fort Worth. Dallas was a possibility. That whole city was lighting up with electricity, and they had a new power plant where I might get a steady job. Indian Territory beckoned, but, if Gentleman Jack was

laying low up there, I didn't want to poke a stick in
that nest. Not yet anyway. Indian Territory would
wait.

There was Birdville just because it reminded me
of Bird. Nacogdoches because I'd never been that
far east. Then there was The Flat. I'd spent a night
or two down there, and something told me I had
more to spend there. Me and Little Cuss headed
off in that direction. There would be plenty time
for talking and lots of stories to tell. I would tell
him, from memory, stories of Axel and Professor
Lidenbrock and their amazing journeys. I would
read from the *Encyclopedia Britannica*, sixth edition.
I'd tell him about Roman, the most noble horse I
ever saw in my life. Greer Lusk who came from a
place called the River Clyde and had the most
beautiful eyes I ever saw. I would tell him about
Long Gun and Lieutenant Hanley. About Reverend Caliber and Madam Pearlie and Sunny, who
I found stayed in my heart, just as Ginny Hay had. I
would tell him stories about Mama and Ira Lee and
the school nuns back in the District.

Yes, in time, I would tell him about Gentleman
Jack too. But for now, whatever the story was about
to be, he wasn't a part.

On our way toward The Flat, we passed through
Meridian. I found Ira Lee's grave easy enough, not
ten yards off the trail. We stopped and paid our
respects.

"Ira Lee," I said, "I hope you found some satisfaction in dying there. Satisfaction seems to come
pretty scarce, this side of the dirt. You were a good
brother and a fine trail boss. That drive, you know,

it should've been the start of something. Not the end. I guess I'm not a brother anymore, and I'm not a husband and I'm not in the Army anymore either. But I'm a deputy Texas Ranger. Ain't that something?"

Later on, I wished I'd told him how I had his Colt and would use it to slay the man who designed our ruin. What did it matter? Ira Lee could no more hear me than the horn on my saddle. I might as well have been talking to it. Or, once again, just to Little Cuss. No question he could hear me. And people who says horses don't understand don't understand horses.

I left Meridian for the second time in a month. On the way out, I passed a man driving a horse and wagon. He doffed his hat as he approached.

"You looking for somebody?" he said.

I tried to think if there was anybody anywhere I was looking for.

"No."

He nodded like it was a good thing I wasn't.

"They just found a guy out there in the desert, wasn't nothing but a bunch of bones and a pair of drawers."

"It can get dirty out there," I said.

Little Cuss passed the wagon, and I saw he was carrying mail. I guess even the few folks wandering around in Meridian get a letter every now and again.

"You know if they found a wagon or horse with the guy?"

I had buried Roman proper, but I had left the man's horse to fend for itself. It was something I wasn't proud of, but I had been preoccupied at the time. The man eyed me with not a hint of suspicion.

"Wagon and horse come in here a week or more ago, loaded down with animal pelts," the mailman said. "Not sure this guy belonged to the horse or not. The bones was found pretty near Fort Worth."

I could still remember that stranger's face clear as the blue sky. I could also remember him pitching forward into the sand with his mouth wide open. Could he have gotten up and crawled that far without kneecaps?

"Suppose he must have been a fur trader," he said.

Little Cuss and me moved along.

"They prefer to be called *furriers*," I said.

I could have told him more, but that would have brought more trouble for him and for me. That's the nature of telling stories. You have to know where to start and, even more important, where to stop. I didn't get to The Flat, leastways not right away. Seems like I'm always headed for one place and then arriving at another.

The bones of the fellow out there in the sand got to poking around in my head and wouldn't let me go. Sure, I told myself, it had to have been the fur trader I shot in the kneecaps. He couldn't have survived out there. Even if he hadn't bled to death, the snakes or wolves or Comanches would have lucked up on him.

I couldn't quit thinking about that other man though. The one who rode alongside Bird and me as we made our way across the desert on that final moonlit night before hitting Fort Worth. Had it been Gentleman Jack? Well, no. That young Henry John Liquorish with the envelope in his pocket? Surely not him either. What had he been doing out there in the middle of nowhere? Had he been looking for the fur trader? Had he watched me shoot him down? The rider remained a mystery in my mind, some kind of thing that represented everything else that I couldn't quite put my finger on. I don't much like mysteries roosting in my mind.

I stopped Little Cuss on a bit of a natural bluff that had a clump of dead trees still standing strong on it and took an early lunch break. By that I mean I fed Little Cuss, but it was more a chance to stop and think. I once had a conversation with an Oriental man who told me if you wanted to go to El Paso, you wouldn't normally go in the direction of Natchez, but you could if you wanted to. I didn't want to.

I looked behind me and saw no one. Looked ahead and saw that same no one. The more I thought about The Flat, the more I wanted to go to Waterproof, Louisiana. Or New Orleans. Even Acorn, Arkansas. Exactly why I gave one whit about this Arkansas horse rider, the lady he left behind and that night train coming down toward the washed out bridge, I couldn't have told you. Maybe it was the fact that I couldn't tell you that appealed to me. Maybe the whole story was beginning to get away from me, like that dream you're having when you first wake up, how it seemed as real as the morning sun but then begins to lose its hold on you.

I hadn't ever been to Arkansas, but there wasn't nothing stopping me. Little Cuss was raring to go. Maybe I could even stop off in Waterproof and say hello.

On one of the last nights I spent with Sunny, I was telling her about my days in the U.S. Army, about how it had seemed that a whole different world was laid out before me, if only for just a brief time.

"When you're out there in that part of Texas, it seems like you're in a completely different world," I said. "It's hard to believe you can be standing in Fort Worth and San Antonio and Mobeetie and The Flat and you're standing in the same Texas in all four places."

I think part of me had already been looking beyond Texas at that point, trying to see what was over the state line, over the border. Before I knew it, I was telling Sunny about Long Gun and his rabbit-killing gun. She waved me down.

"Wait, wait," she said. "His name was Long Gun?"

I told her that his real name had been Dohoson Tay-yah, but they had nicknamed him Long Gun because of his skills with the Whitworth rifle. She squealed with laughter.

"Oh, I thought you said his name was Long Gone."

I remembered a day when I wondered if it had all been for real. If I had been Long Gun all along. Of course, I didn't tell her that. And I was never good enough with a rifle to be Long Gun anyway. I was pretty good at being long gone though. That fit me like a well-worn pair of gloves. And so, Wilkie John Liquorish—Liquor Man—became Wilkie John "Lone Gone" Liquorish. It was that difficult, that easy.

You have to know when to stop telling a story, because every storyteller knows, stories never end. They twist and turn and circle back on themselves like a snake, but they don't ever end. They do have a way of becoming truth through the telling though, and you have to live with them. That is, if they don't get you killed. Riding off with my back to the sunset, I was lucky to be alive and looking forward. What I was looking forward to I didn't know, but at least I was looking forward.

TURN THE PAGE FOR AN EXCITING PREVIEW!

**On the untamed, harsh American frontier,
living wasn't always easy.
On the other hand, dying was.**

Wilkie John Liquorish is a hard-luck young man
trying to make his way in the Wild West.
He doesn't look for trouble—it's usually there
when he wakes up in the morning.

**DEAD AND BURIED
A Wilkie John Western**
BY TIM BRYANT

The Wild West is about to become even wilder.

Coming in June 2018,
wherever Pinnacle Books are sold.

CHAPTER ONE

People who live out in the sea of sand that is West Texas tend to have strong beliefs in God and the devil. It's not really any mystery. When you walk out into the landscape and take a look at the mountains and plateaus, the cliffs rising up dramatically out of the earth in streaks of reds and browns and even a few greens here and there, it's real easy for these people to see God. Even a nonbeliever like myself can be swayed. Walk out farther into that same landscape, try to ride very far across the flatland, into or around one of those mountains or maybe through a pass between them, hang out for a while with just you and your horse and the sun, it gets pretty hard not to see the devil too. You can hear him rattling, cooing and cawing at you. He might show up in the form of a black bear or a javelina. He might even show up as a man.

I found the bones of a guy out there in the middle of nowhere, and I just as well might have been looking at my own self. I was out of water, my horse Little Cuss was down and dying, and I had good reason to think I was following shortly behind.

When I say the man I found wasn't nothing but bones, I'm speaking in the most literal of terms. There was some leather chaps less than ten feet away, and the ripped remains of a shirt pulled over some scrub brush. The only other thing was bones bleached pure white in the sun, gleaming like the teeth of some dust devil.

Of course, everything was starting to look white. The sun was bleeding into everything and washing out enough of my eyesight that I was blind to just about anything farther away than ten feet. I was hoping I didn't step on a rattler or run up on any of the black bears that called the area home.

"Hell's Half Acre got nothing on you," I said.

I had been talking to myself ever since I left Little Cuss back a few miles. I had reason to believe there was an Army encampment just over the hills to the south, and that's what I was aiming for. If I made it by nightfall, there was a chance they could send back for the horse. At least that's mostly what I was telling myself.

I had spent a considerable amount of time in Hell's Half Acre, the area of Fort Worth where gambling dens rubbed up against the most spectacular whorehouses you ever saw and made the sweetest music ever heard by a sinner's ear.

What I was standing in right here was more hell than Fort Worth ever thought of raising. A week out of camp in Fort Concho, I'd followed the

Pecos River down to the Pacific Railway and then turned west. It had been days since I'd seen smoke behind me. I was on the part of the map that was a big blank. And I could see why.

The bones strewn out in front of me weren't me. I was pretty sure who they were. If I was lucky, they belonged to a man known among the Apache Mescaleros as Phantom Bill. His true name was Manley Pardon Clark from Chicago, and he had been on his way to Chihuahua with a sack full of money taken from a train from Santa Fe.

I'd stumbled across the carcass of a horse the day before, so I expected to catch up with the phantom. I just thought there would be more to him.

"The Tonkawa ate your horse like it was a fine steak, Manley," I said, "and, from the looks of things, they got their teeth into you too."

That didn't bother me much. I'd heard tales of the Tonkawa eating captured families and then dining on the family dog for dessert. They were a hearty bunch of people. Great trackers too.

"What I want to know is what you did with the money, my friend," I said.

I knew him well enough to know he would have hidden it before letting Indians get their hands on it. You could tell by a few drag patterns that Manley had been dragged due south, either by the Tonkawa or by bears that came along and took what was left. I walked back north and scanned the horizon. It was all white. If I was going to do this, I was going to have to do it on my hands and knees, a few feet at a time. If I did get down there, I had serious doubts if I'd be able to get back up.

I don't rightly know how long I searched for that damn money. Time kind of bled all together like the light did. I stopped to rest frequently and slept a bit too. Somewhere along the line, my knees and elbows folded up and left me stretched out across a bunch of rocks, another easy meat stick refreshment for a passing band of renegades.

"Wilkie John."

In my dream, it was a woman's voice. Not just any woman's voice. It was Sunny, a colored girl left behind in Fort Worth. Only now I was back there with her in a big house called the Black Elephant, and she was coaxing me into a nice, warm bathtub.

"What are you doing down there? Wake up, you fool."

I opened my eyes to the sensation of lying naked in a place you shouldn't be naked. I reached down and fumbled around for my different parts. My clothing was soppy as a dishrag, but it was there. I looked up into the light like a heathen looking into the face of God.

"I can't see a damn thing, Jack," I said.

Gentleman Jack Delaney. Probably the last person you would expect to see me with. Jack was something to see, if you could see. He was wearing a new blue suit that looked like it was made from fancy brothel curtains. When I questioned the suit's practicality, I was given the speech on wind and sun damage and the importance of shielding yourself. He had proven right about that much, but I had heard it all before.

It wasn't exactly true that I couldn't see anything. I could see the shod front feet of the fastest quarter horse in all of Texas. I was pretty certain of it because she had caught me and Little Cuss even with a morning's head start the previous day, and I took no enjoyment at all in that fact. In my mind, that whole episode had been responsible for Little Cuss cutting his leg. If he hadn't been trying to prove something to himself, he'd still have been right there beneath me instead of the rocks and sand.

"Manley Pardon Clark is lying right over there against them rocks," he said.

Gentleman Jack Delaney waved his rifle, which cut through my white light like an angel of death slicing through fire.

"Think I don't know that?" I said. "I was the one who found him."

I listened to the man swing down from his horse and crunch his way toward me.

"No money?" he said.

I shook my head, and the world seemed to tilt and spin backwards in reaction. I turned away from Jack and vomited a stream of clean water that polished the rocks beneath me. I suddenly recalled that I had done the same thing before. Just minutes, maybe hours or even a day ago, but some earlier time.

"Should I trust you or search you?" Jack said.

I couldn't figure out how he was standing there,

cool and composed, while I lay on the ground, closer to Manley Clark than Jack Delaney.

"Little Cuss hurt his leg," I said. "We need to go back and see if we can save him."

Jack laughed. Not so much like he was laughing at me. Just laughing at the ridiculous situation.

"Little Cuss didn't cut his leg, Wilkie John. Snake got hold of him."

It depended on how you looked at it. He may or may not have run up on a snake, but the bite threw him off balance enough that I came off the tail end and Little Cuss went down. That was when he'd cut his leg. I was sure of it. Somehow, in my fall, I had totally missed the snake.

"Don't worry," Jack said. "I made a tourniquet and cut the bite out. Gave him some water. He'll probably make it."

He bent over and grinned down on me.

"You, I'm not so sure about."

I was just about as happy to see the man as I could have been, generally speaking. He'd spent considerable energy trying to kill me the year previous, and I'd sworn revenge on him for it. Now, back down in the lonesome part of the state, I ran into him when he was running down Manley Pardon Clark, or Phantom Bill, and I was sitting around, trying to decide what to do next. To be specific, Jack had sent word to Fort Concho: he was looking for a soldier or two to help in the capture of the outlaw. Then he sent word again and made mention that the reward would be split in an equitable manner.

When still no soldier was provided, he showed up at the fort, looking exactly like himself. At six and a half foot tall, his legs were long for his horse, and he still insisted on wearing a top hat that made him look odd and even taller. He wore a suit that fit perfectly, even if it didn't befit the situation. Sure, it was important to dress well, to guard against all the things the desert might spring on you, but he was still dressing for a night out on the town, and that didn't appear to be in the cards.

"He was here three days before he held up the train," I said.

Neither of us had any thought that he would be coming back that way, but the stop at the fort had proved helpful. Two different soldiers, neither of whom had a clue who he was at the time, said he'd mentioned going to Chihuahua when he left. That information narrowed the trail enough that I was now just a few yards from what remained of Phantom Bill. Seemed he hadn't been a phantom at all.

Neither soldier reported any mention of train robberies or other plans for misbehavior along the way. In fact, being told who they had been talking to, neither believed he was the man. Not him. He didn't have it in him to do such a thing.

Now I was laying in the desert, half blind and wondering where the money was.

"How hard would ten thousand dollars be to hide?" I said.

I was looking at Jack's suit and counting pockets. I didn't trust him as far as I could see him, and he was moving in and out of eyesight.

"A hundred one hundred dollar bills. Two

hundred fifties," Jack said. "Ain't gonna slow you down a whole lot, Wilkie John."

I scanned the sand between me and Manley, like I was expecting a bill to come fluttering by on the wind.

"Hell, bears could've eat up the money too," I said.

I had no idea how much time had passed, but I knew I was quickly running out of it. We had four more days to find the stolen loot and return it to the railway people in Alpine, Texas. After that, they were leaving for California and half of the reward money was going with them.

Gentleman Jack Delaney had asked me to come along for one reason. He was considerably more likely to find both Manley and the loot with me helping. He knew it, and he knew I knew it too. I also knew something else, and I wasn't completely sure if he was aware I knew that part of the deal. He wasn't planning to split any reward money with me. Not a chance. In fact, he had no intention of taking the loot to Alpine at all. Why would he take ten thousand dollars into Alpine and get five thousand back when he could take ten thousand to Chihuahua?

How did I know what he was doing? For all his faults, and they were numberless, he was too damn much like me. I wasn't interested in some reward money doled out by the railroad or the government. I also had no interest in vacationing in Chihuahua with Gentleman Jack. I would leave his bones with Phantom Bill for the devil to find.

Then again, he had saved my life and maybe even the life of my horse on that day we found the bones in the sand. And there was that thing about me being a Texas Ranger. Damn. Things, as usual, were bound to get complicated.

CHAPTER TWO

Becoming a Texas Ranger had an interesting effect on my life. Womenfolk took more notice of me. Maybe I walked a little taller. At least I didn't think of myself as so small anymore. I wasn't perfect, but it reminded me of something a Fort Worth preacher had once told me.

"Being saved doesn't make me perfect, but it makes my imperfection into something God can work with."

I didn't know about all that, but if you counted that the Rangers had saved me from a life of crime, it certainly did go on to make my weaknesses something easier to overlook. So even if Reverend Caliber had got the letter of the law wrong, he'd at least got the spirit of the thing. There was no question I was a better Ranger than I had ever been a non-Ranger.

I'd had it in mind to visit Indian Territory. In fact, I was in Comanche, Texas, and headed north, stopping only to pay respects at the gravesite of my older brother Ira Lee when word came that the

Colorado and Concho Rivers were flooding and there were German immigrant families stranded and possibly in danger of drowning. I went down there and, with the help of another Ranger from Leon Springs and a soldier from San Antonio, we brought out eight Germans of varying shapes and sizes and two Cherokee women with their children.

The soldier had already set up a camp on high ground by the time I arrived, and we carried our survivors there behind two mules. I call them survivors because we saw more than a few who weren't. A dead boy in a tree that spooked me good, the look on his face so real, I tried to talk him down before I realized he wasn't alive. There were several people washed up in bushes and against fence posts. Most looked like farmers, farmers' wives. We didn't move any of them. Where would we bring them? We didn't have the tools to dig graves, and, if we had, we'd have just dug into more water. The soldier said a solemn prayer over each of the bodies, and I was completely respectful.

"Which way you going from here?" the soldier said.

The rain was gone, but the Colorado had flooded its banks, and the water was still rising. You couldn't make out where the river began and ended. Standing on high ground and surveying the scene, it looked like the whole world had become the raging Colorado.

Half of the Germans wanted to stick it out. I couldn't get over that. With everything underwater or washed downstream, they wanted to stay put. Start over. The other half had had enough. There was nothing left to pack, nothing to save. They were ready to go back east right then.

"All I know, I'm moving upstream," I said.

I was like that half of the Germans. I'd seen enough water. I'd seen enough of what it could do. I was going elsewhere.

"You mind carrying these people over to Fort Concho?" the soldier said. "They'll be okay there until they can get a coach or maybe a train back to where they come from."

"No coach take us back to Bremerhaven," one of the ladies said.

She didn't appear to be talking to us, so I didn't answer.

By then, the Indians had slipped off, never to be seen again. There was no need to look for them, no need to worry. They could look after themselves.

It turned out Fort Concho was less than forty miles away and, if it wasn't in my preferred northerly direction, at least it was out of the flood's path. And it was a direction I'd never taken before. I said yes, and we decided to go ahead and move out that afternoon, so we stood a good chance of arriving in camp the next day.

"Wait until tomorrow," said the Ranger, who turned out to be Roy Lee Deevers from San Antonio. "You don't want to travel by night."

But I did.

"There will be a full moon tonight. Plenty of light, and much cooler for the horses," I said. "Plus, maybe he will sleep."

I nodded to one of the German men who had a badly broken leg. He wouldn't be easy to deal with.

He was a mean son of a gun who didn't seem the least bit happy to have been saved from a more horrible fate than traveling back east.

The San Antonio Ranger cleaned up the break as best he could and made a real decent splint with one of the many sticks scattered around us. When the German argued against it and tried to get up and walk to prove his case, Roy Lee knocked him over the head with the butt end of his rifle.

"I've done just as much good with that end of the gun as the other," he said.

I drug the German and his family off in peace, making good time through the night. Watching the moon come up right in front of me, climbing up into the night even as we climbed into the hills. At one point I stopped and made them all look at the beautiful sight before us, split equally between the valley below us, the sand seeming to glow under the moonlight, and then the sky, so full of stars they seemed to be crowding each other out, trying to get in position to look down upon us. I saw a hundred rabbits and even some hyenas, one of which I drove away with a single shot from my gun. Overall, it was a perfect example of why I like to move at night and sleep during the day. To make it even better, we arrived at Fort Concho in time for a late breakfast of ham hocks and eggs.

Fort Concho was built on a grand scale. So grand, I thought I found it and left it, only to find it a second time. Turns out I had never left and wouldn't exit the grounds for two more days. It was bigger than Mobeetie. Enough men to whip Attila and all of his Huns. I never did figure out who the supreme commander was, but there was one Lieutenant with the name Zephaniah Swoop who seemed to have a pretty firm grasp on the situation. Most of them seemed to bow to him, in spite of his name.

Swoop had a heap to say. Mostly about this outlaw the Indians called Phantom Bill. The Phantom had robbed the Pacific Railway train three times, each time getting more brazen and getting away with more cash. It was embarrassing the railway people, who had put three Pinkertons on the last train. His ability to get away seemed supernatural. That's how he got the name Phantom Bill.

Orders had come down to help some bounty hunter track him down and kill him. Swoop was hesitant.

"I don't mind taking my orders from President Arthur," he said. "These orders are coming from Pacific Railway. I don't work for the railroad."

I could sympathize. I wasn't much of a railroad guy either. And I damn sure didn't take orders from California. He called a few meetings, none of which I was party to. I had delivered my Germans safe into the care of the U.S. Army and was planning to pull out for Indian Territory the following day.

Swoop awoke me while it was still dark. I thought I was dreaming.

"Say again?"

I blinked hard and shook my head, trying to force myself to attention.

"This bounty hunter is named Jack Delaney. He seems to think he knows you."

It was quite possibly the last name I would have ever expected to hear from the man's lips.

"And what exactly does he want me for?"

With a few hard blinks, my vision had come back to me and was focused on this man, tugging on his beard like maybe he would pull the answer out of it. I recall wondering, ever so briefly, if pulling at your beard would make it grow longer like Swoop's. Mine grew to a certain length and then seemed to just stop. I had never pulled on it much.

"Phantom Bill's robbed the Pacific Railroad three times now in two months. This guy's looking for someone to ride with him. I'm not sending any of my guys out there with him. If they get that money, they won't come back. If they don't, they'll be dead. This fella seems rather fond of you."

One of the privates was standing right at Swoop's elbow. He looked like maybe one of the men who wanted to go and didn't get the call.

"Said he's going back to California with a hat made of Phantom Bill's skull," the private said.

Swoop elbowed him right behind the ear.

"It's Gentleman Jack's skull I'd be more comfortable wearing," I said.

The idea of a hat made from a human skull was worthy of contemplation. Hunting down an outlaw with the man who'd tried to kill me only a year before wasn't.

"Why don't you send one of the Germans?" I said.

It was an admittedly weak argument. The only one who might have been up to the job at all had bone sticking through his leg and was delirious from either fever or the medication he'd been given. The only other boy, obviously the man's son, was watching over his father and feeding him water from a canteen. Or maybe it was beer.

"You are a Ranger, aren't you?" Swoop said.

Even if the ladies did look at me differently, and even if I did walk more like five foot and six inches than five foot even, there were times I'd just as soon not wear the badge.

"I'm not afraid of no Indians," I said, "and I'm sure as heck not afraid of this Phantom Bill. But you can count me out of this one. I'm not signing up."

Swoop and his boys watched me for a good while.

"He didn't say he wasn't afraid of this Jack Delaney," one of them said.

I was saddling up Little Cuss just as the Army medic arrived to patch up the new arrivals and prepare to ship them to Savannah, Georgia. My instructions, if I wanted to meet up with Gentleman Jack, were to ride due south. Pass Lonetree Mountain and then proceed thirty miles. There I would join my old foe and proceed to track down and smoke out the outlaw Phantom Bill. Manley Clark. Whoever he was.

I wasn't going to do it. That much I knew.

"You have an alias, Wilkie John?" Zephaniah Swoop said while I checked my supplies.

I thought about it. I'd been falsely identified as John Liquorman, but it hardly qualified as an alias. I'd toyed with calling myself Long Gone Liquorman, but I'd never put enough effort into it for it to catch on.

"People named Wilkie John Liquorish and

Zephaniah Swoop don't have much need for an alias," I said.

Swoop laughed and nodded.

"I never trusted anybody with an alias," he said. "Don't much matter if they're good guys or bad guys."

Swoop had a handle on things all right. He'd had one look at Gentleman Jack Delaney and had taken the measure. All in all, I'd have rather chased the Phantom down with Swoop and told him as much.

"I don't reckon I believe much in phantoms," he said.

I mounted Little Cuss and tipped my hat. "Real phantoms probably don't have to call themselves phantoms," I said. "Same goes for gentlemen."

I left riding south, and I cussed myself for it. It was the one direction I wasn't interested in. I was potentially riding into a trap. Even if I wasn't, I was surely riding into trouble. I wasn't teaming up with Gentleman Jack. He could count on that much. I looked down at the peso badge on my coat. In ways, it had surely changed me, its pin poking through layers to jab at me, prod me. Sure, part of me was a little intrigued. Had Jack really asked for me? If so, why? We hadn't separated on good terms. In fact, I had promised his daddy I was going to shoot him dead. I was more interested in following through on that promise than wasting bullets on some damn ghost.